MW00882988

Eleutheria

— ΕΛΕΥΘΕΡΙΑ —

T.F. Linn

ISBN-10: 1499712073
ISBN-13: 9781499712070

DEDICATION

To the people of Eleuthera. May the sea always provide.
And to my wife, whose patience is broad as the sea itself.

CONTENTS

ACKNOWLEDGMENTS

A special thank you is owed to my sister, Kristina, for her encouragement and support. I am grateful also to the people of Spanish Wells, St. George's Cay, Eleuthera, The Bahamas. Their story writes itself. Last, I am indebted to my fellow travelers aboard the *Grand Mariner* (Blount Small Ship Adventures) for your kind words of encouragement and tireless proofreading.

1 TORRINGTON

We beat them from hedge to hedge into their barricadoes, which our men carried after about an hour's fighting after several repulses, and so forced the enemy into the town whereupon the horse were set in and charged the enemy in the streets and after hard fighting drove them out of the barricadoes at the further side of the town. Many prisoners were taken and put into the church but many more threw away their arms and escaped in the darkness. No sooner were we possessed of the town than the enemy's magazine of about eighty barrels of powder, which were in the church blew up whether by accident or on purpose we cannot yet learn. Many of the prisoners were killed, many houses defaced and the whole town shaken. Some of our men in the churchyard were killed and two great pieces of lead fell within half a horse's length of the General. One whole barrel of powder was blown out into the street without taking fire The enemy seeing the explosion made another charge under John Digby, brother to Lord Digby, but were repulsed by our musketeers and our horse, instantly advancing, began the pursuit at eleven at night and I hope will give a good account of the business. Thus hath it pleased God to rout Lord Hopton's forces foot and horse.

* * * * *

Locked as he was in Torrington church, Joseph Pinder feared painfully for the lives of his oxen. He'd just prayed for the elder, Goliath, and the younger, Simon, but now afterward his mind was troubled by the thought his prayers might themselves constitute a sin. Sorting out what was right from what was wrong was proving difficult this 16th day of February in the year 1646. But hadn't the Reverend Allsap, his brother in-law, recently written explaining with great passion and conviction that God loves the whole world, not only the human souls occupying it? If the whole world and all in it were created and loved by God, then Goliath and Simon were surely proper subjects for prayer.

Cold Devon rain continued to drive upon the slate roof high above and the sound of cannon fire clattered down the belfry in an angry, persistent clamor. The battle on the ground and the storm in the sky raged on, and as the pooling rainwater mixed with the warm blood of Parliamentarians and Royalists alike, Joseph prayed anew for the safety of Goliath and Simon.

The Cornish Infantry, every man loyal to King Charles, were responsible for Joseph's troubled state of mind. Having commandeered the sole means of his family's livelihood, Joseph could only watch as the soldiers loaded his oxcart higher and higher. The cargo was easy to identify, even in the dark of night, and it grieved the drover to know the many barrels of gunpowder would be used against General Fairfax.

Perhaps he should have followed his friend, the village wainwright, John Wilshire, into Cromwell's "New Model Army". But then Wilshire and many others perished in the battle of Naseby more than a year ago. No, Joseph instead heeded his wife, Rose, who begged for his abstinence from the fray on account of the boy. Another year passed with King Charles clinging obstinately to the wrongheaded principles his subjects could no longer abide. Joseph did not go to war, but the war had come to him anyway.

In regard to religion, the question was whether Charles would be king of a presbytery or no king at all. Still the bishops remained and the king continued to believe God Himself was responsible for their power.

In regard to militia, the question was simply whether the king should be permitted to raise his sword against his own subjects. Well, on that point the king's position was clear. Nor would Charles agree to distance himself from the pack of sycophantic counselors who continued blindly to support him in his deceitful attempts to deadlock government and outlast all petitions for political and religious reform. It was clear to all by now that Charles would never work in good faith with Parliament.

* * * * *

Nearing ten o'clock, Rose lifted the boy and his blankets from the small bed by the fire. She ducked through the doorway and stepped out into the dark, bending at the waist to protect her son from the wintry rain as she hurried across the farmyard towards the neighbor's cottage.

Standing there in the cottage doorway, her plea was brief and desperate. Against her better judgment, the widow Agnes agreed that she would keep David with her for the remainder of the night while Rose tried to make her way into town in search of Joseph.

While the road earlier was wholly obscured by the wide ranks of the Cornish Infantry, they were nowhere to be seen now. They'd disappeared and taken Joseph and the oxen with them. As Rose neared the dense cluster of Torrington proper, she realized with a sinking dread and rising fear the terrible noise of battle was emanating now from the town itself. She would certainly be seen if she were to continue along the open road, which carried traffic and goods between South and North Devon. The riverbank, she supposed, would be a wiser means of reaching the George Inn, where she hoped to find news of Joseph.

Though she and her ten year-old son, David, often walked along the River Torridge, parting the thick willows as they made their way, the black night and rain made the passage arduous and frightful.

Within minutes the sharp grasping of riverbank gorse had unraveled a good part of her woolen shawl. Thick mud sucked hostilely at her feet but then graciously soothed the wounds suffered upon her shins by the ragged piles of driftwood.

Rose summoned to her mind a picture the riverbank in the daylight and saw the flow of the river swing westerly just opposite the inn. She flinched at each loud musket report, holding her ears now as she pushed through the reeds and willow branches. The dark was punctured by flashes of blue and white light, suddenly illuminating the edges of smoke clouds hanging sullenly in the rain above.

Ten more paces, she told herself, and then she would make away from the bank and try to find the back wall of the inn. But then a faint whisper came through the rain, repeating itself until its reality was at least tentatively established. Her eyes strained in the direction of the human voice, hushed still, but insistent. In another step she was looking into the face of Abner Walsh, the keeper of the George Inn. His head poked out turtle-like from under a piece of canvas covering the tiny river skiff he and his wife had pulled high up among the reeds. No one remained in the town, Abner pleaded, and any that did were no doubt locked up in the church, which now served as the Royalist stronghold. Abner's wife, Helen, also took up the plea for Rose to join them in hiding in their boat. But Rose was in a state and the not-knowing seemed worse than the danger of proceeding. She would go to the church and be held there by the Royalists if it meant knowing Joseph was alive. She was not as inclined to prayer as her brother, the Reverend Allsap, but she prayed with all her heart now: "Dear God please lift up General Fairfax and give him strength that he might take Torrington away from the king this night."

Not more than twenty steps from the cover of the riverbank thicket, a Royalist sentry wearing a long black cloak, appeared to her like the Reaper himself, barring Rose's passage. Madwomen or spy, the soldier reasoned, the best place for her was the very heavily guarded town church in which the Crown had begun housing prisoners. On the other hand, a loss of the church to Fairfax would inevitably mean victory for the Parlimentarians, as the building held not only prisoners, but the Royalist powder magazine as well.

* * * * *

5

No sleep could possibly come to him, Joseph decided. The guns alone were enough to wake the dead in the church graveyard. Seventeen thousand men and horse now collided in Torrington as if hell itself had burst open and sent its occupants into the narrow streets above.

Royalist soldiers could be seen now and again, each time appearing more and more despite as they through the guards posted at the door and then clattered down the stone steps into the basement powder magazine. Joseph's only companion, there on the floor of the alcove chapel dedicated to Saint Michael, was a horribly injured Parliamentary calvalryman. He sat still as death, back against the damp stone wall. His right hand was missing, as was the better part of the right side of his face. The only evidence he still lived was a growing pool of dark blood collecting against his right flank. His eyes were closed, the right one permanently on account of his wounds.

It seemed to Joseph, therefore, a high miracle that the man now struggled silently to his feet. He leaned painfully against the ornate statue of Saint Michael and seemed to fight for balance. The poor devil would soon fall down, Joseph could see plainly enough, but perhaps in the soldier's mind he wished to die on his feet rather than crumpled on the floor. His remaining eye was still closed tightly.

At least half an hour more passed and still the soldier stood. Then suddenly a change of guard was announced by the captain stationed at the church's enormous front doors. At once the two guards standing on either side of the pulpit separating the dual basement stairwells passed down the aisles toward the front of the church.

"Joseph!" called Rose as she peered down the aisle. "Are you here!"

Joseph was on his feet in an instant. He brushed by the wounded calvalryman and ran down the aisle towards Rose's voice.

In the small alcove in which the stature of St. Michael stood supporting the wounded soldier, a candle flickered to life. The soldier, candle held tightly in his left hand, carefully stepped away from the statue and slipped out of the alcove and into the stairwell.

The tears flowed down Rose's face as she reached out to embrace Joseph.

"Thank God, you're unharmed," she said.

2   TO PORTSMOUTH

"Ah," realized Agnes, "so this was man who'd insisted Rose have the boy schooled in the church." The scarecrow Reverend stood at the door of the cottage as Agnes shielded David behind her skirts. "David is to come with me now Mrs. Cartwright. I am the boy's uncle and my sister's affairs have now been settled."

Agnes reeled, "But Joseph's cottage, the barn, the oxen, these are the boy's now, are they not?"

"The farm and chattel are sold now, Mrs. Cartwright. What remains of the proceeds will go to David after his passage is paid to the island of Bermuda. I shall be joining a congregation of Independents there and David will be placed into the service of a very fine man, Captain William Sayle. The Captain is a devout believer, Mrs. Cartwright, a man of great principle and esteem. He is the former Governor of the colony."

She'd seen the boy grow from a babe and it was too much now to imagine this ruffled magpie of a Reverend taking David away from his home. She looked hard at the boy standing by her now. He was fine looking lad, she thought to herself. He was not large for his age, but the picture of health nonetheless, with sandy hair and his mother's blue-green eyes. The boy's hands were knobby and always felt cold to the touch, but his smile would warm a room.

When the Torrington church exploded, as if portending the end of the world itself, Agnes knew at once David was an orphan at ten years of age. Standing there in the frigid rain watching the fire burn on the horizon, she'd vowed before God in Heaven to look after the boy until she drew her last breath. Now only four days after the death of the boy's parents, her vow was being challenged by this bedraggled, crow-like stranger.

Panic rose in her throat and choked her words into a ragged staccato, "if the Pinder's farm is sold, David is welcome to stay with me as his godmother and I will see my cottage and field pass to him upon my death." Rather than being moved by the plea, the Reverend appeared to be outwardly annoyed. The panic rose still higher and Agnes now bleated "you keep the money for your congregation, Reverend, and I shall keep the boy."

* * * * *

The novelty of sitting in a carriage drew David's attention momentarily, but now the full weight of his sorrow and confusion flooded once again into his heart. He leapt to his feet and poked his head quickly out the window trying to find his father's farm through the thick fog. But nothing could be seen now save for the dual muddy tracks of the Devon road.

"Sit down, boy," hissed the Reverend Allsap. "Any other boy in the world would be grateful to be put into service of a man such as Captain Sayle, and here you are sulking like a wet cat."

In truth, thought David, he *was* sulking, but he gave himself leave to do so nonetheless. Other boys had lost their parents, no doubt, but David was quite certain his had been the finest ever to walk the earth. And now Goliath and Simon too were lost, sold to the fat brewer.

The boy's shivers amplified with the thought. It was cold in the coach, as David and the Reverend Allsap were its only passengers. There'd not been a day in his life when the wisp of a boy had not shivered in the indifferent Devon air and it felt as though the month of February would freeze him solid.

"You must pray for your soul, David. I see you someday as a man of worth, but not unless you abandon your unholy pride and defiance."

True also that David fiercely resisted going away with the Reverend; he'd clung to Mrs. Cartwright like a drowning lad. But in his mind David was merely negotiating a better deal. Hadn't his father always said never to agree with the first offer? Being put into service was one thing, leaving Torrington quite another. Where in England was this "Bermida" anyway?

"Where is Bermida, Uncle?"

"Reverend, if you please, boy, Reverend!"

"Where is this Bermida then, Reverend?"

"Bermuda is an island, boy, in the sea along the way to the Virginia Colonies. We shall voyage there in a ship part-owned by Captain Sayle himself."

Now this was something new, something that might slant the bargain.

"To sea, then?" asked David.

The Reverend turned again from the carriage window and gazed directly at the boy as if the lad had sprouted two horns from his head.

"Didn't I just tell you Bermuda was in the middle of the sea? You are trying my patience before God Almighty, David, but I shall not indulge your vexatious nature. You shall sit there in silence until we reach the inn and you shall pray for temperance of your unruly soul."

Silence it was then, but as for temperance of soul, thought David, if his uncle would not talk of Bermuda, perhaps the innkeeper or a guest would answer the quickly growing number of questions amassing in his mind." Would there be Indians? Was there a river to fish? Would there be boys of his age? Were there wild animals? Upon a sudden thought, he snapped his head forward into a reverent bow and clapped his hands before him in silent prayer: "Please God, let it be warm on Bermuda Island." The Reverend Allsap could scarcely believe his eyes. The boy certainly did look as if he were prostrate before the Lord, his small soul in the balance. Perhaps, there was hope.

* * * * *

If only the Reverend would allow him to stand in the carriage, thought David. The seemingly endless days sitting upon carriage benches since they left Devon for Hampshire had worn upon his woefully thin rear end. To relieve the pain he imagined himself upon the broad muscled back of Goliath. But to no avail. If anything, the image merely shifted the pain to his heart, which seemed to be an altogether worse state of affairs.

That night they would reach the fortress city of Portsmouth and David was told by the last night's innkeeper there would be great warships to see in the harbor. The ship he and the Reverend would board called the William was also moored somewhere within sight of the city.

"Will we walk upon the fort then, Reverend?"

9

Silence.

"Will we go up to the great fort, Reverend Uncle?"

Silence.

"Shall we eat a meat pie broad as your hat and fat as a town-rat Reverend?"

Nothing

The Reverend Allsap was deep in important thoughts of an ecclesiastical and political nature. How things had changed since he'd met Captain Sayle in Cambridge two years prior! Upon their acquaintance, the Reverend Allsap was instantly smitten by the great man. By then, the Captain was a dedicated and influential member of a stalwart Independent congregation in Bermuda, and the congregation looked to Sayle as its best hope for survival. To Sayle's increasing dismay, members of the congregation continued to suffer insult and persecution from the Royalist population, all of whom recognized and belonged to the official Church of England. Sayle, at that time Governor of Bermuda, sailed to Westminster to petition Cromwell's influence for a Charter over the Bahama Islands. He resolved with several partners to establish a plantation colony in the unclaimed archipelago and populate the colony with likeminded brethren. Sayle and his partners commissioned the refitting of a merchantman ship, the *William*, while a six ton shallow draft boat would be built in Bermuda. If the Reverend were willing, offered Captain Sayle, after the *William*'s refitting was completed Allsap was welcome to sail aboard her to Bermuda and serve the growing congregation. "Come join our Adventurers, Reverend," exclaimed the animated Captain, "no doubt you shall suffer hardship and danger, but yea shall have the blessing and support of our Lord and Savior."

The Reverend Allsap, generally taciturn by nature, could hardly contain his excitement at his opportunity to inform Captain Sayle and Bermuda's Independent congregations that flight into the Caribbean wilderness was no longer necessary. Cromwell's army and the victory of General Fairfax at Torrington foretold the inevitable end of King Charles. The strangle hold of his Bishops had since relaxed. The Westminster Assembly, comprised of Church of England clergy who'd finally been maneuvered into hearing out the demands of the Reformers, was called to order in 1643. Now after seemingly interminable debate, the Assembly had produced the Westminster Confessions of Faith.

The Reverend clutched a copy of the Confessions against his chest as the carriage rattled down the Portsmouth cobblestones. While he understood Sayle and his Independent congregation would likely reject certain articulations of the theological position, the Confessions, now adopted as guiding dogma, represented a great leap forward for the Presbyteriate. The tide of persecution against the reformers in Bermuda would surely wane in due course, just as it had in England.

Allsap pictured himself in his mind's eye gallantly stepping off the *William* and immediately handing Captain Sayle the blessed Confessions. He imagined the Captain's relief and his gratefulness that good Reverend Allsap should bring such deliverance. He, Allsap, would of course eschew any credit and instead quietly mutter a demure reference to the grace of God.

Rather than ply the dangerous and uncharted waters of the Caribbean Sea, the *William* would ply a civilized trade between Sayle's Bermuda home and England. The financial and ecclesiastical survival of the congregation would be assured.

* * * * *

No pain is greater to a small boy like David Samuel Pinder than to be burdened with a prolonged wait. His uncle kept him a virtual prisoner in the rectory where they were housed. "Captain Butler" was often mentioned as the source of the endless delay. Butler was to sail the *William* to Bermuda, but he appeared to David to be in no particular hurry to do so. It was now the 20th day of March.

In Portsmouth, David's formal education under the tutelage of his uncle began, the chief purpose being the daunting transformation of boy into a good Christian. Endless hours bent over poorly printed "short" and "long" catechisms were followed by more sermons than a boy his age could count. The Reverend's endless questions bore into David's increasingly desperate mind. Anything would be better than sitting in this cold and unforgiving rectory surrounded by irritable reverends reeking of boiled cabbage. Even if the alternative was religious torture upon a cold and unforgiving sea, at least he would be traveling towards an earthly destination of some sort, rather than striving for a heavenly salvation impossible for the boy to imagine.

* * * * *

St. George's Bay, Bermuda, 20 March, 1646

A young maidservant showed Captain Sayle into the parlor, begged him take a seat, then disappeared in search of Sayle's friend and investor, William Rener. The Captain sat nervously staring at his carefully polished boots. The shutters were open and it was a bright day, but he paid no attention to the luxuriant Bermuda landscape outside.

He was thankful, at least, that all but one of his financial backers was over 3,000 miles away in England. He'd not seen Rener since the his ship, *Triumph*, sailed into port without her sister ship named *Devotion*.

The two vessels were sent from Bermuda in search of an island group south of a place the French called Abaco. In particular the expedition sought to survey an island sometimes called Cigatoo, where it was hoped the environs were suitable for settlement. The French, under the reign of Louis XIII, laid claim to three other strategic islands somewhere to the south of Cigatoo named Inagua, Mariguana and Gilatur, so Sayle believed Cigatoo to be the best bet for him and his shareholders. But then *Triumph* returned paradoxically without success and *Devotion*, having not been seen since the 26th day of February, was presumed to have foundered in a terrible four-day storm blown in from the north.

Rener entered the room and Captain Sayle raised his 55 year old frame from its sitting position into a posture Sayle hoped was at once deferential and determined. The *William* had probably by now set sail from Portsmouth. Given the failure of the expeditionary venture, it seemed doubtful Rener and Sayle would be able to recruit a sufficient number of settlers willing to emigrate to a completely unknown destination. It was true that members of the congregation, including Sayle himself, were exhausted by the constant mockery, threats and insults of the majority of islanders, Royalists and devout members of the Church of England. But Sayle feared that the hostile environment, in and of itself, might be insufficient motivation to flee the relative comforts of Bermuda. He must now, he thought to

12

himself, fire the imaginations of his prospective émigrés not so much on the promise of prosperity, but on the ideal of freedom – that no other place on earth would allow for the worship of the Creator in a way the congregation desired.

"I've just written to John Winthrop in the Massachusetts Colony of the failure of our expedition, Captain Sayle."

Rener's face betrayed neither anger nor disappointment. He appeared to Sayle to be unmoved by the bad news now threatening their venture. Sayle's sense of foreboding eased for the first time in days.

"I hope and expect that upon receipt of my letter, Winthrop will consider means through which our congregation might settle in New England."

Sayle's heart immediately sank at the words and he held his breath, anxious that Rener's position, now apparently adverse, would worsen.

"Captain, your charter for a plantation in the Bahamas Islands seems as yet to be of little value, wouldn't you agree?"

Sayle, resisted the impulse to lean back on his heels and instead edged forward towards Rener.

"Sir", Sayle began, "those who've settled in Barbados have prospered greatly and I should expect our venture on the isle of Cigatoo shall yield equal prospects."

Rener replied without pause, "Captain Sayle, no one of our party has yet laid eyes on Cigatoo and I understand Barbados is a great distance from there."

Sayle paused, paralyzed for a moment by the realization he was losing, or had perhaps already lost, Rener's support. "Freedom," he again thought to himself.

Then on impulse, the Captain suddenly stepped forward and placed his hand on Rener's shoulder, "William, our company shall find the island of Cigatoo and God shall provide for us there. But before then, even before I take leave of you this day, the island of Cigatoo shall be called Eleutheria."

William Rener was quiet for several long moments, Sayle's hand still on his shoulder. Then softly, almost in a whisper, "Well Captain, it has been many years since I was a boy struggling to unravel the Old Testament in the Greek language. But I well know the word for freedom. The next letter I write to Winthrop will be news of your departure with a full company of settlers bound for Eleutheria."

Sayle exhaled and squeezed Rener's shoulder, "and the next letter

I write to you, dear William, shall be brought to you aboard your namesake along with a very fine cargo we shall produce in our new settlement."

3   TO BERMUDA

July 15, 1610, excerpt from a letter written by Sea Venture survivor, William Strachey, to an anonymous recipient.

The shore and bays round about, when we landed first, afforded great store of fish, and that of divers kinds and good, but it should seem that our fires, which we maintained on the shore's side, drave them from us, so as we were in some want until we had made a flat-bottom gondola of cedar, with which we put off farther into the sea, and then daily hooked great store of many kinds, as excellent Mirandafish, salmon peal, bonitos, sting ray, cabally, snappers, hogfish, sharks, dogfish, pilchards, mullets, and rockfish, of which be divers kinds. And of these our governor dried and salted, and barreling them up, brought to sea five hundred; for he had procured salt to be made with some brine, which happily was preserved, and once having made a little quantity, he kept three or four pots boiling and two or three men attending nothing else in an house (some little distance from his bay) set up on purpose for the same work.

Likewise in Frobisher's building bay we had a large seine, or trammel net, which our governor caused to be made of the deer toils (which we were to carry to Virginia) by drawing the masts more straight and narrow with rope yarn, and which reached from one side of the dock to the other, with which (I may boldly say) we have taken five thousand of small and great fish at one haul: as pilchards, breams, mullets, rockfish, etc., and other kinds for which we have no names. We have taken also from under the broken rocks crevises oftentimes greater than any of our best English lobsters, and likewise abundance of crabs, oysters, and whelks. True it is, for fish in every cove and creek we found snails and skulls in that abundance as I think no island in the world may have greater store or better fish. For they, sucking of the very water which descendeth from the high hills, mingled with juice and verdure of the palms, cedars, and other sweet woods (which likewise make the herbs, roots, and weeds sweet which grow about the banks), become thereby both fat and *wholesome; as must those fish needs be gross, slimy, and corrupt the blood which feed in fens, marshes, ditches, muddy pools, and near unto places where much filth is daily cast forth.*

Unscaled fishes, such as Junius calleth mollis pisces, as tenches, eel, or lampreys, and such feculent and dangerous snakes, we never saw any, nor may any river be envenomed with them (I pray God) where I come. I forbear to speak what a sort of whales we have seen hard aboard the shore, followed sometime by the swordfish and the thresher, the sport whereof was not unpleasant, the swordfish with his sharp and needle fin pricking him into the belly, when he would sink and fall into the sea; and when he startled upward from his wounds, the thresher with his large fins (like flails) beating him above water. The examples whereof gives us (saith Oviedus) to understand that in the selfsame peril and danger do men live in this mortal life, wherein is no certain security neither in high estate nor low.

* * * * *

The twenty-first morning of March in Portsmouth England was brisk and clear, the wind blowing with stubborn winter determination from the northeast, although it was the first day of spring. Captain Nate Butler finally arrived aboard the *William* where he'd inspected and approved the stowage of cargo and provisions for the voyage to Bermuda. He was in a foul mood to see much of the space aboard the merchantman, which ordinarily would be used for cargo, converted into space that could be occupied by passengers. It had been difficult, therefore, to secure everything that would be offloaded at their destination. In order adequately to protect the cargo, he'd been forced to use much more line than he would have liked , and the ship's carpenter was still busy fashioning chocks.

At midday, Butler sent word to Reverend Allsap that they would sail upon the outgoing tide early the next morning. The ever-irascible young captain had been delayed in his arrival at Portsmouth by a dispute over wages related to his last commission in Southampton. He was now anxious to be underway to Bermuda and doubly anxious to make for the Caribbean. Unlike so many of those men who toiled upon the sea at the beck and call of ship owners, shareholders and, God forbid, passengers, Butler had long set his mind upon a coarser ambition. He would be a rich man by God or the devil. "Land is wealth without reproach," he thought, and in the Bahama Islands he'd have plenty of it.

Three years had passed since Butler read Sayle's broadsheet published in London. Little matter to Butler that Sayle's investors appeared to be of the religious sort. What mattered was word that the man had been granted a Charter, reportedly aided by the same earl who had helped Winthrop establish his colony in Massachusetts. What mattered was the fact that Sayle had been able to raise sufficient capital to buy ships and provisions. If it were Sayle's objective to populate the new colony with religious Independents, very well, let them waste time in church while Butler built his fortune. He would say nothing to dampen the spirit of the zealots; it was because of their fervor for freedom of religious practice that the whole venture had gotten off the ground in the first place. Butler thought to himself, "best not to say anything about the turn of events here in England in favor of the Reformers." He would keep his mouth shut until the island of Cigatoo was on the horizon.

"Jackson," roared Butler. "You'll see to the passengers throughout this voyage. I don't care to speak a damned word to them, and you make sure they stay well out of the way. Do you understand?"

"That I'll do, Captain. You'll not be bothered by the Reverend and the other passenger is a mere boy, sir."

Benjamin Jackson had served many captains on many seas, and he had a very bad premonition about this one.

"*Boy*," replied Butler, is another name for trouble, Mr. Jackson. I don't want to see that little shoat unless he's tied to your leg, understand? And keep 'em well clear of my quarters. Have Cook bring 'em their meals. The mess is no place for either a boy or a reverend."

"Aye, aye, Captain, I'll stow them well forward and away from ya."

* * * * *

David Pinder felt he would jump from his his skin when the Reverend told him they would sail in the morning. He'd remained wakeful most of the night conjuring visions of the sea and of the island of Bermuda, which some called "Somer Island." Now in the early morning gloom he could scarcely contain himself, and he consciously willed his uncle to walk faster as they approached the pier.

There it was, the *William*. If only his father and mother could see this sight, David thought, as he stood stupefied before the gangway.

"David," spat the Reverend, "wipe that grin from your face, boy, or I shall do it for you. Now up you go and I don't want to hear a single word from you."

A grizzled man with a barrel chest and sandy grey hair stepped lively and bowlegged towards the top of the gangway. "My name is Jackson, Reverend, but the world knows me as Fishy Jack. I'm ta look after ya, show ya your quarters and such like."

"How did you come by that name," blurted David.

It had been only a moment since his uncle sternly warned him against speaking, but the sailor's announcement of such a colorful name seemed to David grounds for deviation, although the Reverend's icy gaze indicated otherwise.

"Well, that's a story for another time, boy. What would your own name be?"

"His name is David Samuel Pinder and I am his uncle and ward, Reverend Allsap."

"You don't say?" offered Jackson, I know a Pinder on the island, Timothie Pinder is his name. Might be kin, ya know. Never can tell."

"I wouldn't know," replied the Reverend, I barely knew the boy's father, killed at Torrington along with my sister."

"Well I'm awful grieved to hear that, Davey," said the sailor, bending down to the boy's level. "But there are many on the island of Bermuda who will welcome ya."

Jackson showed the two to their quarters under the forward ladder. There would be air aplenty explained the sailor, which the two might appreciate once the ship entered warmer climes. Pointing at a narrow berth with two rolled blankets he advised "that'll be yours to have for the voyage, Reverend, and the chest below. You'll find a pitcher and bowl in there, as I understand cleanliness to be of importance to fellas of the cloth such as yerself."

"The accommodations shall be more than adequate, sir. I am accustomed to the simple life and therefore feel assured life at sea shall strongly agree with me," replied the Reverend.

Jackson could feel the boy's eyes upon him and when he turned to look, David appeared bursting to say something.

"What is it Davey? Ya look like ya might be standing on hot coals."

Before the Reverend could stifle the boy's question it was out, "but where shall I sleep, Mr. Fishy?"

"Ah, I nearly forgot, didn't I, lad? You'll sleep same as the crew, in this hammock, see?" As he spoke, Jackson reached aloft and unfurled a canvas hammock from its starboard hook and stretched it to the other. "Let me see ya climb aboard."

With some instructions and the aid of an overturned keg fetched from the galley, David soon had the mount and dismount mastered and was reveling in the exercise until the Reverend's patience wore too thin. Then the sounds of great activity above deck signaled the beginning of their voyage and David was off like a nimble cat up the ladder.

"Wait for me right there Davey, I'll show ya where you and the Reverend can sit forward and not git your heads staved."

With the tide now running swiftly out to sea, the *William* glided quietly from Portsmouth harbor. Less than twenty-four hours later, on the 22nd day of the March, news came to Portsmouth of a slaughter at Stow-on-the-Wold and the surrender of the commander of the Royalist troops, Lord Astley. The war was now finally and unquestionably grinding to its bitter and pointless end. A new day had dawned for those who did not sanction the Church of England. King Charles could do nothing about it.

* * * * *

"Yer uncle may in fact be a man for the simple life, Davey, but I've n'er seen a man take so badly to the sea. Five days now without food and I swear if he heaves any harder he'll turn inside-out."

David nodded in agreement. The only opportunity afforded to the boy to go on deck was to empty the wash basin of bile and saliva vomited by the Reverend every twenty minutes or so, the first time into the wind, every other time to leeward. David's first lesson at sea.

"He's asleep now, Davey, and the way t'ings went for him last night I shouldn't t'ink he'd be wakin' up any time soon. Come on deck. Ya can't stay below the whole voyage. We're on a fine reach to the southwest now with a lively following sea. A boy like you ought to go about in the air."

Once on deck, David's sadness and burden seemed lighter at last. The sea was the deepest blue he'd ever seen and it made the blue sky above look shallow and rather shabby. The wind was cold, but the sun warmed his bones for the first time in a week. Jackson pointed forward to several canvas bales and said, "There's a fine spot for ya Davey, right there in the sunshine and outa the wind for the most. I'll join ya 'til the mate calls my watch. You sit down there now, no roamin' about just yet, and I'll be right back."

It was the grandest bed he'd ever laid upon, David thought to himself as he looked up through the rigging, which seemed to him an incomprehensible puzzle. How could men construct such a confounding thing? He used to be amazed at the manner in which his father's droving tack came together and allowed almost unbelievably heavy loads to be pulled by Goliath and Simon. But this ship was something he could not have dreamed up.

Jackson returned, loping confidently along the deck as if it were dry land. He sat down next to the boy and opened the neck of a sea bag.

"I'll just work a bit, Davey, if ya don't mind. Plenty of time to work at sea, away from the bustle of shore."

He tilted the open bag towards David allowing him to look inside.

"Is it hair, Fishy Jack?"

"Aye that it is, boy, horse tail", said Jackson, "and here is what I make of it."

He drew out from the bag a spindle wrapped with finely woven line, shining in the sun.

"This here, Davey, is the finest line for fetching up fish there ever was. Horsetails being somewhat rare as they are in Bermuda, I always do some 'collecting' in English ports."

"So your name then," asked Davey, "it's because you make that line to catch fish?"

"Well, indirectly, I suppose. The story is a bit more complicated, but I'll tell it if ya want to hear."

David nodded so vigorously it put the image of a pigeon into Jackson's mind.

"Alright, Davey, and I just might've run across a sea name for you as well. The name ya have ashore is rarely the name ya have at sea. You were David Samuel Pinder when ya stepped aboard the *William*, but now me and the crew'll be calling ya Pigeon Davey and there won't be any argument of the point. Rule of the sea, ya might say."

Now the nodding gave way to a smile and the boy asked, "will you tell the story or not?"

"Fine, it's not a bad one if I do say so myself," and he began.

"Far as I know, Pigeon, I was the first Englishman ever to walk upon the island of Bermuda, and then only because I could swim like a porpoise in my youth. Ya see, I'd shipped aboard the *Sea Venture* in the year 1609 under Captain Somers. The ship was the pride of the Virginia Company, don't ya know, and I was the luckiest man alive. I was only nineteen years old and the third officer. We were loaded with provisions and settlers for the new colony of Jamestown, in Virginia its ownself. Well, the fleet was caught in a storm, and the *Sea Venture*, sorely loaded she was, began to founder and we were vastly separated from the flotilla. I come to find out a year later another ship among us, the *Catch*, perished in the same cruel storm that blowed *Sea Venture* off course and poured half the sea into her bilges."

Jackson paused then, apparently gazing back into the past.

"When we spotted reefs to the eastern end of an island, Captain Somers gave the only order with a chance of saving anyone's life. We ran the ship as fast as she'd go upon the reef, all of us fair believin' she'd go to pieces, but at least we'd have a chance at shore."

Jackson exhaled deeply and paused again.

"Did she, Fishy Jack? Go to pieces?"

"Nay, not as ya might imagine. There was quite a commotion on deck, I suppose mostly disbelief, then the old man ordered her pulled higher up upon the rocks. Her stern was still heavin' a bit in the break and if she slid backwards, down to the bottom it would be. Well now, it's one thing to give such an order, it's another to carry it out. By and by, I was sent over the side to swim a line ashore. Then the crew fastened all the ship's hawsers together and I used the first line and the tackle I'd swum ashore to pull the monster to my feet."

Spellbound, David once again started nodding, pigeon style.

"Well then come ashore Captain Somers, and the ship's chippy, Forbisher was his name, and the first mate as well."

"What's a chippy?"

"Ah well, a chippy is what a carpenter is called at sea." Jackson shook his head as a thought crossed his mind. "Our John Forbisher was the finest chippy I ever did see. Could build anything out of nothin."

The old sailor stopped weaving his fishing line and dropped the spool back into its bag.

"To shorten things a bit, Davey, we got her high and dry, high enough to see the great damage done to her poor hull. And there we were, all one hundred and fifty of us, shipwracked. Oh, and one dog as well."

"A dog!" exclaimed David.

"Aye, the finest ratter ever ta terrify the species. His name was Toothy Pete and by God he had a powerful dislike of vermin. Within an hour aboard *Sea Venture*, he'd sent a barrelful of ship-rats to their Maker. He spent the rest of the voyage in awful funk until the ship's sail maker fashioned him a toy rat. Well . . . the first of many toy rats, as Toothy was partial to disembowelment."

"So is Bermuda yours then, Fishy?"

"What on earth do ya mean by dat, boy?"

"Well, you were the first one there, you said."

"Ah, well, you might think that such an act would secure a man a parcel o' land, but I'm afraid that's not how it works. No, before it became known as Bermuda, the island was named after Captain Somers, the 'Somers Islands' ya see. All sorts of papers and charters and contracts and whatnot, but in the end it's Bermuda and a simple sailor like me will never own a blade of grass on the island."

"But you live there now."

"Aye, I surely do. And if you want to hear the rest of the story you'll have to try harder to listen."

The boy's pigeon-like nods affirmed his assent and Jackson continued.

"Alright now Davey, let me tell ya a bit about what it'was like to be shipwracked. We were able to bring ashore all of the provisions, every barrel, every crate, every cask, every bag, every morsel of food. But it wouldn't last nearly long enough for us to get off the island. Besides, the provisions we had aboard *Sea Venture* were meant for the settlers waiting in Jamestown. If we were ever to get off the wee island, the only t'ing for us to do was take apart the *Sea Venture*, and haul every piece of her ashore, as it was the Captain's intent that we should build a new ship. *Two* ships as a matter of fact, *Patience* and *Deliverance*. Every able-bodied man in the party set to work building the vessels exceptin' myself."

"Were you hurt then, Fishy?"

"Nay, as it so happened, I was the only fella amongst the mob who knew anything about fishing, and it was plain to see that eatin' fish would be the only way to save the provisions we'd need to make the voyage to Jamestown. There was hogs on the island, but Somers was awful determined that they should be saved and eaten on the voyage and in the colony. As it turned out, them pigs got their revenge on the fine Captain. Upon his return to Bermuda, he died of eatin' tainted pork, don't ya know! They pickled him in a barrel and sent him back to England. But not before they buried his heart on Bermuda. Oddest thing I ever seen done."

David gulped hard, then commenced again nodding, bird-like.

"Anyhow, day and night, all I did for the next forty-two weeks was fish, think about fishing, and then fish again. I tell ya now, the only real experience I'd ever had fishin' was throwin' a line off the transom at sea. Now there I was trying to puzzle out how to make nets and where to put them, what that fish yonder liked to eat and what he didn't like, how close you could get to that kind of fish and how far you had to stay away from t'other. I tried everything. I even had the smithy make me a couple small harpoons, and by God if I didn't get clever about spearin' the buggers out on the reef. I'd go under the sea after them if I had to. I'd take a fish right out of a shark's mouth if it meant another meal for me and Toothy. Oh, forgot to tell ya, Toothy became me first mate, as he wouldn't believe for a moment there was not a rat to be found aboard the new ships the men were building. He came close to drivin' Chippy Forbisher mad, he did."

"And Toothy didn't mind the fish?"

"Well I can't say as he was cordial. But I don't t'ink he took the same kind of pleasure in bitin' the head off a fish as he did shaking the life out of a rat."

"Almost time for my watch, and look, I've not woven a single inch of line. I'll give ya the end of the story instead."

"Well, it come to pass that *Patience* and *Deliverance* were wholly built and floated. The Captain had the lads haul two cannon upon the hill over the water and set to buildin' a small fort. By then, the folks inclined to farmin' had succeeded in assemblin' quite a stockpile of stores from the island itself, so the ships and the fort were well provisioned. And then a funny t'ing happened, Pigeon. When the Captain asked for volunteers to stay behind on the island to man the fort and generally strut about like we owned the place, I raised my hand. Bein' third mate under Captain Somers was the best t'ing ever happened to me, and there I was mad in love for that small island. I been there ever since, thirty-seven years."

David looked up from his feet into Jackson's face, "and the company or the crown, or whoever, never gave you any land?"

"No, as I said before, they don't hand out land to poor sailors, even the ones who know how to fish."

"One more bit of the story for ya, my old friend Pigeon Davey. Somers got *Patience* and *Deliverance* to Jamestown well enough, but they found a terrible state of affairs. There'd been starvin' times in the settlement, terrible starvin' times. Only sixty folk remained of the five hundred that landed there the year before. That news came as an awful burden to me when I hear'd it told. There we were on Bermuda 'tinkin' we were sorely sufferin' in the wilds. But by the grace o' God we lived like kings compared to those poor pilgrims in Jamestown."

It had been the best day David passed in a long while and the loss of his parents eased ever so slightly. Now back in his quarters, the boy dipped a piece of flannel into the water cask and handed it to the Reverend.

"Try to put the corner of it into your mouth, Reverend, maybe the water will stay down if you take it in real slow like."

The Reverend's throat was so dry he could not respond, and his hand too shaky to grasp the rag. David dipped it again in the cask and placed the lightly twisted corner in the Reverends mouth. His uncle closed his eyes and groaned, then seemed to slip back into his stupor.

* * * * *

On the eighteenth morning aboard the *William*, David was drawn awake by the sound of his uncle's hoarse voice below the hammock.

"What day is it boy?"

"It's Sunday, Reverend."

"Then fetch my hat, my shoes as well. And my bible from the chest. Oh, and also, the Westminster Confessions of Faith, those are the papers wrapped with the ribbon, boy. The sermon cannot wait."

"What sermon, Uncle?"

"Don't start with me, boy. I am prepared. I am always prepared. God's word is always fresh in my mind. This Sunday is no different."

"But we are at sea, Reverend."

"Just leave me at once, David, or I won't stop myself tearing the hide from your back! Out!"

David, shaken by the sudden and strange arousal of the Reverend after so many days of sleep and groaning, scampered up the ladder onto the deck. He went forward to the space Jackson had designated for their meetings and sat down, perplexed. The sun was rising quickly in the east, but it was still chilly on deck and the boy wished he'd pulled on his coat.

Jackson step on deck from the aft ladder and, seeing David forward, approached along the port rail.

"Well if it isn't Pigeon Davey, out for peck around the foremast."

"The Reverend requested as much, Fishy."

Jackson pulled his chin inward rapidly and opened his eyes wide, "the Reverend is speaking is he?"

"Yes, says he's a sermon to give."

Just then a cry came forward from the helmsman, "Fishy! Watch that man!"

Jackson and David turned in time to see the Reverend step up on the rail as if to a pulpit. "Be seated" he said just as he stepped into the air and was gone.

"God in Heaven," whispered Jackson, as he looked over the side and into the waves below. Nothing could be seen but the Reverend's hat, afloat like a toy ship, and a packet wrapped with a ribbon, which soon sank out of sight.

David stood with his mouth open at the rail and reached for Jackson's hand.

"As God is my witness, Davey, I don't know what to tell ya."

4   ST. GEORGE'S BAY

July 15, 1610, excerpt from a letter written by *Sea Venture* survivor, William Strachey, to an anonymous recipient.

It is like enough that the commodities of the other western islands would prosper there, as vines, lemons, oranges, and sugar canes. Our governor made trial of the latter and buried some two or three in the garden mold, which were reserved in the wreck amongst many which we carried to plant here in Virginia, and they began to grow, but the hogs, breaking in, both rooted them up and ate them. There is not through the whole islands either champaign ground, valleys, or fresh rivers. They are full of shaws of goodly cedar, fairer than ours here of Virginia, the berries whereof, our men seething, straining, and letting stand some three or four days, made a kind of pleasant drink. These berries are of the same bigness and color of Corinths, full of little stones, and very restringent or hard-building. Peter Martyr saith that at Alexandria in Egypt there is a kind of cedar which the Jews dwelling there affirm to be the cedars of Libanus, which bear old fruit and new all the year, being a kind of apple which taste like prunes. But then neither those there in the Bermudas nor ours here in Virginia are of that happy kind.

Likewise there grow great store of palm trees, not the right Indian palms such as in San Juan, Puerto Rico, are called cocos and are there full of small fruits like almonds (of the bigness of the grains in pomegranates), nor of those kind of palms which bears dates, but a kind of simerons or wild palms, in growth, fashion, leaves, and branches resembling those true palms. For the tree is high and straight, sappy and spongious, unfirm for any use, no branches but in the uppermost part thereof; and in the top grow leaves about the head of it (the most inmost part whereof they call palmetto, and it is the heart and pith of the same trunk, so white and thin as it will peel off into pleats as smooth and delicate as white satin into twenty folds, in which a man may write as in paper), where they spread and fall downward about the tree like an overblown rose, or saffron flower, not early gathered. So broad are the leaves as an Italian umbrella, a man may well defend his whole body under one of them from the greatest storm rain that falls; for they being stiff and smooth, as if so many flags were knit together, the rain easily slideth off. We oftentimes found growing to these leaves many silkworms involved therein, like those small worms which Acosta writeth of, which grew in the leaves of the tuna tree, of which, being dried, the Indians make their cochineal so precious and merchantable. With these leaves we thatched our cabins, and roasting the palmetto or soft top thereof, they had a taste like fried melons, and being sod, they eat like cabbages, but not so offensively thankful to the stomach. Many an ancient burgher was therefore heaved at and fell, not for his place, but for his head. For our common people, whose bellies never had ears, made no breach of charity in their hot bloods and tall stomachs to murder thousands of them. They bear a kind of berry, black and round, as big as a damson, which about December were ripe and luscious; being scalded whilst they are green, they eat like bullaces. These trees shed their leaves in the winter months, as withered or burnt with the cold blasts of the north wind, especially those that grow to the seaward; and in March there burgeon new in their room, fresh and tender.

* * * *

David stood at the rail transfixed by St. George's bay, bathed in the April sunshine. The scene appeared like nothing he'd been able to imagine of Bermuda. Nothing, he thought to himself, could possibly be so beautiful. And it was warm.

Jackson, stood by the boy and spoke for the first time since they'd nosed into the harbor.

"Well Pigeon Davey, what do ya think of Fishy Jack's wee island?"

David looked Jackson square in the eye, but could find no words.

"I feel the same way, boy," said the old sailor.

"Jackson! Jackson!" bellowed Captain Butler.

The sailor walked aft to the Captain.

"You'll take the boy ashore. Are you certain he is to be placed in service to Captain Sayle?"

"It's what the Reverend told me his self, Captain."

"Then deliver him to Sayle before ya set foot in your own cottage, do ya hear?"

"Ay Captain, t'was my intent."

Jackson walked aft again and down the ladder with the boy.

"Well Pigeon, have you gathered your belongins?"

"I have, Fishy, and the Reverend's as well."

"Aye, that's a good 'ting boy. Then let's get ashore."

David stepped off the *William* onto the waterfront paving stones and into a thick cloud of uncertainty. On the ship, there'd been a singular objective, the constant movement towards a specific port of call. Here in the Somer Islands, in 'Bermuda', David's purpose was far from clear. His uncle had placed him into the service of Captain Sayle, but what that entailed David could not imagine. He could read and write passably well, but he had no other skills to speak of. In another month, he'd be eleven years old, not nearly old enough to understand fully what a fickle place the world could be and how far a man could get blown off course.

Not a hundred paces down the waterfront David suddenly stopped and declared to Jackson, "The island is moving, Fishy!"

Jackson smiled and chuckled softly, "Didn't I tell ya, Davey? This little part of the Somer Isles, St. George's Bay, is a floatin' island. You'll get accustomed to her rollin' just as ya did aboard the *William*, ridin' along the waves."

David looked up at Jackson, awestruck, then followed behind the man as he picked up the pace again, heading for the small hillock to the north. Jackson delighted in showing the boy all the evidence of change the waterfront settlement had experienced in the thirty-seven years he'd called the place home.

"Can ya still feel the island movin', Davey?"

"Only a little bit now. What's it like in a storm, Fishy? Do you have to lash things down as we did on the *William*?"

"Now, Pigeon, I've been havin' a bit of fun with ya, see? The island's not actually movin', it's just ya haven't got yer land legs yet. Yer sea legs is tellin' ya that ye'r still aboard the *William*. T'ings will settle down soon enough and ye'll see these Bermuda islands are as solid a place as any."

David was incredulous, but said nothing in response to Jackson's theory regarding two pairs of legs. The boy and the old sailor now approached a fine whitewashed cottage built into the side of the hill with a splendid view down to the harbor. The water below was a stunning turquoise and the fresh smell of cedar trees wafted through the air as the sun rose higher.

"Fairly sure this is the cottage where Captain Sayle berths when he's in St. George's Parrish. He owns a grander home in Smyth's Parrish further west. Run up to the door there boy and give 'er a thump."

David trotted ahead and knocked several times while Jackson caught up. In the moments before the door opened, Jackson surveyed his feelings about leaving the orphaned boy with a man older even than Jackson himself. He'd never met Sayle's wife, Margery, nor any of their three grown sons. It was common knowledge on the island that Sayle was in possession of a Charter for the settlement of a new colony somewhere south, and that Sayle would lead the settlement himself. Where did that put Davey, he wondered?

"Well, Pigeon, I suppose Captain Sayle, bein' of a pious nature, will likely put ya to work studyin' upon the bible and such. You'll be a right scholar before ya know it."

David nodded, but not in the usual excited, bird-like fashion. He looked a bit defeated to Jackson as the door to the cottage scraped open. Captain Sayle gazed directly at Jackson with a look of recognition on his face.

"I know you, don't I?" Sayle questioned the sailor.

Sayle was a compact and lithe man, dressed all in reverent black with a broad white collar. His complexion was sallow for a man of sea and his dark eyes were deep-set on either side of his sharp nose.

"Aye, Captain, I'm Fishy Jack, wot they call me. Benjamin Jackson my given name."

"Ah Jackson, yes, of course I recognize the longest resident of this colony! I'm pleased to see you Mr. Jackson. Did ya not come aboard the *William*?"

"That I did, Captain, she's just now in the harbor, ye can see her plainly from here," he pointed.

"Ah yes, excellent, excellent. Following the loss of the *Devotion* I've been on edge, you see, but God has delivered the *William* safe and sound. I'm embarrassed by my trepidation, but there you have it."

Sayle now seemed to notice the boy for the first time, standing in Jackson's shadow.

"Well, come in, the both of you gentlemen. I'll have the girl fetch a pot of tea. Have you tried the beverage, Jackson? I'm smitten myself. Can't imagine life without it now."

"No sir, Captain, I've not tasted the brew myself. Seen it advertised in an apothecary back in Portsmouth, but didn't partake. I don't know if the same is true for Davey here," said Jackson, turning to the boy.

David shook his head silently, feeling a bit overwhelmed to have finally, after so many miles, arrived at the place he and his uncle set out for on a cold day in Devon.

"Did ya take aboard a Reverend Allsap, Mr. Jackson? I'm expecting him."

"Yes, Captain, we took the Reverend aboard in Portsmouth on the 21st day of March."

"Fine, and is he ashore now?"

"Well no, Captain. Ya see, the Reverend passed away on the voyage across, I'm sorry to tell ya."

"Oh my word," gasped Sayle, "how did he pass then Jackson?"

"Well sir, he. . . well he'd come upon the deck to give a sermon, ya see. And well . . ." Jackson forged quickly ahead, "he went o're board and was lost."

"Dear Lord bless his departed soul," whispered Captain Sayle "High seas then?"

"Aye, well, yes sir, for him terrible fierce, sir."

"You've brought tragic news, indeed, Jackson. I shall see to it the Reverend has a fine service and remembrance at the next meeting of our congregation. Can ya tell me what was done at sea, Jackson, were there words spoken?"

"Well, no sir, not as such. Ya see, Captain Butler . . . that is to say, no sir, no service at the time, sir."

David shuffled nervously by Jackson's side. He wondered if Captain Sayle held Fishy responsible for the manner in which the Reverend met his irreverent end? The boy grappled as hard as anyone with piousness, and had thought it right at the time to read something from the Book. However, Fishy Jack reported to David that Captain Butler was not enthusiastic on the idea, and the watch proceeded as scheduled. The matter was dropped.

Pointing now at David, Jackson continued.

"This here, Captain, is the Reverend's nephew David Pinder, ready now to be placed into service for yea."

"Service?"

"Well yes sir, as you and the Revered agreed."

"But I had no idea until today the boy even existed. The Reverend told you this? That the boy would be placed into my service?"

"Yes sir, Captain, he did just that. Is it not yer understanding then?"

"Not at all, Mr. Jackson. I'm afraid I'm off balance here. I haven't a clue what the Reverend Allsap had in mind, but I'm in no position to take on a small boy. I've a great task at hand putting my decks in order for a new venture."

Jackson felt his face go numb and he was suddenly washed with compassion for the boy standing by his side fighting back tears. To Jackson, things always seemed to move in inexplicable directions while ashore. Unlike at sea, the winds that moved lives about on dry land could not be read easily and often took a man completely by surprise. He struggled now to find his footing.

"Well, let's see Captain. Let me just t'ink here a minute," Jackson stuttered. "Supposin' I looked after the boy for the most part, taught him my trade while ashore – that is to say, fishing – and you signed on like as his proper ward? Might we not try that arrangement for a while?"

Sayle leaned back in his chair scratching the back of his head. Time seemed to stand nearly still and Jackson took a deep breath weighing the probability Sayle would refuse.

Finally, the Captain raised himself from his chair and spoke. "I reckon, Mr. Jackson, that taking the boy on as legal guardian would be in furtherance of the Lord's work."

Jackson could not prevent the smile from forming on his face. Looking now at the boy, he reached to shake his little hand.

"But you, Jackson, you must keep your end of the bargain, you understand. I and my partners are engaged in a venture that will require all of my time and energy. I intend soon to set sail for Eleutheria and establish a settlement. There are endless preparations to be made, you see, and . . . well, let's leave it at that. You bring the boy here to my house every Sunday, first thing. That day shall be the Lord's and the boy shall be raised an Independent Christian like his uncle, the Reverend Allsap, God rest his soul."

"Aye-aye, sir, you can count on it, sir. You'll see us at your door every Sunday morn rain or shine!" Then in a quieter voice, "Eleutheria, you say?

"Yes, Eleutheria, in the Bahama Islands. The name means freedom, Mr. Jackson."

"Ah, well then, no better place for a settlement, Captain. No better place on earth."

5   A COMPANY OF ADVENTURERS

Walking back down the slope towards the waterfront, David sensed his life had just taken a sharp turn for the better, but he dared not speak such a thing aloud. Orphaned and mismatched with his taciturn uncle, the boy had simply accepted as fact that he would be indentured to Captain Sayle for seven years, as was custom. It never occurred to him that he would be anything but a servant in Bermuda, but now here he was walking toward the wharves with Fishy Jack and a new life as a fisherman. The notion was overwhelming and David could do nothing but walk on in silence as Fishy Jack whistled one of his sea ditties.

"Fishy?"

"Yes boy."

"Where are we going now?"

"I'll tell ya, Davey, since ya want to know. Before I show ya the old Fishy Shack and yer berth, I mean to introduce ya to my little one, my little girl."

David's eyes widened and he darted forward in front of Jackson and came to a stop facing him.

"You never told me all this time!"

"Well, Pigeon, I t'ought it would be a nice surprise for ya, see? Although I wasn't expectin' you two to meet so early like."

The two walked on wordlessly for another few minutes, then Davey spoke up.

"How old would she be then, Fishy?"

"Well now, she's a young t'ing, just turned four while I was away."

From a corner window in a tidy white house set directly along the wharf came a women's shout, "Well, if it isn't Fishy Jack back from another voyage to dirty old England! How many horse tails did you bob this time ya scoundrel? It's a wonder to me how you manage the caper time and time again."

"Good mornin' Mrs. Newbold, tis a pleasure to see you again as well. This here is Pigeon Davey, he'll be bunking with me awhile."

"Hallo there Davey" she called with a wave. "I'll be right out to get a better look at ya."

"That's me landlady, Davy," said Jackson. Her husband, John, has a workshop further down the bay. He makes barrels he do."

Pointing now at a ship being towed into the channel, Jackson explained, "there goes the *Dorset* with the English crew wot sailed with us aboard the *William*. Can you imagine! The Captain of the *Dorset* is a fine man, Davey, but short on patience, I can tell ya. Captain Butler said the man was fit to be tied by our delay out of Portsmouth, but then I don't think Butler much cared. The poor crew never so much as set foot on dry land, and away they go again."

"Well isn't he a little marvel, Fishy!" exclaimed Mrs. Newbold as she burst through her door like a squall over the bow.

She was upon David before he could raise his defenses. She drew him into her grasp like an octopus, inspecting every inch of the unsuspecting boy, prodding, poking, lifting and laughing the whole time.

"Why how did he come to stay with you Fishy, you old coot?"

"A story for another time, Mrs. Newbold."

"Alright, alright. I know who you've come for and I know you don't want to waste any time talkin' to me," she smiled. "Give that little bell by the door a good jingle and she'll come running. She's down with John at the shop."

Jackson bent to lift a little bell, the kind Christmas carolers used on the island, and gave it good shake.

"You'll see, Fishy. She always comes straight away. Such a good girl."

David stood back against the front wall of Mrs. Newbold's home, waiting shyly for the girl's arrival. Aboard the *William*, Fishy volunteered that he'd once been married, but that his wife, Caroline, had died suddenly. The boy remembered the look upon the old sailor's face as he explained further, "the Lord makes a wife particular and special for each man, Davey, but it's a rare thing when the man finds her out there in the wide world. Well, through God's providence Caroline and I ended up on the same small island, though we'd been born in two different countries, I in England and she in Denmark. It would be ungrateful and wicked of me ever to marry another woman after what the Lord done for me."

Just then a nimble white dog, speckled in black with a black cross pattern on its chest came prancing around the western corner of the wharf. The little dog stopped suddenly in its tracks, then like a shot from a musket she was racing towards them. Jackson knelt down on one knee and opened his arms. Mrs. Newborn started to laugh again and clapped her hands to her face. Then the dog leaped like a gazelle and was caught mid-air by Jackson.

There was a frantic tangle of man and dog, wagging tail, lapping tongue and pawing feet. The dog chirped with joy and Jackson, his face smothered by licking, laughed and whirled around like a Dervish. Finally winded, Jackson set the dog down and stroked its silky head against his thigh.

"Pigeon Davey, I'd like ya to make an acquaintance with Toothy Jill. She's the great granddaughter of 'ole Toothy Pete, the fine devil I told ya about when we were at sea."

David extended his hand to the lean, compact little dog, noticing for the first time that she had one pale blue eye and one brown. He smiled as she licked the back of his hand. He was speechless with emotion, thinking how his father would have admired little Jill.

"Well you two drop yer sea bags in the Fishy Shack and we'll fix ya a nice hot meal," said Mrs. Newbold. "I expect to have fresh fish tomorrow," she winked at David, "but we'll have to make due today with mutton."

The tiny dwelling behind the Newbold's house was neat as a pin, but nearly obscured by the nets heaped upon two high crossbars. "Tools of the trade, Pigeon. You'll be familiar soon enough" Jackson quipped as the two ducked through the low door of the diminutive cottage.

"Ya see there, boy" he said pointing to a hammock stowed on a hook hanging from a rafter, "that's where you'll berth 'till we can cypher somethin' a bit more becomin' a man of the world such as yerself."

Jackson threw down his bag on the bunk against the far wall and sat down at the rough carved table by the open window. Toothy Jill rested her pointy chin upon his knee. David looked about the space now, seeing that almost every inch of wall was covered by netting upon which hooks, floats, buoys and all manner of other fishing gear was hung, including two small harpoons that David guessed might be the same as those made by the *Sea Venture*'s smithy. A much larger harpoon rested upright in corner.

"What d'ya 'tink Davey, do ya reckon it suits ya?"

"Why it's grand, Fishy! And Mrs. Newbold cooks for ya?"

"Aye, that she does, and very well I might add. Ya see, the deal is this: I bring the fish in, Mrs. Newbold sells them about town and we split the earnings. I stay in this here castle free of charge, and all mutton bones go to Toothy Jill", he laughed.

* * * * *

No word of Cromwell's success and the growing tolerance of puritans in England reached Captain Sayle's ears. Reverend Allsap's copy of the Confessions of Westminster was at the bottom of the sea, along with the Reverend's earthly hopes and dreams. If anything, earlier news of Civil War had served only to intensify Royalist sentiments among the islanders, most of whom could not imagine threatening the slender vein of support that streatched from their diminutive outpost in the middle of the Atlantic to the mainland.

The English sailors who'd delivered Captain Sayle's refitted merchantman, the *William*, were now aboard the *Dorset*, having shared no news of the world with the island's residents. Captain Butler would not utter any word that might jeopardize his chances of earning his fortune in the Bahama Islands with Captain Sayle's company. No one else on the island save for Jackson knew anything of recent developments in England. And Jackson never spoke of politics or religion, believing the subjects were studded with far too many reefs to navigate successfully. David was too young to understand the complex political landscape and too bereaved to notice in any case. The atmosphere on the island of Bermuda remained unchanged.

* * * * *

Jackson drew himself awake, a bit surprised to find he was not aboard the *William*. It was still dark and early enough that the determined and rancorous roosters inhabiting the village had not yet begun to announce the arrival of a new day. As Jackson's eyes focused in the gloom, he could faintly make out the shape of David's tussled head peering over the side of his hammock.

"Ye'r awake are ya boy?"

"I've been waiting, Fishy. Are we going out in the skiff now?"

"Of course we are. Didn't we agree so last night? We'll go soon enough, but first we'll have our porridge. Mrs. Newbold will have it waitin'. Never go to sea with nothin' in your gut. That's the first lesson. The fishin' we'll do ain't for sport, Davey, ya need yer strength. "

The air was still cool in the small yard behind the Newbold's house. Toothy Jill was already awaiting for the pair outside. As was his custom, Jackson refrained from lighting a candle and made his way toward the cookhouse in the dark. Davey followed close behind, minding the best he could not to stub his bare toes on the rough paving stones. The top of a large square cistern glowed faintly white in the darkness and Jackson squeezed between it and the low eaves of a shed without walls. A tiny orange dot of light flickered in the hearth of a large brick oven. Jackson grabbed a poker leaning against the oven and stirred the one live coal into many. The resulting light revealed an iron pot sitting on a black grill.

"There ya see, Pigeon, Mrs. Newbold makes the porridge at night and it cooks here real slow 'til morning. Sit down there and I'll spoon ya some. Toothy's not much of one for breakfast, least not porridge. She prefers fish livers and such."

The most ambitious neighborhood roosters were now tuning their blaring instruments. In the pale light from the coals, David could now see a wooden bowl full of what appeared to be fat little pinecones. Reaching out to touch one, he discovered the things were not rough and prickly like a pinecone, but supple and plump.

"What are these things here, Fishy?"

"Those would be sweetsop, Pigeon. Some says sugar apple. They're stunning popular amongst boys your age on account of their sweetness." Here, he said, reaching for the knife in his belt, "I'll show ya how to go about eatin' one."

He sliced the fruit in half, exposing whitish flesh punctuated by evenly spaced black spots. Placing the point of the blade on one of the spots, Jackson said, "Them are the pits, boy, but the yaller-white part is for eatin'. Use yer spoon to scoop out a dollop."

David did as he was told and raised a heaping spoonful to his mouth. He deftly nibbled the tiniest portion, and realizing with surprise that the strange fruit not only failed to kill him on the spot but was indescribably delicious, he exclaimed, "Why it's custard, Fishy! But even sweeter!"

"As I said, always a favorite among lads of yer age."

The two quickly finished their breakfast and emerged from the cookhouse. Then Jackson darted back inside and could be heard scraping the porridge pot. He emerged again with a large pewter mug. Rather than walking back to the Fishy Shack to assemble gear for the day, David found himself following Jackson around the Newbold home to the wharf.

"But don't we need to bring nets and such, Fishy?"

"Lesson number two, Pigeon Davey, apprentice fisherman that ya are: always prepare the night before for the next day's fishin'. Ya want to get to the business of haulin' them in early as ya can. Last night John Newbold helped put the skiff in the water and now she's all loaded and ready to go."

In the dim, pre-dawn light, Jackson pointed over the side of the wharf to a lively and elegant little skiff, bow tied to an iron ring in the stone wall and stern held off by an anchor line.

"Down you get, Davey. Use the step wot's carved there in the wall."

The skiff was loaded with gear and David sat down on a pile of gill net draped neatly astern. Toothy Jill leapt without hesitation onto the bow of the skiff five feet below."

Jackson said, "Move further forward, mate. Give ole Fishy a bit o' room to flounder about in the stern."

The two quickly settled with Jackson sitting in the stern and David in the bow.

"Untie the bowline from the ring and we'll be off. We'll move the anchor and its line into the bow when we ship the oars and get the sail up."

Jackson swung the bow out into the channel by pulling hard on his right oar. He then fell into a smooth, seemingly effortless rhythm making way toward to inlet. As soon as they rounded the sea break, a breeze could be felt coming from the southeast. Jackson rowed a few more strokes forward and then turned the skiff sharply out of the deeper channel and along the shoreline.

"Stand by a moment, Pigeon, we'll try to take some bait aboard."

The skiff drifted slowly along the shoreline as Jackson carefully unfolded a light net weighted around the edges with little lead beads. He stood up carefully, holding the net in his right hand and its long thin retrieval line in the other. The very first cast of the net yielded a dozen shimmering little pilchards, which Jackson dumped into a wide basket. The second cast was unsuccessful, but the third, as they drifted closer to shore in the fore-reef, was a winner and Jackson declared the skiff ready to fish. He rowed the vessel back into the channel and a little further out.

"Alright Davey, let's get the anchor forward and tied to that ring there," he pointed. David handed the anchor and line to Jackson and then watched as the skiff's captain tied off the line.

"I'll be asking you to tie that same knot tomorrow, understand?" David nodded, wishing he'd paid closer attention. Jackson told the boy to duck his head, as the old sailor raised the sail and tied off the line. Taking in the mainsheet, making sure it was free of knots, he trimmed the sail and the skiff began to make way in a westerly direction.

"Shift over to windward, Pigeon, and sit on the gunwale as she rises. We'll put a little haste on 'er."

Just then the sun's bright forehead emerged from the sea to the east and gold light suddenly cast upon the skiff and its passengers. David looked back at Jackson, tiller in hand, gazing forward, and thought the man looked like a statue he'd seen in Portsmouth.

"We'll head to a reef I frequent, Davey, and give you a chance to use a hand line o'er one a Toothy Jill's favorite spots. Always somethin' for the pot out there and it's as good a place as any to start your life as a fisherman."

David's pigeon-like nodding was becoming familiar to Jackson now, but the humor of the sight still tickled him. Although Toothy Jill had been fishing with Jackson hundreds of times before, she seemed just as excited as David to be aboard. Her little brow was furrowed deeply as she peered fixedly over the side.

"She can smell a fish two leagues under, she can," Jackson said, pointing to the dog. "She's quite a little fish herself, ya know. I tell ya, though ya won't believe me 'till ya see fer yerself, she can swim underwater and pick a conch off the bottom. She does it all the time back in them shallow shoals," he said, pointing off in the distance.

Before the sun was more than ten degrees off the horizon, Jackson swung the bow into the light breeze and instructed David to drop the anchor.

"Now, you play out the line 'till I tell ya, then tie 'er off on the cleat there."

The boat drifted backward as Jackson and Toothy Jill peered over the transom.

"A little more there, Davey, about the length of man. Alright, tie 'er off."

Jackson set to work preparing four lines he pulled neatly coiled from a finely wrought box divided into handsome little compartments.

"John Newbold made this here fishin' box for me. It's a marvel. Got a place for everything."

Toothy Jill wagged her silky tail frantically and whimpered softly as she peered into the gin clear waters. The sky was bright blue and the sea very gently rocked the skiff like a cradle.

"Alright Davey, now I'll advise ya to wear this pair of gloves, as I don't want ya to feel it necessary to let go the line if she really starts to sing."

Jackson picked up one of the hooks, showing the boy how he'd baited it. He then showed David the small piece of lead fastened to the line about three feet above the hook.

"That's to bring the bait near the bottom, where the fish generally have their meals."

He dropped the line over and handed it to David.

"Now stand by and act sharp. If there's a good tug, you tug back like this," he demonstrated, "and you'll know quick enough whether the fella will be comin' aboard."

Almost immediately the boy was tight as a drum and on his feet with bite.

"Hook 'em, boy, like I showed ya."

And the line was suddenly running through David's gloved hands with a fury.

"That's fine boy. It's not a big fish, so you can wrap the line around your hand, but ya must sit down first."

David obeyed and watched the line zig this way and that, tugging his arm with waning force.

"Don't just sit there like a lump, boy, pull that fish over the side."

Into the boat flopped a fine red spotted rock hind. Jackson had him off the hook and into the basket in a flash. He handed David an already baited line and said, "go get another one Pigeon Davey."

The process was repeated dozens of times. Jackson showed the boy how to play out the line with larger fish, how to judge if there was weed on the hook or the bait had been stolen. Toothy Jill soon had a fine breakfast of fish livers and hearts and the day was still young.

"I'll show ya one more trick before we head back with the catch," said Jackson.

He let the boat drift awhile until he was satisfied with the look of the water over the side. Then he pulled the pewter mug he'd packed that morning from under his seat in the stern. Using the knife in his belt, he finely chopped half a dozen pilchards into a mince, then mixed the slop together with the porridge in the mug. Last he took a handful of sand from a small bucket and mixed that together with the porridge and bait fish. The result was a hard paste jammed into the bottom of the mug. He then tied a small line to the mug handle and lowered it gently over the side.

"That there is to get the attention of a school of snapper, yaller tailed ones," he said. Then he set about baiting every line in the boat, ten in all. He handed David two and pointed, "put one o're the port side and t'other o'er the starboard. Tie one of 'em off on the peg there." Jackon did the same aft, and added a third off the transom. All of the sudden, pandemonium. All four lines jumped about and soon the fifth one as well. Within three quarters of an hour they'd nearly filled the wide basket in the stern. Forward, another basket was full of the grouper and bar jacks they'd caught earlier.

"We'll let's head for port before the sun spoils the catch, boy. That was a fine morning and you did well. Toothy Jill seems much pleased with yer company."

David smiled broadly and blushed despite willing otherwise.

"Now you'll sail her home, Pigeon."

The boy instantly took on a panicked expression and Jackson chuckled.

"She's not a thousand ton merchantman, Davey, it's a simple matter."

In no distance at all, with Jackson's patient instructions, the boy was on his way to becoming a skiff mate. He quickly surmised how hard he could pinch her into the wind before the sail would luff. How to come about smoothly and sensibly, and how to trim the mainsheet to get the most out of the little craft.

Jackson, leaning back against the bows, smiled back at the boy.

"Well now ya pull yer weight, ya see. It's kinda nice being a passenger for a change."

Just then the boy pointed ahead and exclaimed, "What's that, Fishy?

Jackson turned his head slowly at first, then snapped it quickly around. He leapt to his feet and stepped high onto the bow peering intently at the fin breaking the water ahead.

"Well I can hardly believe it! On yer very first day! My boy, that there is swordfish and we're gonna get 'er."
He sprang into action, instructing David to bring the skiff up behind the slowly moving fin and keep Toothy Jill aft at all costs.

"Let the mainsheet out if ya have to, but bring her in careful like, as close as ya can get to 'er."

Jackson was furiously playing out line and laying it carefully in the bow, one elongated coil atop and beside another. Towards the end of the line he secured a large buoy, then another closer toward the end, and yet a third topped with a large knot.

He then stood up in the bow, the large coil of line to the leeward and closest to the great fish, whose shadow he could now see just ahead.

The boy watched as Jackson picked up the long harpoon attached to the head of the line.

"That's good, boy. Now ease out the mainsheet as we come alongside." Jackson leaned forward bracing his thighs against the bow thwart as he raised the harpoon. Suddenly he heaved the heavy iron spear to leeward stopping himself with his left hand against the gunwale as the momentum of his throw carried his body forward. He then jumped back to windward and clear of the line racing over the side.

"Alright Davey, now move aside and I'll take the tiller. But stay clear of that line, ya hear!"

David scrambled past Jackson as he handed him the tiller and mainsheet. The first buoy thudded over the side with a splash, then the second. A moment later the last float skidded along the gunwale and forward into the choppy waves. Jackson trimmed the mainsheet tight keeping a close eye on the buoys ahead and to the leeward. Suddenly they arched to windward and Jackson swore under his breath. Finally forced to tack, he called forward to Davey.

"Keep yer young eyes on them buoys, Davey, don't let 'em out of yer sight for second!"

The skipper brought the skiff quickly around and pulled the mainsheet in tight. The buoys could still plainly be seen but they were rapidly growing smaller.

"Keep lookin' boy, my eyeballs ain't what they used to be."
Holding his steady course, the buoys, at first blurry in Jackson's sight, slowly disappeared from view.

"Do ya still see 'em Pigeon?"

"Aye, Fishy, right back there."

"Point again, boy, real particular like."

David obeyed and Jackson nodded, continuing to hold his course. After a few more minutes, he called "I'll be comin' about now, so keep yer eyes peeled sharp boy."

He swung the bow around and David ducked under the boom, pivoting his gaze to the other side of the skiff.

"Still there, Fishy, but I can barely see."

"We'll get closer now, just keep lookin'."

Sure enough, as David gazed ahead squinting, the buoys appeared to be growing in size. Then moments later they again came into clear focus, bouncing through the chop like portly bulldogs.

"Ah, I see 'em now," said Jackson. "The monster's almost done in. She'll be comin' up to the top for the last time soon. And she was kind enough to move a bit closer to our island as well," he laughed.

In another half hour Jackson had retrieved the buoys and was now heaving in the line, foot by foot, tying it off every few minutes or so to rest. When the fish came into view, David couldn't believe his eyes.

"Fishy, it's bigger than you!"

"Nay boy, it's bigger than me, and you, and both Newbolds all piled together. She'll weigh six hundred pound easy."

Over the next hour, using a small block and tackle secured in the bows, Jackson slowly hauled the great fish aboard, careful not to capsize the boat. David helped when instructed and stayed clear when ordered to do so. Tail-first, the beast had come aboard, now the fish's long sword finally cleared the transom pointing incongruously skyward.

"Well, the belly of that fish weighs as much as a barrel of lead shot, wouldn't ya say, young Davey? That's the first time I've had to use that tackle in while. Look how low we're ridin!"

David grinned and felt along the fishes flank.

"Boy, I ain't never seen any new fisherman have luck such as you brung aboard today. We'll not tell Toothy Jill right away, but I reckon you've been promoted to mate."

* * * * *

The return to port with the catch was greeted with great fanfare. Mrs. Newbold, always the saleswomen, quickly advertised success to anyone with the patience to hear her out. Jackson declared the first order of business would be for David to race up the hill to Captain and Mrs. Sayle's cottage with a dozen fat swordfish steaks, free of charge. The boy reported back that Mrs. Sayle, as pious as she was known to be, danced a little jig in her kitchen house. The reaction provided strong evidence the boy would be left to the task of fishing, rather than formal schooling.

The days proceeded into the warm Bermudan summer. To Jackson, David seemed to grow in spirit and body every day. The boy was a hard worker, that was clear. His sallow English completion slowly gave way to reddish gold hue and his hair turned a careless blond under the sub-tropical sun.

Each day seemed an adventure to both David and Toothy Jill. The two were inseparable now. When the sea was too rough for the skiff, boy and dog roamed the main island, collecting treasures that soon accumulated in the Fishy Shack, prioritized and categorized in a manner that only a boy of eleven could understand. Jackson seemed impervious to Mrs. Newbold's comment that the boy was "going feral." Feral or not on land, when the boy was at sea he paid strict attention to Jackson, regardless of whether the sailor's words were in the form of advice, instruction or warning. David quickly learned the seasonal runs of fish species, the use of various kinds of net, trolling, construction of crab pots and every other craft Jackson had long since mastered.

In July, after David fell overboard frivolously trying to spot starfish and sponges on the seabed, Jackson, much alarmed, hauled him out by the collar and announced that the boy would learn how to swim before he'd set foot in the skiff again. As fond as the boy was of sailing and fishing, and as quickly as he'd mastered the related skills, he was far from enthusiastic about learning to swim.

"Boy, it's always been a puzzle to me why so few sailors can stay afloat unless they're aboard a ship. A boat will do ya no good if yer in the water without one, now will it? I'll tell ya certain, you'll learn to

46

swim and you'll learn to appreciate the fact ya did."

Swimming lessons proceeded according to Jackson's efficient plan. The two would wade onto the shoals carrying a basket and Jackson's casting net. The first order of business would be the swimming lesson itself and the next would be gathering bait. With more patience than Jackson imagined he had, he managed to teach the boy how to stay afloat within two days. Within two months, David could swim hundreds yards, floating passively for a spell if he became winded. Within six months, and largely because the boy would not be outdone by Toothy Jill, he could hold his breath and dive for conch in shallow water. Within a year, the lad could hold his breath and dive for over a minute.

"Davey," said Jackson, "you'll sprout gills sure enough if ya keep up spending so much time under water." He sighed and continued, "But they say the salt water removes the scales from yer eyes, so p'haps you'll start to see the truth better now, and the truth is you're already glad ya learned to swim, just as I said ye would."

Sunday mornings in the Fishy Shack were sad events, though the two never articulated the fact. Jackson had not been able to beg off attendance at Captain Sayle's church, and much to fisherman's dismay, he was forced to apply some of his fishing profits towards a set of church cloths. Captain Sayle himself provisioned the boy in a similar fashion. Jackson was at once uncomfortable being placed in a position that to him seemed outwardly political. Up until then, he'd staunchly avoided taking side in the quarrels between the island's Church of England supporters and the Independents. But it was for "the good of the boy," he reasoned, and so for the first time in his life, Jackson found himself inhabiting a church pew. Jackson had been was a man of autonomy from his first day on the island in 1609 and made it a practice to remain so. Up until the day David stepped aboard his skiff, no other person had accompanied the old sailor on his fishing trips. He'd never gone into business with anyone except Mrs. Newbold, had never taken sides in an argument, and for that reason, together with his intrinsic kindness, he was tolerated by all.

To Jackson's great surprise, he took an instant liking to Reverend Patrick Copeland, a pious Independent who'd renounced the Church of England several years prior. Copeland, now nearly eighty years old, but as spry as a man twenty-five years younger, was similarly drawn to Jackson and an odd friendship blossomed between simple sailor and godly reverend. It was upon Copeland's invitation that Jackson went in June to attend a meeting in which the standing members of the congregation would begin the process of agreeing upon the form of governance to be adopted by the new colony on the island of Eleutheria. By then, Sayle had succeeded in recruiting half of the one hundred persons he'd set out to persuade.

Jackson listened intently as Sayle presented the first paragraphs of what he'd titled The Articles and Orders of Incorporation in language Jackson regarded as a bit grandious, which always seemed the case with legal documents. Nevertheless, Jackson had no complaint that he could conjure regarding the paragraphs' objective that no man should be judged or regarded as an enemy on account of his religious beliefs, and that derision on account of those beliefs would not be tolerated. It did not escape the old sailor's attention that Captain Butler, on the other hand, sat dour-faced with arms crossed the entire length of the meeting, not uttering a word.

WHEREAS experience hath showed us the great inconveniences that have happened, both in this Kingdom of England and other places, by a rigid imposing upon all an uniformity and conformity in matters of judgment and practice in the things of Religion, whereby divisions have been made, factions fomented, persecutions induced, and the public peace endangered. And for that we well know, that in this state of darkness and imperfection, we know but in part,

That there are both babes and strongmen in Christ: And that every Member who holds the head, and is of the body of Jesus Christ, hath not the same place and office, nor the same measure of light, who yet desire and endeavor daily to increase in knowledge. And the mean time walk according to what they have received in all godliness, justice and sobriety. And whereas experience hath also showed us,

That the peace and happy progress of all Plantations doth much depend upon the good government thereof, the equal distribution of justice, and respect to all persons, without faction or distinction the certain knowledge and manifestations of every ones rights and properties, and careful provisions for common defense and safety.

It is therefore ordered, That all such person and persons who are so as aforesaid qualified, shall be received and accepted as Members of the said

48

Company of Adventurers, and into the said Plantation, notwithstanding any other differences of judgment, under whatsoever names conveyed, walking with justice and sobriety, in their particular conversations and living peaceably and quietly as Members of the Republic.

That there shall be no names of distinction or reproach, as Independent, Antinomian, Anabaptist, or any other cast upon any such for their difference in judgment, neither yet shall any person or persons assume or acknowledge any such distinguishing names, under the penalty of being accounted (in both such cases either of imposing or accepting or assuming any such name or names) as enemies of the public peace: nor shall any man speak reproachfully of any person for his opinion, or of the opinion itself, otherwise then in the Scripture Language.

That no Magistracy or Officers of the Republic, nor any power derived from any of them, shall take notice of any man for his difference in judgment in matter of Religion, or have cognizance of any cause whatsoever of that nature: But that their jurisdiction shall reach only to men as men, and shall take care that justice, peace, and sobriety, may be maintained among them. And that the flourishing state of the republic may be by all just means promoted.

Yes, thought Jackson, Captain Sayle had chosen the name 'Eleutheria' very wisely. Save for the taciturn Captain Butler, the idea of freedom was so appealing to the members in attendance, not a single objection was made regarding the next paragraph read by Sayle:

That the present Adventurers, and all other persons, who within the space of one year now next ensuing, shall bring into the public stock, the sum of £100 shall be admitted and reckoned into the number of the first Adventurers, their number not exceeding one hundred persons.

When the meeting adjourned, Jackson walked with Reverend Copeland down the slope away from Captain Sayle's home towards the waterfront.

"Jackson," said Copeland, "I think a man such as you would be of great service to the company. Would you consider joining us when we sail?"

The suggestion came as great shock to Jackson and he struggled for a polite response.

"Well Reverend, I hadn't considered it, truth be told. I'm not sure of what great usefulness I could be to the troupe, and I can't claim to be 'qualified' as the Captain put it."

"I believe you are 'qualified', Jackson," spoke the Reverend without hesitation, "and I believe you know that in your own heart here under God's gaze."

"Well sir, it's kind of you to say so. I'll give the matter some t'ought," said Jackson, not really intending to do so.

But think about it he did. He wondered what would become of David when his *de facto* legal guardian, Captain Sayle, left for Eleutheria. He wondered what would become of David if he remained in Jackson's care on Bermuda. The boy would have little chance of bettering himself, meaning he had no prospect of ever obtaining land on an island where land was already becoming scarce. The boy would lead the life Jackson had led, only worse. Linked as he was to Sayle and his Independent congregation, David would be the subject of derision and prejudice.

* * * * *

Walking up the hill to church one Sunday morning with David, Jackson was joined by Reverend Copeland who confided, "I'm afraid we've had only one additional family join our venture, Mr. Jackson." The old reverend stopped ambling his way up the slope and turned to face Jackson. "My friend, I tell you it puts me in great dread that our plantation may fail if we cannot harvest at least another score of settlers from the flock of Independents here on Somers' Island."

"Davey, you run ahead to church while the Reverend and I parlez a little."

Jackson had grown to admire the old reverend greatly since their first meeting months before. The man's motivations, in Jackson's view, were unassailable. While others may claim religious freedom as their sole purpose for joining the venture, Jackson was worldly enough to understand that many who made such a lofty claims were secretly also motivated by the prospect of achieving wealth. But that would not be the case for a man nearing eighty years of age. Copeland would almost certainly die on Eleutheria long before any earthly wealth ever materialized, but he would die knowing he was free to worship as he believed God had instructed.

"Well," began Jackson, and then paused trying to find the right words.

"Go on, Mr. Jackson, speak your mind."

"The t'ing is, Reverend, £100 is a right princely sum of money, ya know, and . . . well, perhaps ya might consider publishing some particulars about land grants and suchlike. That's not to say I'm suggestin' any of the fine Independents here on the island don't put the good Lord first in all matters, but it might help some folks, those more inclined to cypherin' return upon investment, if ya added somethin' about land to the Articles and Orders ya started writin' up."

Reverend Copeland turned his gaze down to the toes of his shoes and was silent for quite some time. Jackson feared he'd mortally offended the man and began to apologize, "But what would a fella such as me know about . . .."

A loud burst of laughter erupted from Copeland and interrupted Jackson.

"It is providence itself that you slowed your pace this morning and chose to accompany me to up to our little church, Jackson. God's ways are not always clear to me, I admit, but this morning it's clear he sent you to advise me in this important matter. You're right. It is a daunting sum of money, £100, such that our flock deserve some 'particulars', as you say, regarding their prospects for land ownership."

Jackson smiled and responded, "Probably best if ya claim the idea in the Lord's name, wouldn't ya say?"

"That I will, Mr. Jackson, that I will."

* * * * *

Five months after the first meeting to discuss the religious foundation of the prosed settlement, a second meeting was called at the church to introduce additional articles regarding land rights. Sayle read from the pulpit:

That every one of the number of the first Adventurers, shall have three hundred Acres of land, laid out for him and his Heirs forever, in the first convenient place which shall be chosen, by those persons of the number of Adventurers, who shall go to the said Plantation, in the present expedition and shipping.

And that the said quantity of three hundred Acres for each first Adventurer; shall at the end of the first three years, or sooner, if the major part of the said number or Company of first Adventurers shall require the same, shall be divided and set out by lot, unto every particular person.

And that in the meantime, all the same Land shall be employed and improved for the joint advantage of the said Company.

And that for the further and better encouragement of the said first Adventurers, every one of the said Company of first Adventurers shall have two thousand Acres more of land, to be laid out for him and his Heirs forever, in such place or places as shall be most convenient and satisfactory unto him, and least prejudicial or disadvantageous to the public.

And that this shall be effected with as much convenient speed, as the occasions of the Plantation will permit. And that all the adjacent Islands shall be reserved too, or laid out and had for the use of the said Company of first Adventurers.

By a show of hands, the provision was adopted unanimously with the kind of solemn praise befitting that congregation's values. Later, however, in the privacy of their own homes, many would celebrate with an enthusiasm bordering on abandon.

"Brothers and Sisters" called Sayle from the pulpit, "is there any other business to discuss this evening, or shall we adjourn?"

A light cough emanated from the back pew and Jackson's hand rose sheepishly.

"Yes, Fishy Jack, do ya have a thing to tell?"

Jackson rose slowly, imagining now what it must feel like to be a fish caught in one of his nets.

"Captain," began Jackson.

"Go ahead man, what is it?"

"You know I'm a fisherman."

"Yes, of course I know you're a fisherman, and a fine one. Now go ahead," urged Sayle.

"Yes sir, presently sir. The 'ting I'm trying ta say is, well, when I want the fish out there on the reef to join inta a proper tight school and commence bitin' on my hooks, I generally provide them a reward as such."

"What do ya mean by that, Jackson," asked Sayle.

"What I mean is, I been told plain by Reverend Copeland it's of great importance for the success of a colony ta have many a man and women labor towards it."

"Yes, that's right, Jackson, we aim to start with one hundred," answered Sayle.

"But you'll be wantin' more, am I not right?"

"Yes, of course," exclaimed Sayle, now visibly impatient.

"Well then," continued Jackson, it seems like ya might consider chummin' the water a bit like the boy, Davey, and me do out in the skiff. P'haps ya might include in them articles a reward of sorts for them settlers that bring in more souls."

"Reward?"

"Yes sir, land sir."

Sayle could see the meeting attendants were rapt.

"So Jackson, you are suggesting the company grant land to those successful in facilitating additional immigration?"

"If I understand ya, Captain, yes. But I 'tink I'd also give consideration, as it were, to the *attempt* to bring in folks, friends, family and what have ya."

"I think I understand, Mr. Jackson. If the Brothers and Sisters will excuse me while I meet in private with Reverend Copeland, I'll give the matter some thought."

Sayle and Copeland huddled at the front of the church in a whispered sidebar while the audience of 'Adventurers' filed outside to the church steps and cooler air.

It seemed to Jackson and the Adventurers that hours passed before Copeland came to the door and hailed them back into the church. Sayle was again at the pulpit and began immediately to read:

That as well every one of the Adventurers aforesaid, as also every other person, who shall at any time or times, within three years transport, at his own charge, unto the said Plantation, any person or persons, shall have and enjoy to him the said Transporter and his Heirs forever, the quantity of thirty five Acres of Land per person, for every person which he shall also transport;

Much nodding and other evidence of assent spread through the audience, and Sayle continued:

The same Land to be set out and appointed for him, by such as shall be hereafter authorized for that purpose by the first Adventurers upon the place.

Sayle gazed again from the pulpit and seeing no apparent objections he continued.

And that if any Servants or Children, or any other persons who shall be shipped to be transported to the Plantation, shall after their shipping miscarry, or die by the way : yet nevertheless, the person at whose charge any such miscarrying or dying person, Child or Servant, was shipped shall have and enjoy to him and his Heirs forever in the said Plantation, and to be set out and appointed as aforesaid, the quantity of thirty five Acres for or in respect of each one person so dying or miscarrying, in as ample manner, as if he had been safely transported, and come into the said Plantation.

And that every other person or persons that shall adventure, after three years shall have five and twenty Acres.

At this point, Sayle asked for a show of hands for those who approved thus far. Not a hand was withheld and Sayle confirmed the passage of the provision.

"Now," he said, "there is the question of persons arriving to our plantation who're pledged to service. Reverend Copeland and I propose the following:

That every Servant being a Christian, which shall be transported to the said Plantation, and shall serve out his time agreed upon, the use of him who transported him, or of his Assigns, shall at the end of his time of service, have and enjoy to him the said Servant and his Heirs forever, the quantity of twenty and five Acres of Land, to be allowed and set out for him by such as shall be authorized by the Governor and Counsel. And for the better encouragement of the first Adventurers in a work of that hazard; and also for the exciting and awakening the industry of all.

"Do ya all agree to those terms as well," asked Sayle. "It is my desire, and I hope you share it, that *all* shall have the opportunity to better themselves here on earth and before the eyes of God on judgment day."

Again, every right hand in the church was raised, and Sayle

confirmed the adoption of the provisions.

"At our next meeting I aim to introduce additional ideas for governance of our settlement. Until then may God bless our little band of Adventurers and add to our numbers."

As the party dispersed, Reverend Copeland hailed Jackson and joined him on his walk back to the waterfront. Copeland began the conversation. "I think I understand the motivation behind your suggestions regarding land, Mr. Jackson."

"It's a brave venture, Reverend, and many would want it to succeed," responded Jackson.

"That may be so," said Copeland, "but I believe you have the success of someone in particular in mind. When will you tell the boy he's to go with Sayle to Eleutheria?"

"Well, Reverend, ya do have gift for gettin' to the heart of a matter. I plan to talk to the boy when next we're out upon the water."

"Jackson, if it's any comfort to you, I'll see to the boy's religious instruction as best I'm able."

"I thank ya fer that, Reverend. I 'tink such will be important to Davey, him bein' an orphan and all. He should know that God will be lookin' out for him."

The two men shook hands as they parted, Jackson to the Fishy Shack, and the Reverend Copeland for a stroll along the wharf in the cool night air.

* * * * *

July 15, 1610, excerpt from a letter written by Sea Venture survivor, William Strachey, to an anonymous recipient.

In August, September, and until the end of October, we had very hot and pleasant weather; only (as I say) thunder, lightning, and many scattering showers of rain (which would pass swiftly over, and yet fall with such force and darkness for the time as if it would never be clear again) we wanted not any; and of rain more in summer than in winter. And in the beginning of

December we had great store of hail (the sharp winds blowing northerly), but it continued not, and to say truth, it is wintry or summer weather there according as those north and northwest winds blow. Much taste of this kind of winter we had, for those cold winds would suddenly alter the air. But when there was no breath of wind to bring the moist air out of the seas from the north and northwest, we were rather weary of the heat than pinched with extremity of cold. Yet the three winter months, December, January, and February, the winds kept in those cold corners, and indeed then it was heavy and melancholy being there; nor were the winds more rough in March than in the foresaid months, and yet even then would the birds breed. I think they bred there most months in the year. In September and at Christmas I saw young birds, and in February, at which time the mornings are there (as in May in England) fresh and sharp.

* * * * *

David and Jackson sat together in the dark cookhouse eating the porridge Mrs. Newbold left warming in the pot. As was custom for the two at breakfast, they asked Toothy Jill whether she wanted to go fishing. The ritual inevitably sparked laughter, as the dog danced and leaped about in circles stopping now and then to stare into Jackson's eyes for any additional sign they were going to sea.

"Alright then," Jackson would say to Toothy Jill, "if it's so important to ya, Davey and I aren't opposed to haulin' in a few fish for yer sake."

David and the dog ran ahead to the skiff while Jackson walked alone behind the pair. It was the first time he could remember that he didn't look forward to heading out in his skiff for a day of fishing.

As he reached the boat, he called down to David, "We'll spend the morning trollin', boy, I t'ink them Spanish Mackerels might be runnin' a bit early this year."

"Should I ready the charmers then, Fishy," asked Davey?

"Aye, ya know where the fishin' box is, set to work on three lines," Jackson responded as he climbed aboard the skiff.

David carefully withdrew from the box three handmade lures. As he carefully tied the lures to the lines, they caught the rising sun, creating little reflections that darted around the boat and against the stone wall of the wharf. As far as Jackson knew, the lures were his own special invention and he was proud of them. Each one took many hours to complete with the rudimentary tools Jackson possessed.

The morning passed well with the two hauling in six large specimens, four Spanish Mackerel and two Bonita. Toothy Jill was elated by the success and now settled down to a breakfast of livers and a piece of cheese smuggled to her by David.

"Well, let's try for a couple more, Pigeon, then we'll take 'er in and run these fellas up ta Mr. Sands' smokehouse, what d'ya say?"

"Might we also visit the blowhole, Fishy, as it's not that much further on?"

David never grew tired of watching the ocean swells approach the north shore, then duck under the limestone promontory with mighty groans, followed by a monstrous exhale and huge plume of white foam and water shooting into the air, sometimes fifty feet or more.

"Well I don't see why not," Jackson replied, "but see here, before we go back to shore there's somethin' wot I need to discuss with ya."

The boy looked instantly uncomfortable, "What is it, Fishy?"

"Well, ya know that Reverend Copeland invited me to listen in on them gatherings Captain Sayle organizes on account of the big venture, right?"

The boy nodded and continued to stare at Jackson with a troubled bearing.

"And I know ya don't understand much about all the bad business between them folk wot go to the Church of England and them wot go to Reverend Copeland's church, or some other independent place of worship. But here's the t'ing boy. Ya been baptized by the Reverend and ye're now part of his church, which is fine t'ing for any man in the eyes of God, but in the eyes of most folk here on the island, ye're somethin' of a blight, ya see? Them wot's loyal to the king don't much approve of anyone who don't go to the king's own church."

"But I know that Fishy! It's alright. I don't care what them others say. Let's just go back to fishin' now."

"We'll be fishin' soon enough, but now you ain't heard but the half of it. Ye're a fine mate, Davey, and you've become a fine fisherman, but you'll never be able to better yerself just by fishin'. All my life I've also had to sign on to ships now and again just to make ends meet. I want ya to have better."

Jackson held up the palm of his hand before the boy could respond.

"Now let me finish, Pigeon. You'll be goin' with Captain Sayle to Eleutheria in the Bahama Islands and you'll be given land, Davey, land all yer own. It's all been settled. You'll be of service to the Captain for six years, and when ya turn eighteen, you'll have twenty-five acres and the means to acquire more if ya work hard."

David's eyes filled with tears and soon they were streaming down his face. In reaction, Toothy Jill quickly propped her paws upon the boy's shoulders and began licking him.

"Why," sobbed the boy? "You told me I was good! You said we were partners!"

"Aye, Davey, I said both them t'ings. But then Captain Sayle, ya see, well he promised to give land to everyone wot joins the colony. I know ya understand that ownin' land here in Bermuda is impossible for ya. So goin' to Eleutheria will help ya along in life. T'will provide ya with opportunity ya won't have here."

"But why do ya not come yourself, Fishy," the boy wept?

"Ah, little Pigeon Davey, I'm not a planter and I'm far too old to take up farmin' now. It'll be different for you, boy, ya have yer whole life ahead of yea. There's nothin' for me there in Eleutheria, least not now, and by the time the place claims enough settlers to support other occupations, like fishin', I'll be an old man."

For the second time in his short life, David's world turned upside down. He said not a word as Jackson sailed the skiff back into port, and once at the wharf, the boy climbed ashore and ran off alone.

Jackson sat for long while in the skiff, speaking silently in his mind to his dead wife, Caroline. "Girl, I don't know rightly what to do. But then I do: I'm to act in the boy's best interest and the best t'ing for him is to be a landowner. I can't go with him, how on earth would I make my livin'?"

He unloaded the skiff slowly and instead of hauling the catch to Peter Sands' smokehouse, he brought them in the handcart to Mrs. Newbold.

"Catch o' the day, Mrs. Newbold," he said quietly, stopping the handcart at the front door.

"Where's your first mate then, Fishy?"

"Ah well, he's runnin' about as boys his age will do. I'll be in the back working on them crab pots now," Jackson said, walking stoop-shouldered to the back of the house.

Mrs. Newbold stood examining the fish in the cart for only a moment when Jackson reappeared.

"Changed my mind. I've some business with Reverend Copeland and then I'll be back presently."

He walked quickly away down the wharf with Mrs. Newbold gazing after him.

* * * * *

Captain Sayle called the third meeting of the Company of Adventurers to order, noting with great pleasure the addition of twenty-one new members. As Jackson surveyed the crowd, he noticed Captain Butler absent for the second meeting in a row. "Butler will not take kindly to any agreement among the party that stands between him and his ability to maximize his gain," Jackson thought to himself. He'd seen many men like Captain Butler in his day, and he prided himself in his ability to spot them for what they were.

As with past meetings, Sayle read from his proposed additional articles:

That the Government of the said Islands and Plantations shall be continued in a Senate of the number of one hundred persons; and that the company of the first Adventurers aforesaid, shall at present be the same Senate.

And whensoever any of them shall die or sell away his Interest in the said Plantations; then there shall be another elected in his room from time to time, by the major part of the said Senate, out of the other Adventurers and Planters Resident in the said Islands. And the same election shall be made in this manner, (viz.) First, 20 fit persons shall be nominated. Then those

20 reduced to the number of 4 by scrutiny and out of those 4, one to be chosen by Ballotines.

And so from time to time, as often as any Member of the said Senate, shall decease or shall alien or discontinue his interest in the said Plantations, or shall be removed by the said Senate, upon just cause or complaint. And that the same Senate from time to time, make election of all Officers, for doing of justice, and distribution and setting out of Lands, and for the care and over sight of all public works, and shall have the ordering and disposing of all public monies.

That after the first three years expired, there shall be yearly a Governor and 12 Councilors chosen out of the said number of 100. Senators, who shall take the daily care of all things necessary for the prosperity of the Plantation and that it in nothing suffer detriment or decay. And that the public peace be maintained between man and man, and speedy justice done unto every man that shall seek it at their hands.

And that the said Governor and Council, shall have power to call together upon any emergency, to the said Senate or so many of them, as shall then be upon the said Islands, and to act and execute what shall be by the said convention of Senators ordered and referred, or committed unto them.

That the first Governor and Council shall be elected by the first Adventurers when the number of Adventurers who will transport themselves is once known. And that the same first Governor and Council shall continue in their Office three whole years, from the first day of their arrival in the said Islands or Plantation.

That all succeeding Governors and Council shall after the afore-mentioned term expired, be yearly chosen on the first Tuesday in December, for one whole year to come, beginning the first day of January following, by all the free-men of the said Plantations, by way of scrutiny and Ballotines, in such manner as is before expressed.

That every person that shall transport himself to the said Plantations, or desire to become a Member of the same Plantation, shall before his admittance thereunto, acknowledge his allowance, and consent unto all and every one of these Articles; and by subscribing the same, bind himself to conformity thereunto for the future, And this is to be done before he be admitted into the said company and before he hath any-share or proportion of Land set out and assigned to him according to these Articles.

A couple hands raised among the spectators. With no sign of irritation, Sayle deftly addressed the questions posed by Peter Sands and David Albury, and confirmed with the attendants that his explanations were understood. Then the provisions regarding governance were put to vote, as had become custom. Upon their passage, Sayle asked if there was any further business. Reverend Copeland rose to his feet and approached the pulpit and began to speak.

"Most of you are aware that last year I asked Mr. Jackson here," pointing to the sailor, "if he would lend us the benefit of his years and of his unbiased opinion. Indeed, Mr. Jackson has lately shown in diverse ways that he is a friend to us, despite not being baptized into our midst. He has suggested a means for supplemental support of our efforts, and at this point, I will ask him to provide you with background. Mr. Jackson, will you rise?"

Jackson rose from his seat and nodded in the direction of Captain Sayle.

"Good evenin' to ya Captain. I don't mean to butt into the company's affairs and I hope ya know I wouldn't do so 'cept for the invitation of Reverend Copeland."

"We're glad to hear your thoughts, Fishy, go right ahead."

"Well sir, ya know I'm a sailor," he started.

"Yes, I know you're a sailor and a fisherman too. Now speak your mind."

"Right. As ya know sir, sailors are apt to speak of their ramblings around the globe and they share tales about all manner of t'ings. I've had occasion, sir, to hear tell of ships' commerce in and about the Caribe Islands. I hear'd tell about how them Spaniards first make to the island of Cuba after they sail from New Spain and and other such ports to the south."

"Yes, go on, Jackson," encouraged Reverend Copeland.

"As ya like, sir. The Spaniard, I'm told, is a man half crazed by gold and other such treasure and he'll do all manner of t'ings to get at it. Way I understand it, they got scores and scores of ships sailing through the Caribe Sea, only they ain't wot ya might call expert sailors, p'haps maybe on account of them always bein' in a terrible hurry to get at more gold, ya see."

Sayle was clearly getting impatient, and Jackson plunged quickly ahead.

"Well the point bein', sir, I hear'd tell from sailors wot been in them waters how them Spaniards do run ships upon the rocks with shockin' frequency. Then they run others in right up alongside and overtop, stackin' 'em there like firewood, don't ya know? So I was thinkin' to m'self, might'nt it be an idea to help the colony along if the wrackin' business was part of the venture?   At least 'til yer plantations start yielding some revenues?"

To Jackson's immense discomfort, Sayle stood behind the pulpit silently gazing up at the ceiling. In the process of sitting back down, the old fisherman said a few more words: "Well I don't know that I explained m'self well at'all, but Reverend Copeland's got it writ down all fine and proper like."

Copeland approached the pulpit and stood facing Sayle.

"Captain, with your indulgence, I'll read to you and any who care to listen, proposed articles regarding shipwreck salvage and other potential means of ancillary support of the colony."

Sayle nodded and stepped aside. "Yes, of course, Reverend Copeland, I'm sure I speak for everyone here tonight when I say I'd be pleased to hear what you have in mind."

"Very well then, Captain," Copeland replied, and then he began to read:

It is further ordered and agreed: That whatsoever Ordinance can be recovered of any wraks, shall be wholly employed for the use of the public, and serve for the fortification of the Plantation.

Many in the crowd nodded their assent, so Copeland moved along.

That all other wraks which shall be recovered upon, or near the Islands, or upon or near any the adjacent Islands: And also all Mines of Gold, Silver, Copper, Brass or Lead, Ambergris, salt; and all rich woods, either for tincture or medicament, which shall be had or found upon or near the Islands or territories aforesaid, in any Land not divided, or set over to any particular proprietor, shall be delivered into the Custody of two such persons, Merchants or Agents for the said Company as shall be yearly chosen by the said Company for that purpose, and the same Mines, Wracks, Ambergris, Metals, Salts and Woods, shall be by the said two Agents, made fit for sale, and be by them with all convenient speed, sold for the best price and advantage,

And the whole price and value thereof (the Charges and wages for the procuring and fitting of them for sale, being first deducted and discharged) shall be divided into three equal parts and shares; and the first of the same three parts, shall be unto him or them, who shall be the undertaker or finder thereof:

The second part shall be paid or distributed unto, and among the first Adventurers, their Heirs, Executors and assigns, equally and the other third part shall be paid and delivered into the public Treasury of the said Plantation, to be employed and laid out for the use of the public, by order and warrant from the Governor and Council there, for the time being.

Copeland again surveyed the crowd. He then took a breath and added:

But if the same shall be found in any of the Lands already appropriated, the first third part shall be to the owner or proprietor of the same Lands, and the other two thirds as aforesaid: That when the Plantation shall sufficiently be fortified, and all necessary works finished and the general Magazines sufficiently stored, then what shall be spared of the public third in works of mercy and charity, and for the transporting from England and other places such godly people as shall be willing to go unto the said Plantations, and are not able to bear the charge of their transportation and settling there.

"Well," interrupted Sayle, "no doubt it's the Lord's will that we should include such charity in or articles and I thank you, Reverend, for making the suggestion. Please continue if there is more."

Copeland answered, "Yes Captain, there remains an item or two:"

That no person shall pretend unto, or claim any Wracks, Mines, Ambergris, Salt, or rich woods, as aforesaid; for, or by reason of their growing, or being in or upon his lot or share of ground, which shall be appointed to him as above said; but all the said particulars shall be disposed and employed , as before is expressed.

That none of the said rich Woods growing upon Land, not appropriated, shall be cut down by any person, but by warrant first had and obtained from the Governor and Council for that purpose; and if any shall do otherwise, then he that shall cut, or cause to be cut any of the said Woods without such warrant, shall loose and forfeit all that share which he might under any qualification whatsoever, pretend unto in the same Woods: and the same forfeiture shall be to the use of the said Colony.

That if any places shall appear fit for making salt, which yet makes it not naturally, then the salt-works shall be perfected at the public charge, and the revenue thereof to come into the public Treasury, and be employed for ever for the public service, as aforesaid.

Copeland looked up from the pages and met Sayle's eyes.

"I tell you now, Reverend Copeland, without any further consideration that I approve of what you have presented before us. A show of hands now, do we have agreement?"

As one right hand rose after the other, Copeland and Sayle smiled and shook hands.

Captain Sayle then exclaimed, "Very well then! Now let's get back to our homes as the hour is growing late. Is there any other business, Reverend Copeland?"

Copeland stepped forward once again. "Yes there is one small matter remaining."

"Let's hear it then, Reverend, we're all listening."

"I propose and put forward that Mr. Benjamin Jackson be appointed as chief surveyor of wracks and be put in charge of salvage operations, acting, as it were, in behalf of the colony. I've drawn up here for Mr. Sayle's review Articles of Indenture wherein Mr. Jackson will agree to pledge his service to the colony for a period of three years. However, any wraks he discovers himself, he shall retain a third as aforesaid."

Sayle nodded his approval and approached Jackson sitting in the first pew.

"Well, Fishy, I'll be pleased to have you join us. I must confirm that you understand the terms just now described by Reverend Copeland."

Jackson nodded, "Yes sir, I understand and I'd be right honored to serve the company and yerself sir."

"Will you also be baptized into Mr. Copeland's congregation?"

"Yes, Captain, the Reverend has already asked as much and I've agreed with pleasure."

Sayle smiled, "Well don't forget, Jackson, you'll also be granted twenty-five acres upon completion of your service."

"Oh yes sir, I t'ank ya for that, Captain."

Shaking hands with Jackson, Captain Sayle added, "I also expect you'll agree to serve as crew during the voyage?"

"Of course, Captain, t'was my intent."

* * * * *

Jackson trotted down the hill away from the church at rate a of speed he'd not reached for fifteen years or so. As he approached the Saunders' dry-dock, he could see John Saunders sitting on the front step of the establishment.

"Hallo Fishy Jack!" called Saunders, "I missed the meetin' on account of my sister Jane takin' ill."

Jackson sat down on the step next to Saunders. "Oh no, I'm particular sorry to hear Jane's ailin'. How is she now?"

"Oh fine, fine. Twice this week she's fainted, but she come around just like before. But tell me, Fishy, I'm dyin' to know. Are ya a wracker then?"

"Aye, Johnny, that I'll be as soon as Davey and me reach them islands. Here's hopin' them Spaniards don't learn how to pilot their ships no better!"

Saunders smiled broadly. "I don't suppose they will any time soon, Fishy, so ya ought to have a little business now and again. When will ya tell the boy you'll be joinin' us to Eleutheria?"

"Well I won't wake him tonight. I'll let it be known when we're out fishin' in the morning."

Jackson leaned back on the palms of his hands for moment. Then he turned his face to Saunders, "Say Johnny, I know you can write good and proper, do ya t'ink ya could write a little note for me now?"

Saunders nodded, "Aye, Fishy, no worry at'all."

The two entered the dry dock office where John lit a candle. In a few minutes he and Jackson finished the note and it lay on the table, ink drying slowly in the humid air.

Jackson spoke up again. "Would ya happen to have an empty bottle and a stout cork I could borrow for a day?"

"I do," said Saunders, I'll fetch it now."

* * * * *

Jackson bid Saunders good night and left with the note and bottle. He walked quietly down the wharf and climbed into his skiff, marveling at the reflection of stars on the calm water. He placed the oars in the locks and began steadily rowing out the channel. With each pull of the oars, two phosphorescent swirls ignited in the wake. "Well, Caroline," he said out loud, "tonight I done what ya told me."

* * * * *

"Make sure ya bring extra water fer Toothy Jill, boy. The cask was almost dry when last I looked."

"I already filled the cask from the cistern first thing, Fishy."

"That's a good Pigeon, then let's get movin," said Jackson as he stood up from the cookhouse table.

Before long they were sailing in the light easterly breeze along the north shore of St. David's Island. In a few minutes, the first in a line of crab pots could be seen, its white float reflecting the early morning sun.

"Are ya ready, Davey? I'll bring 'er in on the windward side of the float and you reach off the port bow and grab 'er, alright?"

"Aye, Fishy, it's the same as we do every time."

"Well, true enough. But I feel lucky today, Pigeon, I t'ink that pot might be a winner."

The boy crouched in the bow with his eye on the float as it approached to leeward. As the skiff drew nearer, Jackson let the mainsheet out and the slim craft slowed its approach. David was well accustomed to the maneuver and easily grabbed the float. He braced his knee against the gunwale and drew up the pot, hand over hand. As it broke the surface he paused to take a look inside the pot. There were at least four crabs scuttling about and something else, something greenish and opaque. He hauled the pot over the side, staring intently at its contents.

"There's a bottle tied in there, Fishy!"

"Ya don't say! Dump them crabs out in the basket and let's have a look."

Kneeling in the skiff's tidy hull David quickly shook the crabs out of the pot and then untied the slipknot holding the bottle to the bottom of the pot.

"There's a paper in it," the boy exclaimed in hushed voice.

"Hand it here boy, I'll study on it."

The old fisherman squinted at the bottle, making a great show of turning it this way and that.

"There's a string tyin' that paper together, Pigeon. See if ya can tease out the end of it with this splicin' needle here."

Handing the boy the long needle, Jackson sat back against the thwart to watch. It seemed an eternity before the boy teased the end of the string out of the neck of the bottle.

"Nicely done there, Davey. Now see if ya can pull that paper out without losin' hold of 'er."

The boy, tongue poking out of the corner of his mouth, slowly worked the scroll out through the neck of the bottle. Once he had it in hand, he held it out to Jackson.

"No boy, ya know *I* don't read whereas you yerself read like a scholar. Open 'er up and let me know if there's anything writ in there."

David slid the string off the little scroll and carefully unrolled it. He began to read:

To whomsoever it may concern. The proclamation writ down in this document is of grave importance.

Jackson nodded soberly and said, "Go on boy, let's have it."

David continued.

In the coming days, a company of brave and Godly souls shall sail from Bermuda for the Caribe Islands in search of Eleutheria, an island named after freedom. Them settlers shall endeavor to better themselves before the eyes of the Lord and them that trades in goods as well. Known to all men is the clear fact that many a Spaniard vessel runs afoul of the reefs and shoals which populate that part of the world. On account of such frequent catastrophe, said company of Adventurers shall bring with them unto the Isle of Eleutheria, a man right familiar with the ways of the sea and the ships that wrack upon them. He shall be appointed Chief Surveyor of all Wracks. The man will take aboard as first mate in all things having to do with wracking and fishing a capable lad 11 year of age.

David's eyes shot up to Jackson and then back down to the page. He read the last line and flew forward into Jackson's sun-spotted arms.

Jackson broke into raucous laughter, clapping the boy on the back.

"What else did it say, Pigeon Davey. I'm dyin' to know!"

"It says you're gonna be that very same wracker, Fishy! It says you're coming with me to Eleutheria!"

* * * * *

During the final weeks before the *William* was to sail for Eleutheria, the Adventurers added other provisions to their Articles and Orders, including Reverend Copeland's guidance with regard to natives:

> *That no Inhabitant of these Plantations, shall in their converse with any of the Natives of any of those parts, offer them any wrong, violence, or incivility whatsoever; but shall deal with them with all justice and sweetness, so far as may stand with their own safety, thereby to work in them a good opinion of love, unto the ways and knowledge of God, which everyone shall endeavor to hold forth, and communicate unto them in the best manner that they can.*

With his great heart and unequivocal piety, Copeland also convinced the party they should do what they could to assist any natives who'd been captured by others and sold into slavery.

> *And whereas the Company is informed, that there are some Indians have been taken and sold at some of the Caribe Islands : It is therefore agreed and ordered, that the Indians shall be sought out and redeemed: and after they have some time continued in those Plantations, for their instructions, and make them sensible of the benefit. They shall be then returned to the places from which they were taken.*

Through a committee comprised of Peter Sands, Benjamin Sawyer, David Albury, John Knowles, Henry Rowan and Captain Sayle, rules were established for defense of the Eleutheria.

> *That every Planter shall himself provide Arms and Ammunition sufficient, for his own persons (going to the said Plantations) and for every Male that he shall transport thither, who is or shall be from time to time able to bear Arms, and that such Adventurer shall not have his share of Land set out unto him for any Male person, unless he be as aforesaid, provided of sufficient Arms and Ammunition for them,*

That all in the said Plantation from the age of sixteen to sixty years shall be ready to come to the several Rendezvous appointed them, upon any Alarm, ready and armed for the defense of the Plantations;

That none shall be compelled to take Arms, or to go to war out of the Country unless it be for the necessary defense thereof, and to expel or divert an eminent invasion, neither shall any be suffered to take any depredations or invasions upon any either by Sea or Land, unless upon a War first begun by them and open War by the said Plantations, first denounced against them.

* * * * *

"Captain Butler, sir, you may recollect young Pigeon Davey here," Jackson said as Butler stepped off the gangway onto the deck of the William. "He's been a great one for crawlin' into tight places below as we provision for the voyage." Butler ignored the re-introduction and asked, "Where's the powder been stowed, Jackson? I don't want to have to send a boy for powder when we need it."

"Why no sir, Captain, all the powder's in the magazine same as when we sailed from Portsmouth."

"Then you'll make damn sure you don't block the way to the magazine with all manner of farming flotsam, do ya understand? I tell ya now, Jackson, I won't stand for passengers or their belongings interfering with the operation of this vessel."

"Well sir, if you'll forgive me saying so, they aren't so much as passengers as they are partners in this here venture."

Butler's jaw clenched and he drew in a sharp breath through his sharp nose.

"I'll say this once," Butler growled slowly, "the man among them who regards me as an equal will find my boot upon his throat. I've paid my £100 into this venture, and I'll do my duty aboard this ship, but I'll not play nursemaid to any man who can't take care of himself once we're ashore."

Butler abruptly turned his back and the thudded away in his large boots.

"Well, Davey," Jackson said, looking down into the boy's worried face, "I t'ink I best have a word with Captain Sayle about our man Butler. Don't ya worry yerself about what he said. He's only one man amongst the whole group of us. Surely he can't do too much harm."

* * * * *

The morning of July 2, 1647 came suddenly to exaggerated life as a line of dark thunderstorms cracked and boomed overhead. The early morning light, ducking under the black clouds, turned the harbor bottle-glass green. A gusty southeast wind could be seen throwing white-capped waves against St. David's Island in the mouth of the harbor. Only eight days remained until the *William* would begin her voyage to the south. Jackson and David agreed to meet Captain Sayle that day at his estate in Smith's Parrish to help close up the the graceful estate Sayle called Verdmont.

"Where will we land the skiff, Fishy?" David asked as Jackson raised the mainsail.

"We'll take 'er right in to Devonshire Bay. There's good shelter and we'll just tuck the 'ole girl in behind the headland. Put yer slicker on now, boy, we'll be in the spray soon as we clear Higgs Island."

David pulled on the oilskin coat that once belonged to Mrs. Newbold's son, Abraham, now a full grown man working at the Saunders' dry-dock.

"Toothy! Here girl," said Jackson, patting the deck grate under the tiller, "You come on back here and sit down for the ride."

The dog jumped effortlessly over David's legs and sat immediately down, gazing for a moment into Jackson's eyes as if to confirm she'd done what was asked.

"Good girl, Jilly. Now you be still and mind ya don't knock yer head on the tiller."

The three bounced along the waves to the southwest, passing Annie's Bay, then Neptune Rock and the string of tiny islands guarding Castle Harbour. As they left Canton Bay behind, the sun broke through the swiftly moving clouds above, casting a narrow beam of gold light on the pink sands beach of John Smith's Bay.

Jackson took his eyes off the shoreline and turned to David, "Do ya remember where Devonshire Bay is, Davey? That's the one where we skinned that shark wot we caught in the net."

"I think I know," said David, "It's right before Cox's Bay."

"Aye, that's that one, lad. Did I ever tell ya about the mermaid I seen perched upon the headland rocks as ya look into the bay?"

David's eyes widened and he lost his balance for a moment in the choppy sea. "Was she singin' like they say?"

"The singin' is what drew my attention to 'er, Davey. It was a foggy mornin' and the sun was breaking through only now and again between the banks. Well, as I get near Devonshire Bay, I t'ink I hear this voice cryin' Arthur! Arthur! Then nothin' for a while, then I hears it again real faint like. Arthur! Arthur! Well I'll tell ya, my eyes was strainin' to see who it was. Then all of the sudden, I get a hasty glimpse of her sittin' there right by the water with her hair slicked all back, leaning on her side she was."

As was his custom when listening to a good story, David began to nod energetically, tapping his foot on thwart. "Was she still crying out for Arthur?"

"Nay, all was quiet now, but I approached best I could in the fog 'til I reckoned I must a been fairly close to them rocks. Then out of the fog, I see what I t'ink must surely be her tail against the rock! Then the fog again. I tell ya it was vexin'. Well I took the mainsail down and drifted there with my eyes peeled wide open.

David interjected, "Mr. Sands said mermaids will draw boats right up onto the rocks. Weren't you feared she was trying to do that with you, Fishy."

"To tell ya the truth, Pigeon, the t'ought never entered my head. I just wanted to get a good look at her that bad. And sure enough I did."

"You saw her then plain and clear!"

"Aye, as clear as I see you sittin' there right now."

"Well what did she look like! Why aren't you telling me!"

Jackson straightened his back a little and looked Davey in the eye, "Are ya sure ya want to know?"

"Of course I'm sure!"

"As ya want to know so badly, I'll do my best to describe her. She had big shiny black eyes set in a charmin' face. Her hair was kinda brown and gold, mottled in a nice way. Her tail was small and elegant.

Jackson paused now, a nostalgic smile forming on his brown leathery face.

"What a face she had, Davey! As pretty as could be with that little black nose and them long whiskers."

"Whiskers?" asked the boy.

"Aye, I could see them plain as day. And her flippers too."

"Mermaids don't have flippers; they have *hands*."

71

"That's right, Pigeon, they do."

"Well then what you saw wasn't a mermaid," said David.

"No, it weren't a mermaid at all, it was a harbor seal."

"But you told me you saw a mermaid!"

"I did see a Mermaid, as God is my witness."

But you just said it was a harbor seal."

"It was a harbor seal only I *saw* a mermaid."

"You're driving me mad, Fishy Jack, and I'm only twelve."

"Nay boy, I'm just tellin' ya that ya can't always believe yer eyes and ears at sea, especially when there's fog about," Jackson laughed.

* * * * *

Captain Sayle, his wife, Margery, and the couple's eldest son, Thomas were in the garden of Verdmont manor. Mrs. Sayle directing the task of collecting various cuttings, bulbs, and seeds to take with the family to Eleutheria. The sun was out now, the wind quickly settling into a soft breeze. Verdmont sat upon the slope like a dignifiedt matron in a pastel gown, comfortable in her favorite seat overlooking the sea.

"Hallo Captain Sayle," called Jackson from the road.

"Ah Jackson!", replied Sayle, "come on through the gate!"

With Toothy Jill daintily trotting ahead, Jackson and David passed through the gate set in a limestone wall then up the brick path, which was partially blackened by tropical mildew and lichen.

"Good mornin' to ya, Captain and Mrs. Sayle. And you as well, Thomas," Jackson said as he approached the three.

"Well, so this is the Toothy Jill you've been telling me about, David," said Mrs. Sayle, smiling at the little dog.

"Yes ma'am," answered David, "she can dive conch."

Mrs. Sayle put on a surprised visage, exclaiming, "She swims under water then?"

"Oh yes ma'am, she and I both."

"I suppose we have Mr. Jackson to blame for that mischief, am I not right?" Mrs. Sayle said, turning to Jackson.

"Aye, it was teach the boy to swim or wear myself out fishin' him out of the water every time he fell overboard playin' the fool."

"My husband claims the ability to swim, though I've not once seen a demonstration and fear I've been misled," quipped the Captain's wife.

Sayle, still digging bulbs from the garden looked up and spoke. "Thanks to the grace of God, I've not had any reason to paddle about the water for a very long time and I pray no occasion shall arise in the future."

Jackson and David spent the day shuttling the Sayle's barrow to and from Verdmont to the skiff in Devonshire Bay. Jackson sailed the first load back to St. George's bay and personally saw that the cargo was stowed aboard the *William* according to Sayle's instructions. David stayed behind at Verdmont and helped Mrs. Sayle and the servants cover furniture and roll up the rugs.

In the afternoon, Jackson returned to Devonshire Bay with the skiff and walked back to Verdmont. As he strolled up the brick path, he could see Captain Sayle sitting on a garden bench alone with his thoughts. Jackson approached, letting his presence be known with a polite cough.

"That was a rapid trip, Fishy."

"Aye, the 'ole skiff moves slick as a porpoise when the wind's astern, so the run back to St. George's was swift.."

In this setting, with Captain Sayle alone, Jackson saw his opportunity to broach the subject of Captain Butler.

"Sir, I don't make it my business ever to speak against my superiors."

Sayle, turned quickly from the view of the garden and looked directly at Jackson.

"I'm not speaking of *you*, sir," Jackson quickly clarified, "I'm referrin' to another."

"What is it, Fishy, does it concern our Company of Adventurers?," Sayle asked.

"Yes sir, truth is I feel I need to speak to ya concernin' Captain Butler. He strikes me as a fish that don't care much about swimin' in a school. Seems he'd rather slide around the reef more like a shark, sir."

Sayle, nodded his chin slightly and said, "He strikes me as a very determined man, Fishy, but I don't yet know what it is he's so determined about. But his determination may be exactly what we need to make a success of the colony."

Jackson, looked down at his shoes and replied, "I don't know, sir, seems to me he might be determined to raise himself up by stepping on the backs of others. Is there no way he could be replaced?"

Sayle shook his head, "Even if you're right about the man, we cannot delay further. The worst of the hurricane season will be upon us soon and we must be safely established on Eleutheria by then."

"Aye Captain, ye're surely right about that. Thirty-seven years I've lived on this island and I've seen my share of frightful storms. I won't be botherin' ya about Captain Butler again."

"No, Fishy, it was right of ya to speak up. We're forming a *republic*, and that's the kind of arrangement where all men are free to say what's on their mind."

Sayle rose from the bench and shook Jackson's hand. "I believe I'll walk with ya to Devonshire Bay, if ya don't mind. I admit, I'll miss this island of ours sorely, Mr. Jackson, but I'll not miss the rancor and persecution that's been sent against us for the manner in which we worship our Lord."

Jackson nodded, "Aye, my landlady reported to me yesterday that a man come callin' to collect a *tax* from me for being baptized into Reverend Copeland's church."

Sayle nodded his understanding, 'Yes, we've all been taxed for our beliefs, Fishy. I'm sorry they're on to ya now, but we'll be free soon enough."

6 THE DEVIL'S BACKBONE

Excerpt from the letters and papers of John Winthrop, first Governor of the Massachusetts Colony.

In the way to Eleutheria, one Captain Butler, a young man who came in the ship from England, made use of his liberty to disturb all the company. He could not endure any ordinances or worship and when they arrived at one of the Eleutheran Islands, and were intended there to settle, he made such a faction, as enforced captain Sayle to remove to another island.

* * * * *

John Saunders checked to see that the leeboards, mounted on both sides of the 6-ton shallop, were firmly locked in place before ordering his dockhands to lower the boat down the dry-dock skids and into St. George's bay. Saunders had overseen the construction of the craft from the laying of its keel to the setting of its rigging, a single mast onto which a square sail would be raised. The flat-bottomed, shallow draft boat, built from Bermuda Cedar (Juniperus

Bermudiana), was about thirty feet in length with an eight foot beam. She could accommodate a crew of ten oarsmen and hold around twenty-five souls in all. When under sail, her leeboards, looking much like seal flippers lying along the flanks of the boat, could be lowered on the leeward side of the boat to help prevent the craft from drifting sideways. The boat was much like that which was used by Captain Smith in his explorations along the Chesapeake in the American colonies.

With an elegant 'swish', the shallop glided into the clear waters of St. George's Bay.

"She could balance on the head of a pin, Mr. Saunders!" cheered Captain Sayle.

"Thank you, Captain," answered Saunders, "I think she'll go just about anywhere you ask her to."

"Daniel!" called Saunders to his brother sitting at the oars in the shallop, "go now and bring her around to the wharf!" In a softer voice he turned to his other brother standing nearby, "You, Nathaniel, you run along and help yer brother tie up the boat by Fishy Jack's skiff."

"Can you join us for a trial, John?" asked Sayle.

"Of course, Captain, but ya won't find a thing wrong with her," he laughed. Saunders turned then to David, who stood smiling by Jackson at the water's edge. "Davey, would ya fancy taking the tiller when we get to sea?"

"Aye, Uncle John, I'd be pleased," the boy responded.

Ever since the day Jackson introduced David to Saunders, explaining the boy was an orphan, Saunders had insisted the boy call him 'uncle,' which suited David well. John Saunders was the eldest of three brothers and one sister, Jane, and family meant a great deal to the man.

With Daniel, Nate and John Saunders at the oars and Jackson readying the sail as they rowed, the shallop glided out of St. Georges Bay past St. David's Island and into a stiff breeze. John Saunders quickly lowered the leeboard as the boat heeled over slightly to starboard. The boat, although she had a flat bottom, handled the waves well, if not quietly. Captain Sayle smiled at Saunders as he manned the tiller, pointing aloft to the taught rigging.

The shallop was soon over two miles offshore and the men were enjoying the relatively cool air on the open sea. Milk-white cumulous clouds blossomed above and cast the shallop in and out of shade as if the craft were making its way through a forest of great oaks. Then suddenly to the windward side of the boat, no more than thirty yards away, an explosion of blue water and white foam jolted everyone's senses awake. A huge humpback whale breached leaving behind a large circular wake. The men cheered spontaneously as the leviathan disappeared in a plume of ocean froth.

"Lest we ever forget the majesty of God's creation" called Sayle, "we've been reminded today!"

"Aye, Captain," responded Jackson, "and a rare thing that we should see such a sight in July, as them whales generally pass Bermuda on their way north between April and May."

Just then a calf appeared, nudging up to its mother's enormous flank.

"I see it as a sure sign from the Almighty, Mr. Jackson. That whale must have calved very late in the warm waters to the south so she could be sent to us now on this 3rd day of July as a sign that God is watching our venture and will provide for us along the way."

Upon their return to St. Georges Bay, the men tied the shallop alongside the *William*, now almost fully prepared to sail. Over the next week, several times per day, John Saunders would check the shallop as her timbers swelled in the sea water, making her seams even tighter.

Aboard the *William*, each family handed over into Captain Butler's care the provisions and matériel they would depend upon, including the powder, shot and firearms required by the Articles and Orders.

The time had finally come to find freedom.

* * * * *

It was Tuesday, the 9th of July, 1647. As the early morning sun stretched its warm fingers over the waters of St. Georges bay, forty-one heads of family and seventy souls in total gathered on the wharf to pray.

Reverend Copeland spoke, "We are diverse in our beliefs, but we are as one that such diversity should be, and must be, the cornerstone of our settlement. We are as one against the man-made strictures of the Church of England. I ask you now to bow your heads and share with me a prayer that should offend no one of us."

Lord Jesus Christ, You said that You
are the Way, the Truth, and the Life.
Help us not to stray from You, for You are the Way;
nor to distrust You, for You are the Truth; nor to rest
on any other than You, as You are the Life. You have
taught us what to believe, what to do, what to hope
and where to take our rest. Give us peace to follow
You, the Way, to learn from You, the Truth, and to
live in You, the Life.

Captain Sayle, uttered amen and then stepped up beside Reverend Copeland, standing upon the *William*'s gangway.

"Most among us have been aboard our ship and have seen for yourselves her diminutive proportions. She is but eighty-five tons and her holds are severely cramped, packed as they are with the provisions that shall help sustain us when we reach Eleutheria. I ask you to pray with me now that with the Lord's hand upon our shoulders we shall humbly suffer each others discomfitures at sea ad on land. While we sail, each one of us shall share a single berth with two others, each to have his rest in such berth in shifts of four hours. Each child shall share a single berth with two others, each to have his rest upon the berth in shifts of *eight* hours. Let us pray for the forbearance of others as we move about the ship and attend to our daily ablutions. Let us pray above all for safe passage to the island of Eleutheria. And let us pray that we shall serve our Lord upon our arrival there and for every day to follow. Amen."

Other prayers were shared out loud, and a silent prayer was offered by a Quaker among them. All the while, Captain Butler remained on the ship's bridge.

"As you board the vessel," shouted Captain Sayle to the men, women and children gathered along the wharf, each head of household shall place his right hand upon our Articles and Orders and shall pledge to abide by and uphold them, as we have agreed."

Jackson looked down at David who'd been tugging at the sailor's shirt.

"What is it Pigeon?"

"What shall I do, Fishy? About the Articles?"

"Ah, I see what's troublin' ya. I'll pledge for ya Davey, it matters not that yer Pa isn't here with us. You and I are a household and I'll pledge for the two of us."

Sayle called to Jackson and directed him to make his way onto the ship first in order to help settle the passengers. Butler and the four men he'd arranged as crew, stood silently by. The last head of household stood beside Captain Sayle and pledged upon the Articles and as the minutes ticked past, it became obvious to Sayle that Butler would not of his own accord make the same pledge.

* * * * *

As the *William* tacked east out of St. George's harbor and the rocky islets and reefs disappeared from view, Jackson saw clearly in his mind the day in 1609 when he'd first laid eyes on the same forbidding coastline. That day aboard the *Sea Venture* almost thirty-eight years past was the day Jackson assumed he would die, cut to ribbons by the jagged reef or drowned in the pounding surf. But the island had saved them all, that and Captain Somer's decision to drive the foundering vessel as fast and as high as he could upon the reef. Jackson had come to know with an abiding certainty that the notion of paradise was the exact same notion of freedom. Strange, he thought, that Bermuda could be partitioned to the highest bidder without a thought to its original inhabitant. Strange that paradise would be populated by persons so unwilling to tolerate freedom.

"Ya look as though ya might swim for shore, Fishy." Peter Sands looked his old friend in the eye and then gazed back at the disappearing shoreline.

"Nay, Peter. The first time I swam ashore 'twas to save my life. I'd be doing just the contrary were I to make the swim today. Nothin' for me and Davey back there now. I'll be free again in Eleutheria and Davey will have his first taste."

Sands nodded. "Well I never forgot any of stories you told me about your first years in Bermuda, havin' the place all to yourself without so much as single customs agent or tax collector!"

Jackson smiled and added, "Aye, but the few of us who was there worked hard for each other, only somehow that didn't seem like a duty or a law so much as a privilege. As bound as we were to each other, we were free."

Captain Butler's loud bark cut through the wind and made its way forward to Jackson and Sands. "Tell the men forward to come aft at once!" he shouted to a fidgety man who'd introduced himself to Jackson as "one of Butler's men." Butler, it seemed, had taken it upon himself to assemble his own crew, despite the fact that the ship's company of Adventurers was adequately populated with men born to the sea. The three Saunders males were master seaman, as was David Albury, Stephen Higgs, Jonathan Lowe, Nathaniel Harris, Benjamin Sawyer, Paul Harris and Christopher Johnson. Captain Sayle himself had spent a good part of his life at sea and would have no problem commanding a ship many times the size of the *William*.

Standing stiffly on the quarterdeck, Butler remained uncomfortably silent as his eyes bore into each man assembled on the lower deck before the mainmast. When he finally spoke, he did so looking directly at Captain Sayle, who was standing by the helmsman.

"You'll find I don't tolerate passengers interfering with the operation of my vessel. You men with families aboard make damn sure the decks are clear at all times. When I order one of you to a station, I expect you to take that station at a run without askin' for some women's leave to pass by."

No one spoke, so Butler, a man for whom belligerence had always paid returns, continued his indoctrination. "Redding! Come up here!" he shouted to one of the strangers he'd brought aboard.

Sayle looked towards Butler, but the man had turned away, seemingly dismissing Sayle as irrelevant. Butler suddenly spun the man he called Redding around to face the crowd assembled below on the deck. "This here is your First Mate. My orders will pass through him and only him. Anything you need to say to me will pass through him as well."

Sayle was visibly shaken now as he stepped away from the helm and moved closer to Butler.

"Mr. Butler . . .." began Sayle.

"*Captain* Butler, if you please Mr. Sayle."

"Very well," continued Sayle, "*Captain* Butler. The Company of Eleutheran Adventurers has amongst is ranks more than enough capable seaman. The position of First Mate has already been assigned to Benjamin Jackson."

Butler, whirled around to glare at Sayle. "You forget that I sailed with Jackson from Portsmouth, Captain Sayle. He's a fine nursemaid to small children, but I've seen nothing in the way of evidence that he can control grown men."

Sayle's jaw grew tight and he struggled to hold his composure. "Captain Butler, I would suggest we take up this matter in our quarters at the very first opportunity. I do not expect a lengthy voyage, but it must nevertheless be conducted in accord with our company's fundamental republican precepts."

Butler immediately roared his response, "So you say a ship is a *republic* then? I tell you captain we shall most certainly meet in your quarters as soon as I finish my shift upon deck."

Butler then whirled back to the sailors below the quarterdeck. "Well my dear *republicans*, you're welcome to your high notions when you're ashore and out of my sight, but on this ship I make the decisions. When it's my watch, you'll follow the orders I pass to Redding here. If you don't, you'll wish you had."

Butler then ordered Redding to dismiss the men. As they dispersed, he spoke to Sayle again. "At four bells then. I expect we'll conclude our business quickly, Captain Sayle, so your watch shall not be unnecessarily delayed."

Sayle nodded soberly, "Yes, I suspect we shall quickly put to rest any ambiguity regarding command. I note that you have not yet pledged to the Company's Articles and Orders, Captain, so I expect you to use our meeting as an opportunity to review the same."

"I'll read whatever your party has writ, Captain Sayle. That much I can promise you."

* * * * *

Jane Saunders was fond of the boy, Davey Pinder. During the voyage south, her three older brothers would alternately slip in and out of their cramped quarters every four hours with the change of watch. The three would share one hammock with Jane, who would rest in the berth during the fourth shift. Jackson and David would share the neighboring hammock with one other crew member, Stephen Higgs. David was allowed to rest through the duration of two four-hour shifts, while Jackson and Higgs would be allowed a single shift. Toothy Jill, accustomed to making herself small aboard any vessel, curled up into a neat little bundle wedged into a corner to brace herself against the pitch and roll of the ship.

"Davey," whispered Jane, "are you asleep?"

"No, I don't think I shall ever sleep again. What if we miss something?"

"Well I think we did, in fact, miss something terrible this morning, Pigeon. Did you hear my brothers speaking about Captain

Butler's address to the crew?"

"I heard," responded Davey. Fishy told me to make sure Toothy Jill stayed clear of the man. Do you think he'd kick her, truly?"

Jane sighed and responded so softly that the creaking of the ship nearly swallowed up her words, "I believe Captain Butler capable of worse, Davey. We'll just keep a sharp eye out for little Jilly. Let's agree between us that we'll keep her always on the forecastle deck when she's above, alright?"

"Alright Miss Jane. I think that would be best. And I like to stay clear of Captain Butler as well."

As the sun slipped beneath the sea the 9th of July, 1647, the *William* slowly pulled her way southward towards a place none of her passengers had ever seen and towards a life no one could accurately imagine. The hot fetid air below deck amplified the abstract desire to set foot on Eleutheria into a desperate need. The *William* would require at least ten days to reach her destination, but the soft southeasterly winds on this first day at sea whispered of a longer voyage.

* * * * *

Captain Butler did not knock when he entered the small cabin he and Sayle would alternatively occupy during the voyage. Nor did he wish Captain Sayle 'good evening.' Nor did he report on the condition of the ship as he sat down at the small table affixed to the transom bulkhead beneath a row of little windows.

Sayle began, "And how do you find the ship, Captain Butler."

Without looking away from the view astern, Butler replied curtly, "I find her much the same as she was when I brought her from Portsmouth, but for the overcrowding."

"Well the voyage will be short enough. I am confident in our headings," Sayle responded as he joined Butler at the table. He continued, "You expressed to me an eagerness to review our Articles and Orders, Captain Butler."

"I expressed a *willingness*, Captain Sayle."

"Very well," Sayle conceded, "I am aware that you attended but a single meeting of our Company of Adventurers, so you no doubt require a full briefing."

Butler, now shifted his gaze to Captain Sayle, and as he did so he reached for the hanging lantern, then adjusted the wick to cast more light on the table. "As I said, Captain, I intend to read your Articles and Orders. I'll do so now, if you please."

Sayle laid before Butler the pages he and Reverend Copeland had carefully assembled. "I'll see to the watch as you read, Captain Butler. Please allow me a quarter of an hour."

"There is no haste required, Captain Sayle. I assure you I left the bridge only when the watch had been successfully changed. You met Redding earlier, Captain. I brought aboard three others for each watch, just as capable as he."

Sayle stood and made his way past Butler. "Yes I'm sure they follow your orders dutifully, Captain Butler. As I said, I shall return within a quarter hour."

Once on deck, Sayle paced nervously fore and aft, fore and aft, never speaking a word to any of the crew. He passed Jackson and Peter Sands emerging from below-decks, each with a bowl of potage and a spoon.

Sands cheerfully addressed the captain, "The mess is a bit short of space, Captain, so Jackson and I shall take our meals on deck, with your leave."

Sayle nodded silently, standing very still before the men, his gaze absent and troubled.

"Is there some service we can do for ya, Captain?" asked Jackson.

Sayle looked up slowly from the deck and gazed first at Sands then at Jackson. "I fear that I may be asking for your assistance more than I had expected would be necessary. For now, I ask that you and the rest of our company be forthright in your assessment of Captain Butler. The man was quick to buy into our venture, but his motivations may be quite diverse from ours. Jackson, I wish to express my appreciation, too late it seems, for your words to me back at Verdmont. As quick as Butler was to invest in our company, I was just as quick to abate your observations of the man."

"Well sir," Jackson suggested, "per'aps the burrs will wear off of Captain Butler when we arrive at Eleutheria."

"Maybe so, Fishy, God willing. Now I must return to quarters where our Captain Butler is reading the company's Article and Orders for the first time."

Sands spoke up again. "Fishy Jack and I are behind ya, Captain. If there is trouble with Captain Butler, we'll help in any way we can."

Sayle nodded his understanding, shook hands with the two

sailors, and walk aft, seemingly oblivious to the deep roll of the ship. As he approached his cabin door, he heard laughter behind it. Somehow he did not expect to see Butler alone, but he was – still sitting at the small table.

"Ah Captain Sayle! I've not enjoyed such a fine read in a long while. It seems you may be more a student of Pericles than our Lord Jesus Christ."

Sayle reeled backward against the cabin door as if struck. He slowly shook his head, looking steadily into Butler's eyes. "You make a grave error, Captain Butler, in assuming I place an ancient Athenian politician in equal stead with our Lord. In all things, I am guided by my faith. And my faith is placed solely at the feet of the One who died for my sins."

"I meant no offense . . ." began Butler.

"I believe you did mean offense, Captain, but no matter, as your slight does not change my opinion of you, merely strengthens it."

"Hear, sir! You misunderstand me. I have read your Articles and, as I said, I am pleased to have done so. You are a man of the broad world, Captain Sayle, surely you can respect that I might at once enjoy your philosophy *and* declare it unfit for my tastes. That I shall have nothing to do with your ordinances does not diminish my admiration of your idealism."

Sayle nodded slightly and responded, "You understand that all who have joined this venture have pledged to abide by our Articles and Orders?"

"I understand full well, Captain. But there you are wrong. I joined this venture and paid the same amount of consideration as all others, yet I never agreed to your ordinances nor was I informed of them at the time I tendered £100 into your very hands. The impetus behind the venture, you expressly informed me, was freedom to worship without prejudice. That, sir, is a fine motivation and I harbor no animosity toward it. I choose to worship as the need arises. Thus far it has not."

"Captain Butler, you were invited to the company's meetings and given opportunity to object, yet you did not."

"Ah, well sir, I should have made myself clearer: At the time I tendered my £100 pounds into your very hands I was *neither* informed of your intended ordinances nor advised that my £100 obliged me to attend meetings of any nature. I am frequently *invited* to church and other gatherings but seldom attend. Contrarily, I routinely attend meetings and satisfy other obligations when I am *paid* to do so."

Sayle breathed a sigh and paused for several moments, "Captain Butler, what, may I ask, do you object to specifically?"

"Ah, now there is a straightforward question easily answered. I object, no I *refuse*, to support any man, women or child whom I do not wish to support of my own accord. The fruits of my labor shall be my own. Let me share with you the irony of this venture, as you fail to see it yourself. We are bound for an island you and your settlers call "freedom," yet you intend to yoke every man to his neighbor. Take them back to England, Captain, let them pay taxes and tithes and duties *there*."

A wave struck squarely upon the quarterdeck sending water cascading down the ladders, sounding just like a Lakes District waterfall. Sayle, stooped and looked aft through the transom window.

"Captain Butler, the sea is rising and I must soon attend to the watch. Our conversation must end for the time being. I cannot believe, however, that you refuse to play no part in the defense of our new colony."

Butler interrupted, "I did not say I would not defend the colony against attack. I have no objection in joining with my neighbors to repel a foreign enemy. But I shall not pay a farthing for an improvement to anyone's land but my own. If I wish to enter into contract with one or more men to further a mutual business objective, I shall do so. But I will not willingly enter into a contract with your government and its republican ideals."

Sayle approached the cabin door and took the latch into his hand, "Let us now at least agree that we shall work together in good faith to deliver this ship to its destination."

"Of course, Captain Sayle. Of course."

* * * * *

Captain Butler remained in his quarters the morning of July 13, 1647, a Sunday. The four crew members recruited by Butler were similarly below deck, perhaps upon Butler's orders. The remainder of the ship's compliment crowded onto the deck beneath the wilting sun, with no apparent concessions to the heat in regard to puritan dress.

Reverend Copeland's sermon was energetic despite the swelter and, uncharacteristically, he gave no quarter to those in the congregation exhibiting discomfort, either from the unremitting sun or the motion of the sea. Copeland welcomed the adversity as an opportunity to bind his flock together through shared perseverance. The elderly reverend had traveled wide and had seen much in his 77 years, but he could not know then how severely he and his fellow Adventurers would be tested.

When the service finally, if not mercifully, concluded, Jane Saunders, David and Jackson made their way together below decks and only then removed some of their stifling Sunday clothing. Hats were dispensed with first, as the deck overhead was so low most of the adults moved about bent at the waist even with naked heads. Coats were the second concession for most aboard, with the exception of Copeland and a few others whose piety was of a particularly determined variety.

Jackson placed his hand on David's sweaty shoulder and said, "You go upon the deck, Davey. Forward and in the shade of the canvas we're flyin'. I must have a little kip here in our hammock, as the next watch is mine."

Jane turned to the boy and smiled. "I'll join you, Pigeon. Captain Butler is below decks and we've no concern of encountering the man."

Once again on deck, and tucked among the cargo lashed almost everywhere on the small ship, the two surreptitiously lowered a deck bucket to the bow wake and pulled aboard a few gallons of water that felt barely cooler than the air as they dipped their bare feet into it. Toothy Jill had not moved from her shady spot at the base of the foremast since the evening before. She was a dog well accustomed to hunkering down in the heat.

Eventually, for both Jane and David the shade and the light breeze moving stealthily along the rail, dissipated the assault of discomfort brought on by the long sermon.

"Let's put one of your line's overboard, Davey. T'will give us something to pass the time. Butler won't notice if we're quiet upon the quarterdeck."

Davey smiled, but then almost immediately looked startled. "But what if Captain Butler looks out the transom windows and sees our line?"

"Well, I think it's noise and traffic upon the deck that vexes him so. He'll be in his quarters for at least another two hours so he can't complain of us being in his path. And we'll be silent as night."

David slipped below and crept silently to his berth among sleeping and dozing shipmates. He gathered a long trolling line and one of Jackson's clever lures and met Jane at the transom rail.

"I forgot to bring the gloves Fishy has me wear, but we'll be alright." The boy stood wedged against the portside corner in the railing and carefully trailed out the line to the leeward of the heavy towline attached to the shallop, which bobbed along behind.

The breeze was rising now in the early afternoon and it breathed more life and color back into Jane's cheeks. "What do you reckon the fish do away out here in the sea, Pigeon? All that blue all around, no bottom, no reef, it must be like time stands still for them."

David started nodding in his namesake fashion. "I think they're flyin' out here whereas on the reef it's like they're in a nest."

"Aye, there you have it, Pigeon."

As they looked astern, the lure skipped every now and then as the line cut through the crest of a wave like a knife through jelly. During his first crossing aboard the *William* from Portsmouth to Bermuda, David did not notice the absence of birds. But now on his second long voyage he was keenly aware of they were missing. The gulls back in Bermuda had been constant companions to David and Jackson as they fished along the coasts. Here in the open sea, David felt the nagging emptiness that can come upon a soul accustomed to the cacophony of nature's birds, insects and terrestrial animals. To Davey, the sounds far away from land were somehow mournful, the creaking of the ship's timbers and rigging, the swish and sigh of the bow parting the sea. Even the smells were troubling for their harsh juxtaposition: the fetid and complex assault of human odors against the sterile, alkaloid and simple scent of the open sea.

As David peered over the transom rail watching the clever lure jump tantalizingly through the crest of a wave, a sudden flash of silver caught his eye followed by the slice of two little black dorsal fins. He tightened his grip on the line and whispered hurriedly to Jane, "Mind you don't get your toes too close to the line – there are tuna readying a strike."

Like an arrow shot, the line suddenly raced through David's right hand. He shifted the line to his left hand and quickly wrapped the right in his shirttail. Taking the line again in his right, he tightened his grip on the line as much as the heat generated by friction would allow.

Jane smiled broadly and patted David on the shoulder, "You look like a boy who's done this a time or two before, Pigeon. Is it a tuna then?"

"Aye, it's a tuna but hopefully not one too big to pull aboard. I don't want to lose Fishy Jack's line and one of his best lures. He toils most of a day just to make one of them."

"Then don't let that fish make off with it, Davey! Bring her in and we'll please old Cook to no end. There'll be pudding for you tonight if you carry that fish into the galley."

When little more than twenty feet of line remained pooled on the deck, the fish suddenly stopped it's mad dash towards the bottom. Slowly, hand over hand, David began to retrieve the line, drawing the fish nearer to the *William*'s transom. When the fish was clearly visible below, it made another desperate run to the depths, forcing David again to surrender most of the line. Now he was sweating so heavily his eyes burned with salt and his hands turned slick. Bringing the line back in took twice as long as it had the first time. But the fish was tiring rapidly.

Jane whispered a scream, "You've got him now, boy, get him up against the transom and I'll help you haul him over the rail."

Four more arms' lengths of line and the fish was clearly in view beneath them, a nice blackfin tuna of about twenty pounds.

"Alright, Jane, let's try to haul now," panted David.

The two stood side by side, Jane reaching down the line for a grip and pull, then David taking the next length. Suddenly the fish broke the surface of the water wildly twisting and flicking its tail from side to side, slamming like a sack of potatoes into a transom window. The two stood paralyzed for an instant, looking into each other's panic stricken eyes. Then Jane lunged again for the line and within a few seconds the two of them had the fish over the rail, flapping loudly on the deck.

A withering roar emanated from below and Captain Butler's head suddenly appeared out the broken window. His gaze swiveled upward and fixed upon Jane and David's startled faces.

"What in the devil's name have you two gutter snipes done! I'll see you flogged, do ya hear!" Butler howled, before drawing his head back into his quarters.

David reached quickly for a belaying pin and with two quick blows clubbed the fish silent. Butler burst through the door to his cabin and flew up the ladder in no less of a rage than he'd been in below. He caught sight of the tuna lying at David's feet.

"So you're having some sport at my expense then! I carry the responsibility of every soul on this ship, including your own scurrilous one, and this is the kind of respect you provide in consideration? I should throw you both to the sharks and be done with it."

Jane struggled to regain her thoughts as her eyes filled with tears. "We're very sorry to have troubled you," she managed to stutter, and then fell silent again under his scalding gaze. David could do nothing but nod, nervously confirming his joinder in the apology.

Then the sound of boots on the ladder broke the spell of fright and Captain Sayle appeared on the quarterdeck. "Captain Butler, you could be heard throughout the ship and, I daresay, throughout the Caribbean Sea. What has happened?"

Butler pointed to the fish lying upon the deck.

Sayle looked again into Butler's red face, "This tuna has evoked such ire? I had no idea you harbored unbridled animosity against God's sea creatures."

"I care not the *least* about the fish, Captain Sayle, but I will see these two flogged for hurling the devil through my window as I try to sleep!"

Sayle slowly shook his head, "There will be no flogging of women and children aboard this ship nor will there be any such conduct in our new colony. The solution here is simply to order David and Jane not to enter upon the quarterdeck while you are retired in your quarters."

Sayle then turned to the two perpetrators. "For the sake of us all, and to preserve the peace among us, neither of you shall set foot upon this deck without my express permission. Do you understand?"

David nodded in his characteristic manner while Jane quietly uttered "Yes, Captain Sayle. We're awfully sorry, Captain."

"Take the fish to the galley now, David, and leave Captain Butler and me to speak."

Jane preceded David down the ladder and the two quickly made their way forward with the fish.

Sayle began, "Captain Butler . . . ."

But before he could continue, Butler turned his back and stepped quickly onto the ladder. In two great steps he was out of sight.

* * * * *

"It is almost assuredly the island of Abaco," Captain Sayle said as he looked into Reverend Copeland's tired eyes.

Pointing westward, Sayle spoke again. "This island and the barrier islands off its eastern shoreline are reportedly claimed by the French. Although I've heard nothing that leads me to believe the French have established a permanent settlement."

The starboard rail was crowded with the ship's company, all straining to see the island assumed to be very similar to their destination, the island of Cigatoo, renamed Eleutheria by Sayle. A gull appeared overhead, the first of the Bahama Islands to visit the small ship. Stretches of rocky shoreline, obstinately facing down the crashing Atlantic swell, were punctuated by coves and sheltered beaches as white as snow. Eventually, what seemed to be unbroken shoreline, gave way to a view of several smaller islands lying closer to the ship than the larger mainland. The water closest to shore was a brilliant aquamarine, while the sea under the ship's keel was a deep, unearthly blue.

As afternoon drew towards evening, and the wind shifted slightly more to the west and off shore of Abaco, a large cave appeared along the shoreline. The cave, christened 'Hole In The Wall' by the crew, signaled the southerly end of the island. At the close of his watch, Captain Sayle ordered the ship to ease several more points to the east and the southwesterly wind obliged. Abaco was now out of sight behind. With the last of the light, the *William* would proceed cautiously onward, bringing down most of the sail during the night. The waters ahead were unknown, but assumed to hide shoals and reefs. The crew strained throughout the night to see or hear waves breaking upon hazards lurking in the darkness ahead.

Though the winds blew from the southwest, a large swell rolled in from the opposite direction. Most of the ship's crew remained on deck, nervously peering into the night. Jackson, sitting beside John Saunders by the starboard rail, watched as a band of thunderstorms, like a long string of electrified pearls, flashed beneath the westerly horizon.

Saunders spoke first. "I fear that line of squalls is the sou'westerly edge of a spinning storm that first called up this heavy easterly swell."

"Aye," answered Jackson as he reached down to stroke Toothy Jill's head, "we'll see if the wind starts to shift more and more to the west and north. God willing, we'll be settled at anchor in a safe harbor tomorrow morning.".

* * * * *

Morning came at last with a calmer swell, but the sky to the west was black and the winds had, in fact, continued to shift away from the south. As the sun pulled itself free of the deep blue waters to the east, there was no mistaking the sight of land ahead. The *William*, now under full sail, lunged forward on a stiffening breeze. Word quickly spread among the ship's complement that the islands of Eleutheria, of freedom, were finally showing themselves. Reverend Copeland, standing on the quarterdeck, called down to the flock, "Let us pray!"

He closed his eyes, and clutching his bible to his chest began:

God of the guiding star, the bush that blazes
Show us the way.
God of the stormy seas, the bread that nourishes
Teach us your truth.
God of the still, small voice, the wind that blows where it chooses
Fill us with life.
God of the elements, of our inward and outward journeys
Set our feets on your road today.
May God bless us with a safe harbor today.
May your Son and your Grace travel with us.
May we live this day free in our worship of thy glory.
Amen.

Captain Butler huffed audibly, then punctured the reverent air with a loud order to his mate, Redding. "Send a second man aloft. Tell 'em to keep a sharp eye and if I catch either one them blinking I'll have their hides."

Peter Sands was sent scrambling up the rigging to join Jonathan Lowe. The two greeted each other and Lowe pointed to the black western skyline, which now offset an eerie emerald green light to the north.

"I think the squall line is approaching, Peter. And I can see whitecaps pushed ahead of them black monsters."

Sands nodded agreement with Lowe's assessment. The two men strained to see the features of the approaching shoreline, but the distance was still too great. Another hour passed before the land ahead began to reveal its profile. The easterly end of the shoreline seemed to end in a rocky point after which a narrow expanse of water gave way to a small islet. Looking west from the eastern point, the grey rocky shoreline was punctuated by dazzling beaches, some that appeared like small white flowers, others stretched broad and languid like sleeping cats. A highpoint above a wide beach could be seen about two-thirds of the way along the shore to the west, between low stretches of rock. The *William*'s heading would bring them slightly west of the highpoint.

Further to the west, Lowe and Sands could also make out a perfectly proportioned little cove cupping another small tidy beach. Further still to the west, a cliff rose above the water, then a bay, then a final beach, and the westerly point of the middle island in view. The total distance between the eastern point and the western point appeared to be about three or four miles. A narrow channel separated what appeared to be another island to the west, perhaps two miles long.

Now mid-morning, the wind rose noticeably from the west northwest. At around eleven o'clock Lowe spotted breaking waves dead ahead, perhaps a half of a mile offshore. Then more breaking waves both to the west and to the east.

Sands yelled below to Redding, who was standing just aft of the bowsprit, "Reef dead ahead! Half mile offshore! She looks wide as the shoreline itself!"

Captain Butler peered at the two men aloft and nodded. His watch had ended, Captain Sayle was in command, but Butler bellowed another order nonetheless.

"Hold the course, helmsman, we'll explore this northern shoreline for a channel. That bay there," he pointed, "may be suitable."

Captain Sayle walked briskly over to Butler and immediately addressed him.

"Captain Butler, the weather to the west and north is fouling rapidly. Ya can see for yourself those squall lines are roiling the seas before them."

"I can see that, yes, Captain Sayle. But before we hastily hold off from land and make to sea again, we would profit from surveying that coastline."

"The day is still young, Captain Butler, let us make to sea *now* and allow these squalls to pass. I've sailed tropical seas for many years now and I can tell you the weather you see over our starboard rail will play itself out in no more than a day. Contrarily, each of those dark apparitions has a cruel life of its own and there is no telling how wicked any one of them will prove to be. "

"Be reasonable, Captain Sayle, we are making way fast and another half hour will permit us the opportunity to confirm or deny the existence of a safe harbor. When those thirty minutes elapse, I'll have no objection to you ordering the ship back into open waters."

Sayle sighed deeply, then nodded slightly. "Very well, thirty more minutes then. But we are far too close to those reefs for my comfort and we have come too far in our efforts to take unnecessary risks."

Butler seemed not to hear Sayle's retort. He called upward to Sands and Lowe. "I favor the bay farthest to the west so look sharp on that heading!"

He then ordered the mate, Redding, to send a man forward and one aft with the leads. We'll take a sounding as we come about!"

Redding sent a man forward with a long thin line to which a lead plum was affixed, and another man aft with a second line. Jackson, Davey, and all four members of the Saunders party stood bunched together amidships by the starboard rail.

"We'll no sooner pass through that line of reef than we would over da devil's backbone itself," whispered Jackson into John Saunders ear. "This is folly and I'm strained to comprehend why Captain Sayle agreed to even another minute on this heading."

A violent gust of wind swirled angrily down the deck from stern to bow. Almost simultaneously, a deafening volley of lightening erupted just off the starboard beam. At once, it was clear to all that the squalls were approaching at breakneck speed borne upon a wind that was now almost due north. As a second volley of lightning crashed into the sea behind them, a wall of wind laden with droplets of salt water cuffed the ship's transom and whirled over the length of the deck.

"Come about to the east helmsman!" shouted Sayle. "Jackson! Bring down as much canvas as ya can and have Saunders ready the kedge anchors as well."

Sayle gauged the distance to the east, beyond the tiny island, to be about three miles. With the wind now howling from the north and the fat spatters of rain peppering the deck, the *William* was slipping rapidly southward despite coming about to the east.

"Rowan!" called Sayle, "Organize the men aft and start hauling in our towline, I want the shallop brought alongside the port rail! Load the kedge anchors aboard her as quickly as ya can."

Jane Saunders patted David on the back – the boy was visibly shaken – then shuffled quickly astern with her brothers Daniel and Nate. One of Butler's men fell in behind and the four men began to haul in the towline.

Now the squall was fully upon them and all but a few of the women and children had taken shelter below.

"Keep everyone upon the deck, Reverend Copeland! I want no one out of my sight!"

Sayle glanced for a moment at Butler, standing over the shoulder of the helmsman. "He must surely know," thought Sayle to himself. It was clear they would go upon the reef well before reaching the eastern end of the shoreline, past the little islet and into the open sea. It was nearly as clear that any attempt to hold the ship off the reef by rowing kedge anchors out to the north would likely fail. In order to use the anchors, they would need to come about into the wind and lose all forward momentum. At that point the ship, and all aboard her, would be at the mercy of the anchors and the speed in which they could be set.

Sayle prayed the ship would survive a grind over the coral reef and remain water tight enough to beach her on soft stretch of sand that now appeared tantalizingly close. But in the meantime, he would draw the shallop alongside the windward rail of the ship and prepare her for boarding, whether to attempt a kedging maneuver or abandon the ship, either way, the shallop was their only hope.

The squall then revealed the full extent of its anger, screaming through the rigging and shredding the canvas that remained aloft, tatters slapping about in the gale like cannon fire. It was over. Almost all momentum to the east was quickly spent and the ship's starboard beam bore down on the brown jagged back of the devil. The roar of foamy waves on the rocks was now deafening. More men leapt aft to help with the towline, heaving desperately to bring the shallop around to the side of the ship that faced away from the reef.

"Captain Butler!" screamed Sayle. Organize the women and children along the windward rail. I suggest you get your man, Redding, into the shallop immediately!"

To Butler's credit, he hadn't waited for Sayle's orders to begin assembling the women and children for escape into the shallop. But to his infamy, Redding was below with another of Butler's men struggling up the ladder with the huge sea chest Butler ordered them to bring on deck. The trunk contained Butler's cache of weapons and other personal effects, including a small library of books, charts and writing materials.

A scream broke from one of the women still lingering at the leeward rail.

"Hold fast, everyone!" yelled Captain Sayle, just before the ship heaved onto a coral head with a nauseating screech. The deck almost instantly pitched to the leeward, then, carried upon the next round of frantic waves, the *William* pushed closer to land. A long cry of dying timbers gave way suddenly to relative silence as the wounded vessel crawled over the southern wall of the coral head and into blue water again. She righted herself, swung slightly around to the west, but then her beam again presented to the full force of the gale. She was taking in water fast, and headed directly for a thicket of brownish coral heads crowned with frothy waves.

Redding, staggering closer to the windward rail with the heavy chest, heard Butler call out an order, "Get over the side and into the shallop, man! Ready the oars first then begin taking the women and children aboard!"

No sooner had the words left his mouth then the ship's hull met the next vertebrae in the devil's backbone. Again, she screamed as her timbers scraped along the razor sharp bones of the reef. Again, she clawed her way into another patch of blue water, her momentum gaining anew as the wind pushed her broadside. A few minutes of relative peace, then a pitiable moan followed by a sudden crash. She rolled at once to leeward and many on the deck fell upon each other, some of them now murmuring the Lord's prayer. This time, the ship stuck fast, the relentless waves thrashing at her tattered side. The wild pennants of shredded sail slapped out a chaotic rhythm, and the howl of the wind through the taught rigging sounded like the devil himself, unable to contain his mirth.

Butler's mate, Redding, was now aboard the shallop directing the crewmembers onboard the larger vessel to lower a boarding net over the side. Three men were chosen to man the shallop's oars and Jane Saunders volunteered to pull the forth pair. By ones and twos the women and children were helped down the net into the shallow draft boat until she could accommodate no more passengers. Redding, crawled back over the side onto the *William*'s deck as Butler ordered the shallop away.

Once around the William's bow, the small vessel shot towards the shoreline, riding fast on the wind and the following sea. In minutes she was spilling her passengers onto the beach. The three oarsman turned the boat's bow into the stubborn chop and pulling hard at the oars. Soon they reached the *William*, horrified to see how severely she'd suffered in less than a half hour. A gaping hole revealed itself on her starboard side, and most of the starboard planks were sprung. The sea flooded into the ship's compartments, arrogantly staking its claim on the *William* as it had done with thousands of ships before her. Already, bits of flotsam danced about in the foam, a belaying pin here, a cask there. The ship was dying fast, bleeding her battered cargo into the warm waters.

The steeply sloping deck was a scene from a captain's nightmare. David Albury, without Sayle's knowledge, was below decks up to his waist in seawater, desperately throwing through the hatch above whatever he could grab. Yet another fierce squall piled in on top of the first, and now sheets of windblown rain were slapping into the men as they tried to secure the shallop to the windward side of the ship. Jackson, together with Peter Sands and Jonathan Lowe, were scrambling about on the quarterdeck trying to cut free the dinghy lashed on its side against the leeward rail. As the chocks were pulled free, Jackson yelled, "stand by while I fix a longer line to her bow!" Lowe, Sands, and now David, struggled to hold the dinghy steady against the wind until Jackson had the line secure. Toothy Jill pressed her flank against Jackson, sensing his struggle.

"Alright boys, over the side with 'er!"

The men loosened their grips on the dinghy's gunwale and let her flip into the water, now merely four feet below the tilting deck. Then Jackson waved David over and asked Sands to help the boy and Toothy Jill into the bobbing little boat. Sands quickly seized the boy by the right hand and lifted him like a toy over the side and onto the seat below. Sands then gently lowered the dog into David's outstretched arms.

"Alright Davey," cried Jackson, "I'll be playin' out this line here and you make sure the dinghy don't swing back to the *William*, ya hear?"

David nodded as the tiny vessel sprang away in the greenish surf, moving towards the shore. Jackson tied off the bow line and shouted, "I'll be back presently, boy, you holler if that dinghy starts takin' water down there."

Sayle spotted Jackson scrambling forward and hailed him, "Jackson, you, Lowe, Rowan and Sands cut away everything you can on the deck! Whatever we can send over the side has a chance of making the shore!"

Lowe, a cutlass in each hand threw one to Rowan and the two men started hacking away at the lashings that bound the cargo around the foremast. Sands clawed his way quickly to the large carpenter's chest amidships. Jackson scrabbled along the leeward rail towards Sands, looking down on the tearing reef as he moved aft. Just as he stopped his progress and began to climb towards Sands the huge chest broke free, speeding down the incline and straight through the railing with a splintering crash. Sands reached for Jackson and helped him up to the hatchway. Looking down the ladder into the hold, the two men spotted Albury still trying to hurl items up through the hatch despite the fact that he was now up to his shoulders in water.

"David, for God's sake get out of there!" sang out Sands, "give me your hand!"

Albury heaved his way through the floating mass of debris and managed to grab the side of the ladder. An earsplitting *boom* reverberated through the ship as the stout keel finally gave way. At once the decking around Sands' feet exploded into long splinters and a huge crack opened across the ships raised port side. Jackson and Sands reached down the hatchway, and grabbed Albury's outstretched hands. As Albury's legs emerged from the water, a finely wrought box swirled into view under the ladder.

"Wait!", shouted Jackson, "grab that box through the rungs there, Albury, it could save our lives. That's the fishing tackle box Joseph Newbold made for me."

Albury's left hand let go Jackson's right and he snatched the box quickly, turning it gently so it would fit through the rungs. He then handed the box to Jackson as Sands helped Albury through the hatchway.

Captain Sayle was now halfway over the windward rail standing upon the boarding net signaling frantically to the men to board the shallop with him. A long, jagged bolt of lightning cracked into the sea off the port bow.

"I'll go ashore in the dinghy, Captain!" cried Jackson. "Davey's holding her off the stern!" The bandy-legged sailor then pulled himself aft along the lower rail, now periodically awash in the boiling sea. Sands and Albury, were among the last to climb over the high starboard side into the crammed shallop.

Sayle stood precariously in the shallop's bow, Sands trying to hold the captain steady. "Where's Butler and Redding?" Sayle shouted into Sand's ear.

Lowe overheard and called out to Sayle, "I just saw them not a moment ago on the quarterdeck!"

Suddenly Butler and Redding appeared above, leaning over the rail.

"Shove off!" Butler called to the shallop's oarsmen. The sailors quickly pushed away from the boarding net and began pulling on their oars.

Butler shouted from above, "Fast as you can now, boys, Redding and I will be right here when you get back . . . that is if we're not in the water by then!"

The shallop was so packed Sayle had to sit in Lowe's lap, and as Sayle looked about, he could see that many had resorted to the same seating arrangement. He looked back up at Butler, clinging to the port rail of the *William*. Sayle thought to himself, "Perhaps God is making His way into the man's heart through this tragedy."

As the small vessel battered its way towards the shore, Sayle spotted Reverend Copeland squeezed into the stern. The old reverend's right foot was shoeless and his stocking was nearly off, exposing a thin, chalk-white ankle.

"Reverend," called Sayle, "you've lost your shoe."

"I may have lost my shoe, Captain, and a great deal more," he cried, pointing back at the broken ship, "but I've not lost my faith in God to deliver us from this calamity. He shall provide the strength we need to persevere."

Sayle smiled and then turned his gaze toward the beach. Those already ashore were bathed in an otherworldly green-gold light spawned by the fragmented line of squalls pierced now and then by the sun's rays.

* * * * *

As Jackson lowered himself into the ship's dinghy, he tossed the bowline at his feet and handed his tackle box to David. He pushed hard off the shattered hull of the *William* as another lash of rain spattered all around them.

"Not like the first time I was wracked, Davey, not at'all."

There were no oars in the boat but it rocked quickly towards shore, blown like a leaf on a pond. The leaf's two passengers sat side by side, silenced by the roar of the wind and waves thrashing over the reef. Half way to shore, the shallop passed by on its way back to the ship, rowed hard by the crewmen Butler had taken aboard in Bermuda. From a distance, the oarsmen and oars looked like the legs of an overturned cockroach.

Jackson spotted one corner of the carpenter's chest barely breaking the surface off the dinghy's port side.

"Davey! Keep a sharp eye on that chest, as ya did with our swordfish. If we can salvage her, we'll be the better off for it."

David did as he was told for several minutes, but then suddenly announced to Jackson, "It's gone under, Fishy! Just there," he pointed.

"Alright, alright. We must remember that spot, Pigeon. Ya see it's right square in the middle of them two coral heads. Hopefully the chest went straight to the bottom and isn't wanderin' about under the waves."

Finally the dinghy surged bumpily onto the beach. Jane Saunders and her older brothers rushed to the water's edge to help drag the little boat onto high ground.

Jane ran a hand through David's hair and managed a wan smile. "There's a cave, Pigeon. A grand castle of a cave just beyond the duns, I'll show ya and we can move out of this wind."

Jackson nodded and watched as the girl led David through the wet sand and sea grapes. A vast branch of lightening flashed far out to windward, signaling yet another band of squalls stacked around the swirling tropical storm. The women and children were all now off the beach, huddled in the cave, as the men wandered the shoreline straining to see any cargo that might wash ashore. Peter Sands was in the surf up to his chest, dragging a tangle of rigging ashore.

Jackson watched as the shallop maneuvered around the piece of reef holding the *William* in its teeth. The ship was now wholly over on her starboard side, masts lying on the reef. What remained of her rigging was quickly being chewed up by the jagged reef and washed down with foaming sea water.

* * * * *

Redding and Butler clung to the port side of the ship as the shallop approached. The two men had managed to shift Butler's trunk over the rail, and it was now precariously tied to the boarding net. The forward section of broken keel of the vessel jutted northward and away from the rest of the hull, making it difficult for the shallop to come snuggly alongside.

"Fend off right where you are!" Butler yelled to his crew. "We'll step on the keel and board the shallop from there."

Butler turned to Redding then, "Slide on down first, then I'll lower the trunk to you and the men."

Redding moved across the nearly horizontal boarding net. Then holding the fringe of the net, gingerly lowered himself down the splintered belly of the ship. Stretching as far as he could, his foot barely reached the keel. He was forced to let go of the net and struggled to maintain his balance. The men in the shallop were fending off as best they could by pushing their oars against the remnants of the ship's hull.

"Alright," called Butler, "let the shallop come closer to the keel and I'll lower the end of the chest to Redding as you approach."

Redding looked uneasily up at Butler. "I'm not sure I can balance here, captain," he called. The sea's tuggin' hard at my feet."

"You'll only need to stand there for a moment. Just take the end of the trunk and let the men help ya aboard."

It was madness. "Why," thought Redding, "don't I simply refuse? The man is standing on the broken ribs of a ship that could be ground to pulp in a moment and he's determined to save his creature comforts."

Butler began to lower the heavy trunk into Redding raised arms. Redding's hand met the trunk's bottom and he cried, "I've got it!"

In an instant he wobbled backward, straining to regain his balance. Butler jerked hard on the line before he could properly brace himself, and to avoid spilling headlong over the side, grabbed at the boarding net with both hands. As the trunk came crashing down, the men aboard the shallop let go their oars and lunged out of harm's way. Redding's feet slipped off the broken keel as the trunk tipped off his upturned hands. The crash of the trunk into the bottom of the shallop was accompanied by the nauseating sound of Redding's body being crushed between the two vessels. Butler looked down to see his first mate's right hand clutch briefly at the gunwale. Then in a swirl of his own blood, Redding slipped under the surface and was gone.

7 REMNANTS

July 15, 1610, excerpt from a letter written by *Sea Venture* survivor, William Strachey, to an anonymous recipient.

But even then the tortoises came in again, of which we daily both turned up great store, finding them on land, as also, sculling after them in our boat, struck them with an iron goad, and sod, baked, and roasted them. The tortoise is reasonable toothsome (some say), wholesome meat. I am sure our company liked the meat of them very well, and one tortoise would go further amongst them than three hogs. One turtle (for so we called them) feasted well a dozen messes, appointing six to every mess. It is such a kind of meat as a man can neither absolutely call fish nor flesh, keeping most what in the water and feeding upon sea grass like a heifer in the bottom of the coves and bays, and laying their eggs (of which we should find five hundred at a time in the opening of a she-turtle) in the sand by the shore side, and so covering them close, leave them to the hatching of the sun . . . .

* * * * *

Few were able to sleep soundly that first night in the cave. Butler was vague in his announcement of Redding's demise. Copeland assured the flock that God had been merciful in sparing all but one life.

The morning broke gently and the beach was calm as a churchyard. Before the sun fully appeared on the horizon, Jackson and David set off from the cave to comb the beach in search of anything they might salvage from the wreck. As the first ray of sun suddenly reached out along the pinkish sand, David stooped to pick up a lone shoe.

"Fishy", he called to Jackson further up the beach, "it's Reverend Copeland's shoe."

Jackson walked back to the boy, "So it is," he gasped, shaking his head. "We'll take that as a sure sign from the Lord himself, Pigeon."

During the day, other such bits and pieces of life before the wreck were discovered along the shoreline. Out on the reef, the only thing that appeared to remain of the *William* was a piece of her mainmast, propped up by a stubborn yardarm driven deep into the coral. The rest of the ship was either flotsam along the beach, or lying at the bottom of the sea.

The 'Miracle of the Shoe', as piously appropriate as it was, soon was overshadowed by the 'Miracle of the Grog.' All four of Butler's casks of strong spirits were found completely intact within twenty yards of each other. Butler was quick to claim and sequester them in a small chamber in the cave, which Jackson dubbed 'Butler's Tavern.'

Notwithstanding any disagreement there might be among the party concerning the validity of 'The Miracle of the Shoe' and 'The Miracle of the Grog', which Copeland identified as the work of the Devil, *not* the Lord, all agreed the cave itself was a Godsend.

Merely steps from where the Adventures shipwrecked, a cathedral-like cave had been provided. Its high arched entrance, as tall as the *William*'s mast had been, opened onto a sandy-bottomed gallery, lit not only by the cave's soaring entrance but also by several finely wrought skylights. These long chimney-like holes cast neat round pools of light on the sandy floor. Even the farthest reach of the cave was reasonably well lit by a wide hole through which sky and the tropical canopy could easily be seen. In Copeland's mind, the best evidence of God's hand in the matter was a rock formation that looked all the world like a pulpit set slightly back from the entrance and squarely in the middle of the cathedral grotto. Large bees nests were scattered about the sides of the arched entryway. If nothing else, the survivors would have honey.

By mid-afternoon, the beach was picked clean, as well as the razor sharp stretches of rocky shorelines to the east and west. The sum total of the salvage effort was pitiable. Many of the barrels aboard the ship had been breached as they were torn for the ship's holds. Most of the grain and seed was spoiled, the dried fish and meats were nowhere to be found, and only a scant supply of household goods and usable clothing had thus far washed ashore.

Families, including the Sayles, politely and deferentially set up camp as best they could on the broad floor of the cave, which at least provided five times the space the *William* had. Sayle's posting on the cave of his ornately stamped Charter seemed preposterous to all, but none said a word. Using the shallop oars, some of the men discretely dug two temporary latrines, one on the west side of the cave for the ladies and children, one on the east side for the men. Throughout the night, Peter Sands doggedly collected as much rain water as he could, using anything and everything to contain the water, bits of sail set into holes in the sand, one side of a broken barrel (looking very much like a cradle lying beneath a hole in the cave), even large flat leaves gathered from the trees then cupped into the forest floor. The first order of business, in Sands' way of thinking, would be the construction of some kind of cistern capable of holding enough fresh water, if used sparingly, for the entire company.

Not far to the east, the men found a reasonably good shelter for the shallop in a tight little cove they at once named 'Governor's Bay.' Meanwhile, with leave of Captain Sayle, Jackson, Lowe and David set out in the dinghy in search of anything that might be salvaged from the sea floor. By late afternoon, the three located the huge carpenter's chest. Jackson's first attempt to reach the chest did not succeed and the failure plainly upset him.

"Twenty years ago I could have dived to that chest as easy as I could stroll along the beach. Now I just don't have the breath. Even if we get a line around the box, we'll never be able to haul her to the surface. We've got to empty the box under the surface and bring the tools up one at a time."

Lowe, though he could barely swim, bravely offered to give it a try. Jackson shook his head and turned to David. He'd first refused the boy's request to make an attempt, but now it seemed that no choice remained.

"Davey, I'll let ye have a go, but I'm gonna put a line around yer ankle. Ya sink like a stone, skin and bones that ya are. I don't want ya runnin' out of breath ending up like a flounder on the bottom. I doubt I'd be able to dive fer ya."

David slipped over the side, the bulky hemp line tied around his left ankle. He took a few deep breaths then plunged under the surface, flinching briefly at the initial sting of the salt water on his open eyes. His first dive was a failure. Half way down he turned for the surface realizing his nerves were preventing him from preserving his breath.

"It's alright, Pigeon. Here, let me give ya a hand back aboard."

David shook his head as he tread water, "no, it's just that I was nervy. I want another go."

He repeated the deep breaths, taking much longer than he had the first time to prepare. With a final long and deep breath, he dove downward with Lowe and Jackson peering over the side. They watched the boy descending rapidly upon the chest, which was lying on its side, the hinges of its hatch in the sand and the latch plainly visible through the gin clear water. David tugged hard on the pin threaded through two brass eyelets and it finally pulled free. He immediately lifted his feet up to the lip of the chest's lid, then with his toes pushed violently off for the surface. The hatch cracked opened under the force of his kick and the weight of the tools slowly pushed it agape.

Throughout the remainder of that first afternoon, David dove again and again to the chest tying a line to heavier tools and bringing smaller ones to the surface by hand. Jackson and Lowe wilted under the hot sun of late July, and David's strength finally drained away for lack of food and fresh water. With the dinghy riding low in the water from the weight of the recovered materials, Lowe rowed the little craft ashore.

The success of the first day's salvage greatly cheered Captain Sayle and the company. Stephen Higgs immediately set to work cleaning the tools of salt as best he could. Margery Sayles, together with Rebecca Sands led an effort to prepare some semblance of dinner, but there was so little to be found, and no practical means of cooking. The best they could do was to mash up and mix with rainwater some of the sea-tainted hard tack recovered from a broken barrel washed up on the beach.

As the sun set and David napped on a piece of canvas spread on the cave flour, Jackson appeared with two large conch and a hat-full of rose colored cockles gathered from pools along the rocky shoreline to the east. Margery and Rebecca greeted the find with thanks to God, reserving some for Jackson as well. Jackson begged their understanding in regard to the conch, explaining that it would be best if they were saved as fishing bait or the next morning. Henry Rowan prepared a bed of coals from the fire lit by the cave entrance and the women were able quickly to bake the cockles open. Once cooked they were added to the hard tack mush for a little flavor. Hunger still prevailed, without exception, but at least the effort spent preparing a group meal lifted spirits at the close of a traumatic day.

Butler said not a word to Sayle of the wreck and he now, together with his three remaining sailors, sat drinking rum tucked away in 'Butler's Tavern.' He'd been noticeably absent when Sayle, late in the afternoon, organized an inventory of all the goods recovered that day. It was clear, however, that Butler had at least one musket; he'd been spotted cleaning it earlier in the day. What else he had in the trunk that had cost Redding his life, no one could say.

* * * * *

The following morning, like many to come, began with Jackson, David and Toothy Jill standing together on the beach appraising the weather and the sea. Many times during the previous night, Jackson took stock of the items in his tackle box, which had survived only because of David Albury's bravery. There was precious little in the small box to bet more than seventy lives upon. No nets had been recovered thus far, and Jackson realized they might never be. The harpoons were likely strewn upon the sea bed and the storm may very well have covered them with sand forever.

"Davey," he said as the boy peered out to the reef, "I want to talk serious to ya while we're alone here on the beach."

The boy turned to Jackson and nodded.

"I'm going to tell ya somethin' and you'll likely t'ink less o' me when I do. But I want ya to t'ink of it as an order, such as wot Captain Sayle would issue. Da ya understand?"

David nodded again, now looking outwardly worried.

"I don't see any way we can catch enough fish to feed seventy folk. We don't have enough tackle, no nets, no harpoons. So, every day we go out fishin', we must feed ourselves, away from the cave. We must feed ourselves *first*, da ya understand? It's for the best, Pigeon. Once we're nourished, we can provide as best we can for the others."

David said nothing, his toe nervously digging in the sand.

Jackson continued.

"Soon there'll be turtles comin' upon the beach to lay their eggs, and the company will have some meat and eggs. But it will be hard, Davey, frightfully hard on all of us by and by."

The rest of the second morning was spent in the shallop out on the wreck site. Between Jackson, David and Sayle, who, much to Margery's surprise actually *could* swim tolerably well, vital materials were recovered, chief among them a large iron cauldron and other assorted cookware. Anything the three could lay their hands on was saved, even if it was simply a bent nail or a scrap of iron band from a yardarm. Lengths of line at first hopelessly tangled among the coral heads, were eventually worked free. Odds and ends, scraps and morsels, fragments and remnants all were brought to the surface, even if no specific use could be identified.

In the dinghy, slightly east of the site Henry Rowan was having some luck fishing, as was David Albury. When one of Jackson's precious fish hooks snagged on the reef, David was able to retrieve it and in doing so spotted a huge spiny lobster peering out from its hole. Using Rowan's long knife, the boy dispatched the creature and flung him into the dinghy. Ashore a ragtag pack of young children excitedly gathered the coconuts some of the men were able to knock out of the trees. The company's only meal of the day would be more bountiful than the last.

By the afternoon, a thunderstorm moved over the wreck site kicking up high winds and the salvage operation came to a close for the day. Again, a careful inventory was taken of the recovered goods and it was determined that at least two muskets found on top of the coral head itself would be operational. Gunpowder and lead, on the other hand, were scarce. One partial cask of powder had made the beach, but thus far, no lead shot or ball had been found on the sea floor or the reef.

* * * * *

A loud bellow startled David awake. Then another echoed from the back of the cave. In the dim light of a small fire lit under the rearmost natural chimney, he could make out the shape of Captain Butler seizing a man by the throat. Then two other men stepped quickly past David towards the ruckus. Jackson appeared in the dim firelight, leaning over the boy.

"Go back to sleep Davey, it's just Butler mad with the drink."

Earlier, Butler and his men wandered drunk into camp after sunset with two slain animals that looked like a cross between a rat and rabbit. Much later, the Adventurers would learn the animals were called *hutia*.

Sequestered in 'Butler's Tavern' at the back of the cave, the hunters built a fire and rowdily continued to drink while cooking their prey. The debauchery continued unabated after they'd finished their private meal. Now nearly midnight, a fight had broken out. Although Butler grudgingly agreed to release his crewman's throat, he railed against Sayle's pleas for temperance, a scene that would be repeated almost nightly for many weeks to come.

* * * * *

While the summer heat and humidity climbed to a nearly unbearable apex, Jackson and David's days oddly fell into an almost comfortable routine. As the first rays of light appeared to the east, they'd drag the dinghy into the water and slowly row out along The Devil's Backbone in either direction searching for promising fishing spots. Toothy Jill could always be seen riding in the bow, her front paws propped upon the gunwales to allow her a better view. Henry Rowan accompanied them now and then, as did Jonathan Lowe, a man possessed with a passion for exploration.

None of Jackson's harpoons were ever recovered from the wreck, and the only net found had been hopelessly shredded on the razor sharp spikes that made up the rocky shoreline. So the fisherman relied solely upon the few lines Jackson brought from Bermuda, and a couple he'd fashioned by the light of the company's camp fires. Jackson also managed to craft a tidy little sail for the dinghy which could be raised upon a diminutive mast held in place by a latched slot cleverly carved by John Saunders into the dinghy's thwart seat.

Captain Sayle, exasperated by Butler's interminable outbursts and disrespect, spent most of his days constructing a small dwelling for him and his family a short distance to the east of the cave. Butler, meanwhile, regularly requisitioned the shallop without asking, disappearing with his private crew all daylong then reappearing drunk and boisterous that night or the next morning. Jackson, David and Rowan discovered one of Butler's camps in a beautiful crescent moon bay to the west. Half of the pig Butler shot was rotting in the sand, enough to have provided a meal to the families trying desperately to fend off starvation back in the cave.

True to his word, Jackson made sure he and the boy ate from their catch at least once a day before returning to the cave. He'd also established caches of plum-like fruit and sea grapes, which the two managed to dry upon patches of dark-colored rock. The conch they harvested almost every day from among shallow fields of sea grass were no longer simply used for bait. Jackson, the two-time shipwrecked sailor, would frequently extract a slimy specimen from its shell, remove its tough, elephant-like skin, and eat slices of its raw meat dipped in seawater. They'd then use the 'slop' for bait.

The remainder of the torrid month of July, slipped away into a sweltering August and it seemed unlikely September's autumnal equinox would bring relief. There was little industry among the Adventurers, as the unremitting heat, hunger and thirst beat down both young and old. Those of the company who were born to the sea fared far better than others of farming stock. Noble attempts were made to clear a patch of land in which to plant the scant handfuls of seed salvaged from the wreck, but the effort took an exacting physical toll upon the would-be farmers. The land was as cruel as the native vines and shrubbery were luxuriant. At best, a few square feet or so of arable soil could be aggregated in the natural potholes found in the limestone landscape. Seen from far above, the pitiable little plots would have looked like craters in the dusty surface of the moon.

Captain Sayle grew despondent as he realized with greater and greater clarity that Butler's rebellious and venal behavior would not temper with time. During Butler's latest diatribe he'd accused Sayle and Copeland of a calculated and sanctimonious hypocrisy. "The entire purpose of this settlement is that every man be free to serve God as he sees fit!" he screamed. "I wish to serve God by playing my viol!"

And despite pleas from the cave's exhausted occupants, Butler continued to play his instrument until the break of day, only then mercifully passing out from the copious amount of rum he'd consumed during the night.

8 TO SPANISH WELLS

"May I have a word, Jackson?, asked Sayle as the two stood on the beach bathed in rose-colored early morning light.

Jackson smiled gap-toothed and warm-hearted. "Ya may have as many words as ya like, Captain. They're yours for the takin.'"

"I am considering removing from this place," began Sayle. He met Jackson's eyes, perhaps to gauge the level of the old sailor's surprise. Jackson nodded, as he noticed David and Toothy Jill approaching from the cave.

"David," Jackson called, "go ask Mrs. Sayle if she needs any assistance before we shove off for the day. I need ta speak with the Captain for a moment."

The boy trotted back towards the towering entrance to the cave, Toothy Jill romping ahead.

Jackson turned back to Sayle, "About leavin' this piece of shoreline, Captain . . . I been meanin' to speak to ya on that point as well."

"You have?," responded, Sayle.

"Yes sir."

Sayle was taken aback. "I thought perhaps I was the only one who could no longer tolerate Mr. Butler and his men. I am pleased to know you are of a similar mind, but sorry for my foolishness in ever engaging the man."

Jackson fidgeted a moment before answering. "Well, yes sir, I suppose in a manner of speakin' I am of the same mind. But it's not so much my dislike of Butler that makes me think we should leave this place. It's the shallop that I'm thinkin' about."

Sayle's brow immediately creased and he gazed questioningly back at Jackson. "In what way, Jackson?"

"Well, we can't say what the coming year will bring, Captain Sayle. Maybe good, maybe hardship, that is to say, more hardship than we have already. Perhaps another ship will come from Bermuda and we'll be well provisioned, or perhaps not."

Sayle nodded his agreement and then pressed Jackson on, "Yes, you're right about that Jackson. So what is on your mind?"

"As I was sayin' before, sir, the shallop is on my mind. The shallop could someday be the difference between life and death for us, Captain. And I see two terrible t'ings might happen to her. I'm powerful uneasy that Governor's Bay might prove an inadequate harbor for her when the winter winds blow in from the north, and I'm nearly as uneasy that Butler will take her and never come back."

Sayle nodded, "You're right, Jackson. You are undoubtedly right."

Jackson continued, "Sir, I know the sea and I know men like Butler. The sea will have our shallop in her teeth if we don't find her a safer harbor for the winter, and if a ship doesn't come soon upon which Butler can make his escape, he'll take the shallop and sail away. The man will not be a part of our godly settlement, Captain. The kind of fortune he wants is the kind that can be made without sacrifice and labor."

"There is no need to convince me, Fishy. I agree with you in every aspect. I am certain we should leave Butler here in the cave to stew in his own sins, and I am certain that if we leave many of our party will follow us. I am certain also that the shallop must be preserved above all else. We are less than three months shipwrecked and we've already grown noticeably weaker. In another year or year and a half, if we have not by then been provisioned by the arrival of a ship, we will almost assuredly need to send the shallop for help."

The two shook hands then, just as Toothy Jill bounded over the dunes and onto the beach. David appeared on the path carrying fishing tackle for the day.

"But where?" asked Sayle, "To where shall we remove?"

"Ay, well Captain, on that question Davey and I have been thinkin.' If you are able to join us today in the dinghy, we'll show ya what we have in mind by way of a safe harbor. It's over around the south side of the Spanish wells."

Sayle looked puzzled, "Spanish wells?"

"Aye, the island just to our west has signs of wells them Spaniards musta sunk some time ago. Probably accounts for all the pigs we see around these parts. As ya know, Captain, a Spaniard can't pass an island wot he don't feel obliged ta maroon a pig or two," Jackson chuckled. "But I ain't complainin' in the least about that particular affliction of the mind."

Sayle, greeted David then, "David, Fishy has offered to allow me aboard for the day, if you and Toothy Jill have no objections. Shall we see these 'Spanish wells' of yours?"

Pigeon-like, David nodded his excitement at the prospect of showing the Captain around the island he'd come to regard as a sanctuary from the omnipresent sense of dread that pervaded the cave settlement.

"I'll show Captain Sayle that strange pod tree!," exclaimed David. "And there are sugar apples too. You'll see."

Jackson nodded his assent, but added, "I don't know that any of the sugar apples will be ripe yet, Davey, but we'll see soon enough. Ya can't pick them 'til they're ripe, ya know, or they'll simply rot away and go to waste."

Jackson turned again to Sayle, "we best shove off before the sun gets too high, Captain. Pigeon Davey and I shall provision the dinghy while you inform Mrs. Sayle and Thomas that you'll be away for the day."

* * * * *

The offshore breeze was just barely sufficient to plump the dinghy's small sail. Jackson took heart that Captain Sayle appeared to be relaxed and contented for the first time since the *William* struck the reef. Sitting on the bottom of the boat, Sayle leaned casually back against its ribs admiring the scene both above and below the water. Looking over the leeward gunwale, the crystal clear waters seemed not to exist at all, as if the boat were flying above an enchanting terrestrial landscape where fish swam through the air rather than water. The pristine shoreline similarly appeared enchanted, pinkish sand beaches nestled in perfectly carved turquoise bays. For the first time, Sayle looked at his surroundings not as a hardship to be overcome, but as a stunningly handsome gift from God.

Sailing close into shore, Jackson piloted the little craft past a set of grey cliffs embracing an immaculate little beach dotted with colorful shells. Toothy Jill, braced in her spot in the bow, joyfully barked at a small flock of terns circling about the steep walls. The highest of the cliffs overhung a cerulean pool gently lapping against two large coral heads. Once through the heads, the shoreline gave way sharply to the south into a broad shallow bay ringed by a ridgeline standing above a bone white beach below. The neighboring island could now be seen dead ahead, shallow sea flats to the north.

Jackson spoke for the first time in an hour. "You'll see, Captain, that island has some height to 'er. From atop 'er spine ya can see right the way 'round the whole compass, sir. Back at the cave, we're blind to what approaches from the south, and our sight is limited to the east and west. We cannot defend against what we cannot see. Whether pirate or Spaniard, any ship wot didn't approached from the north would take us by surprise."

"Yes," replied Sayle, "that goes without saying, Fishy. But what of shelter for the shallop? What is your idea there?"

"Ay, yes sir, that will become clear presently."

The tiny bathtub of a boat glided along more rapidly now as the breeze gathered strength over the wide bay. Jackson passed the westward point, crossed the deep channel, then just before striking the sandy shoal covered in sea grass lying to the west he tacked back to the southeast. Sayle could see now that even within this broad, deep channel, good shelter was apparent here and there along the shoreline. The eastern end of the island, which was rapidly assuming the name "Spanish Wells," was flat and close to sea level, but further west the land rose into a ridgeline, partially forested in braziletto trees and other hardwood.s

"We'll be comin' in on the south side of the island, Captain," said Jackson pointing across the shallow grassy shoals. "There's not much of a channel there, but it's deep enough to float the shallop. Further along to the south it's deeper and there's a little harbor of sorts where even the angriest weather would be calmed."

Sayle held his hand up to his brow to shield the sun and looked hard at the island ahead. Coconut palms, gracefully bending away from the prevailing winds, lined the southern shoreline. The forest floor among the trees was dotted with small palmetto trees and a few sea grapes in the more open spaces. A large, spindly legged crane stepped elegantly among a patch of mangroves, its spikey bill poised to strike the tiny silver-sided fish darting about in the sunlight. The sail began to luff. Jackson lowered it and took up the oars.

"I'll row right alongshore so ya can take a closer look, sir. Davey and I generally land about half way down the island where the land starts to climb."

Sayle nodded silently, still staring intently up and down the south shoreline of Spanish Wells. David chatted away, pointing out every little aspect of the shore, whether self-evident or not. Each nondescript tree and every lifeless rock seemed to have deep meaning to the boy. He was beside himself with excitement when a coco plum tree or a guava came into sight.

Jackson landed the dinghy in his usual spot, and the three made their way slowly up to the highest point of the island. A small clearing along the ridge, probably the result of a lightening strike, offered up an unobstructed view out across the reef to the north, and the sound to the south. The channel separating Spanish Wells from its larger sister was also plainly visible.

"Well you were certainly right, Fishy, we'd have warning of almost any approach."

Sayle turned slowly around admiring the lush green canopy spreading out before them in all directions, the shallow waters to the north a brilliant aquamarine and a deep, soothing blue father out. To the south, the narrow channel up which they had rowed was greenish in hue, intersecting another channel to the south that spilled into a broad sound. Turning east, Sayle looked again at the narrow stretch of water separating Spanish Wells from the main island.

Jackson spoke up again. "We'd be well served to place a gun there on the point. There must surely be a passage somewhere through this end of the reef and once through it's only natural for a boat to head for the channel."

Sayle nodded. "You prefer this island to the one we coasted aboard the shallop the first week of the wreck?"

"Yes I do, sir. The other, wot we called Harbour Island, is fine enough, but it's not as protected as Spanish Wells, and yet it takes longer to reach the open sea. It's the better part of a morning to sail north to the Devil's Backbone and no boat could be kept safely on the east side of the island, facing the whole of the Atlantic as it is."

Sayle appeared to agree. "And I believe this island's proximity to the cave may also be an advantage. The cave provides us a place in which to cache supplies, and a place in which to convene should we be forced to scatter under attack."

* * * * *

Sayle's exploration of Spanish Wells continued throughout the day while Jackson boarded the dinghy again to fish. Toothy Jill remained ashore, content to chase lizards, while Sayle patiently suffered through David's tour of sugar apple, guava, and pigeon plum trees. The botanical walkabout culminated at the foot of a giant tree dangling thousands of brown pods.

"This is it, Captain Sayle, the pod tree I spoke of this morning. Have ya ever seen the like of it?"

"Yes, as a matter of fact, I have," replied Sayle. "It's called a tamarind. The Spaniards brought them from New Spain. This one here was probably planted by one of the pigs released on the island. That is to say, the pig was fed tamarind fruit while aboard the galleon and then . . . well, you understand me, I'm sure. We must gather as many of the pods as we can, David. They're called 'legumes' and can be eaten not only by pigs but by man."

By the late afternoon, the explorers had covered the entire island, which was about two miles long and half a mile wide. Earlier, Jackson asked to be met in the narrow channel to the west that thinly separated Spanish Wells from another island of roughly equal size to the west and slightly south. The eastern end of this partner island stretched for about a mile in front of Spanish Wells, forming the western end of the Spanish Wells 'bay'. It extended past Spanish Wells to the west for another two miles.

Jackson pulled the dingy up on the beach under the shade of a cedar tree when Toothy Jill spotted him and ran to his side. Sayle and David appeared a moment later, strolling along the beach as it curved from around the north end of the island and met the channel.

"Ah!" exclaimed Sayle, "I see you've had God's blessing today."

The stern of the dingy was littered with yellow tail snapper and a mammoth black grouper lay below the oarlocks at Jackson's bare feet.

"This big fella swollered one of them yeller-tails wot I'd hooked and was just pullin' to the surface. He come up and *whoosh!* Instead of a small fish I 'ad me a monster on the line. Nearly cap-sized the boat when first I tried to pull him over the side," he laughed.

The trip back to the cave was as peaceful as it had been in the opposite direction. The sun set by the time they pulled the boat high onto the beach, David ran back and forth delivering the smaller fish, while Jackson and Sayle together dragged the grouper up the trail after having gutted him in the surf.

By the time Sayle retired to his shelter for the evening, he'd made up his mind. Tomorrow he would announce his departure with any who would join him.

* * * * *

"You *cannot* leave us here without a boat!" roared Butler. He'd listened to little of what Captain Sayle said in his address to the seventy-three souls gathered around the cave's stone pulpit. However, the mention of removing the shallop to another island instantly piqued both his attention and his ire.

Sayle calmly responded. "If the shallop remains here on this north shore, she is at risk of loss. Surely we can agree that such a loss would be grave. While it was surely providence that we came ashore at this place, we must, listen to God's direction for the future."

"So *God* is instructing you, is He? The Heavenly Father is directing you to make off with the shallop?"

"Captain Butler," Sayle continued, "God speaks to us through our experience. God endows us with the ability to reason. He endows us with the ability to learn from our successes and from our failures. He instructs us every day in ways in which we may be of better service to Him and to our fellow man."

Many in the assembly muttered a respectful 'amen.' Others looked outwardly worried by Sayle's sudden announcement. The slow but ever mounting hunger and exhaustion among the party was taking a profound toll among some of them. To most, making *any* decision was difficult. To some, making a decision to leave a shelter that appeared in every respect to be a miracle was crippling. How much of Sayle's decision was motivated by concern over the shallop's preservation? How much of it was motivated by the unrelenting tension between him and Butler?

John Saunders stepped forward and addressed Sayle. "Sir, I would propose a compromise in regard to the shallop. Let us leave the dinghy here at the cave and shelter the shallop in the harbor you describe."

Staring directly at Butler, Sayle tried to gauge the man's mind. Several long moments passed without a whisper from anyone in the crowd. No response from Butler appeared to be forthcoming, so Sayle began again.

"The dinghy is superior for the purpose of fishing and coasting, Mr. Butler. She is maneuverable and draws only a few inches of water. Most importantly, she can be pulled up and over the dunes if a norther strikes the coast. The shallop weighs over six tons, cannot easily be pulled ashore, and has only the scantest protection in Governor's Bay."

Butler stood silent, his arms crossed over his chest, glowering towards the pulpit. His plans were short-term now, no longer tied to the prospect of owning a large tract of land on or around Eleutheria. It was plain to him now the land was poor in comparison to Bermuda or Barbados. In his mind, the clearer path to riches would be through privateering. The Bahama Islands were tailor-made for preying upon the Spanish or the French, it mattered little to Butler. Let them decide in London who would be fair game on any given day. With a little more knowledge of the countless hiding places and escape routes scattered throughout the island chain, he would be master of his own fate. Let Sayle and his pack of bible-bound planters toil away in fruitless labor all they wanted. What was needed was a ship, not a patch of rocky ground barely fertile enough to support a sour orange tree.

"Leave the dinghy and I shall have no further objection to you removing from this place." Butler spoke out over the crowd. "Those who wish to stay are welcome and you shall have no ordinances or edicts from me."

Eleven weeks into their ordeal, the group was divided into two factions, those too overcome by hunger, heat, sickness, and thirst to expend energy on anything other than merely hoping for the arrival of a relief ship, and those more naturally born to the sea, possessed of an unshakable faith that it would provide all that was necessary to survive the hard times.

Throughout the day, the party solemnly divided itself, like a single cell quietly dividing into two. The larger group went about preparing for an exodus, the smaller group shyly avoiding the larger. No judgments were made, no castes were created. But somehow they all knew the Company of Adventures was now divided into the strong and the weak.

* * * * *

The tenuousness of the company's existence was drawn into sharp focus by the meager supplies and possessions loaded aboard the shallop for the first crossing to the new island. Aboard the boat the next morning, Sayle turned to his wife. "The name Spanish Wells defers too much to Spain, wouldn't you say, Margery?"

"Well, yes, I suppose sinking a shallow well or two hardly warrants the island's association with Spain for time immemorial. Had you another name in mind?"

"Yes," answered Sayle, smiling, "I favor the name St. George's Cay. We left persecution behind in St. George's Bay, it seems fitting we should repay the saint by naming our new island after him."

"Or perhaps you believe that by removing to the island you slay a dragon as did Saint George," joked Margery.

Sayle chuckled softly and whispered into his wife's ear. "Butler may be irritating, but I do not believe him to be a dragon. More like a case of the piles than a dragon, my dear. And I do not believe sainthood is awarded to those who suffer through piles."

Jane Saunders, sitting next to Margery, heard Sayle's riposte and was now struggling mightily to restrain a smile. She, like her brothers was anxious to take leave of Butler and his mercenaries, and her mood was higher this morning than it had been in many weeks. She twisted around to face David sitting on the next bench aft, "You shall remember your promise to me David, won't you?" she smiled.

David beamed in response. "I'll show you straight away!", he answered. I know there will be ripe ones this time."

Jackson patted the boy on the back, "First you'll help unload the shallop, Pigeon. When we shove off for the second run, ya can show Jane the sights wot we have around the island, includin' the sweetsop trees."

The passage was quick with six men rowing the stretch southward through the deep channel and then westward through the shallow shoals. Sands, the Saunders brothers, Jonathan Lowe, Joshua Roberts and Edward Harris immediately set to work building a preliminary camp on the northeastern point of the island. Within yards of the locale, Harris discovered a fresh sea turtle nest and soon dug up many dozen eggs. The party's first moments on St. George's Cay were proving to be propitious.

* * * * *

Toothy Jill's wet nose poked into David's ear and snuffled him one step closer to wakefulness. Parting the slowly dissipating mist of sleep, he gathered his thoughts together as best he could, but

117

something was confusing him. Something was very different. He pulled the dog to his chest and curled up around her, then it struck him: he was *cold*. It wasn't just him, the air was cold, Toothy Jill's nose was cold. For the first time in many months, not a drop of perspiration dotted the boy's brow.

Industry took root on St. George's Cay and sprang from every square inch of the two-mile long island. Trees were felled and arduously sawn into planks. The scarce supply of precious sweet potatoes that survived the wreck of the *William* were anxiously planted and carefully tended. More than a dozen shelters were built, as well as a dwelling that looked all the world like an actual cottage, dubbed 'the Governor's Palace' by Jackson. In the space of four days, John Saunders wondrously managed to build a functional 'dinghy' – granted, one that required frequent bailing, but it was more than adequate for fishing the close along the shorelines in calmer weather.

Under Peter Sand's careful eye, two large and ingeniously designed cisterns were carved out of the limestone rock exposed along the southern shoreline. Sands chose the site carefully, using a steep slope of rock like the graceful pitch of a large Bermuda roof to channel rainwater into the tanks hewn out of the flat surface below. Although the topmost limestone crust was hard and difficult to work, once breached, the newly exposed rock was very soft until it too hardened like concrete once exposed to air and sun. The cisterns could be filled to capacity with a single downpour of rain.

Still curled up on his piece of sail stuffed with coconut fiber, David called to Jackson. "Fishy, are you awake?"

Jackson poked his head in through the opening that passed as a doorway, "Of course I'm awake. I've already been to the beach collectin' bait. What in the devil are ya doing in there? Are ya ailing?"

"I'm warming myself up next to Toothy Jill. It's cold."

"*Cold?* I never seen such a boy. How you ever survived in Devon, England I'll never understand."

Despite his waggishness, Jackson was concerned. The boy, always slender, was now thin as a reed. Their diet was dominated by fish. Fat was rare, and starch appeared only in the settler's dreams. Breakfast this morning was tepid tea made from leaves called 'strong back' and a piece of parrot fish wrapped round and round with palm fronds then buried deep under the coals of last night's fire. Jackson knew the boy would merely pick at the fish. When there was fruit, David ate all that was presented him, but it was harder to convince the boy of the necessity of eating less palatable fare. The tamarind tree was a blessing. The settlers soon discovered the still unripe fruits, which they called 'swells', could be eaten if specially prepared. When roasted in coals, the pods burst, exposing an acidic, sour pulp that could be neutralized and made savory when dipped very lightly in wood ashes. Later in the season, fully ripe fruit could be eaten out of hand.

Two months earlier, in October, the turtle egg season was over, though a number of men in the settlement continued to stalk adult green turtle along the reef and in beds of sea grass. Two pigs were captured on a neighboring floodtide island, named in jest after King Charles. 'Charles Island' , it seemed, was good for nothing but foddering a few ragged hogs.

The first Christmas on St. George's Cay was a sober occasion dedicated wholly to prayer and thanks for surviving not only the wreck itself, but also the loss of virtually all of the party's foodstuffs. The next Christmas might be a merry affair with the arrival of more settlers aboard a well-provisioned ship, but for the time being, all were content merely to be alive.

* * * * *

As the air grew hot and the late April sun warmed the turquoise waters around St. George's Cay, the pace of industry slowed in the settlement. Hunger was never far away. There was only so much planting that could be done without seed stock. There was only so much construction that could be accomplished with rudimentary tools and materials provided by the island itself.

Work generally began at sunrise, but then paused for six hours starting at nine o'clock. Waiting became everyone's primary occupation. There could always be found a small gathering of settlers perched upon the ridgeline straining for a glimpse of a ship approaching from the north. There had been practically no communication between the cave settlement and the Spanish Wells settlement. Yet they were intimately united in unrequited anticipation of a relief ship.

On the 4th day of June, Captain Sayle called a meeting at his house among the men in the company who were experienced seamen. Reverend Goulding led a prayer at the insistence of the elder Reverend Copeland. Sayle addressed the group without prevarication.

"If we are not relieved by a ship by the first of the year, 1649, I shall lead a volunteer crew to the Virginia Colonies aboard the shallop."

Sayle looked enquiringly into the eyes of David Albury, Stephen Higgs, Jonathan Lowe, Nathaniel Harris, Benjamin Sawyer, Edward Harris, Christopher Johnson, Joshua Roberts and Benjamin Jackson. The men were silent at first, furtively glancing at each other. Stephen Higgs softly spoke up.

"Captain, we here have already discussed this eventuality amongst ourselves. Ya need not ask for volunteers, as each of us has pledged to the other our promise to seek assistance for *all* of our families. We've agreed that all of us here, save for Fishy Jack, should crew the shallop when it's time to seek help."

Jackson stepped forward, clearly meaning to object, but Higgs intervened.

"Fishy, ya've got to stay and provide for our families while we're gone. You're the best man for the job and ya know it. You pledge to us now that the you'll do what ya can to see them fed and looked after."

Jackson looked down into the fire pit crackling away in front of the Governor's Palace. He said nothing, but approached each of the men, shaking their hands one by one. When he was finished, he walked quietly away into the moonlit night.

* * * * *

Large flocks of white crowned pigeons and black-billed whistling ducks were discovered in the mangrove stands to the southeast. Despite having only one functional musket and virtually no shot, one of the settlers, John Knowles, proved remarkably talented at trapping them with a number of clever contrivances. Bird hunting was hard and patient work, the caloric reward was limited, but Knowles' persistence ultimately resulted in a modest Christmas dinner bearing some legitimate semblance to bygone Bermudan dinners.

For David, Christmas was made painful by the flood of family memories. While the death of his parents would forever lodge a shard in his heart, for most of the year the boy's appetite for life and exploration dulled his deep-seated inclinations towards sorrowful introspection. He was and always would be resilient, if nothing else.

Jackson's Christmas gift to the boy was a small miracle of

innovation. David had long since outgrown his shoes and his feet wore the constant evidence of open combat with the rocks, plants and insects of St. George's Cay. Jackson presented the boy with a new pair of boots with tightly woven sisal fiber soles and luxuriantly tanned sharkskin uppers. For many years to come, Jane Saunders would greet Jackson with the same felicitation: "Have you made me a pair of those fancy sharkskin boots yet, Fishy?"

* * * * *

On December 27, Sayle and Reverend Copeland, with a shallop crew of 4, set out for the cave settlement. He did not relish confronting Butler again, but he felt deeply obliged to inform the settler's who'd remained behind that a relief expedition would be launched.

As the shallop's bow pushed softly onto the pinkish sand beach laid out before the cave, a thin shroud of smoke hovered at treetop level. No one greeted the landing party and the scene was completely silent but for the gentle lap of boot-high waves upon the sand. Sayle stepped from the bow onto the beach and, without turning to the crew, walked immediately up the beach and over the dunes towards the cave entrance. A strong sense of dread tapped him on the shoulder as he walked, still seeing no signs of life but for the taint of a campfire permeating the air. The day was overcast and cool, calm for the time of year.

As he neared the entrance, he made out the shapes of several figures, prone before the fire pit. One of them spotted Sayle approaching on the path and climbed slowly to its feet. Sayle's eyes adjusted to the darker light around the cave and he saw now that the figure was a pale, disheveled women. Her posture was stooped and her head tilted slightly back and to one side.

"Mrs. Davis?," Sayle softly spoke as he looked into the women's sunken, blinking eyes.

"Yes, Captain, Sarah Davis," the women finally responded in a croaking voice."

The two other stick figures lying in the sand by the fire pit now climbed to their feet and shuffled forward. Many others, by ones and twos, silently emerged from the shadows deep within the cave.

Sayle's crew, Jackson, Roberts, Albury and Sands drew up behind Sayle, having secured the shallop on the beach. Roberts spoke softly, almost to himself, "God have mercy." It was clear to the Spanish Wells contingent that an expedition to Virginia would be the only way to save those who'd remained at the cave settlement, content to place their fate entirely in the hands of God.

Sayle finally spoke with a wavering voice. "Where is Captain Butler and his men?"

"He is seldom here," responded a tall stem of a man standing with bent knees along the forward boarder of the crowd. "He hunts the wild pigs but does not provide for the camp. When the turtles no longer came, we fished, but Butler will not allow us use of the dinghy. He portends the loss of the craft if anyone but he sets her to sea."

Albury, clearly angered, began to speak, but Sayle gently silenced him.

"Can everyone hear my voice?" the Captain asked loudly. A general nodding of heads followed.

"In a week, or as soon as the weather permits, I shall sail for the Virginia Colonies in the shallop. I intend to seek aid there and return aboard a provisioned vessel."

Many in the assembly weakly applauded, some began to weep.

Sayle continued. "If we do not return within a month you must assume the expedition lost. You then must make your way westward, all the way to the point and build a signal fire there. We have built a small craft and it can ferry all of you, by twos, across to our island, St. Georges Cay. Before we sail for Virginia, I shall bring the shallop back here with as many provisions as we can spare."

Nothing further was said. Uncharacteristically, no prayer was offered. Shaken, Sayle and the shallop crew turned and walked quietly back to the beach.

＊ ＊ ＊ ＊ ＊

No sooner had the shallop nosed into its mooring than Sayle requested Jackson, Roberts, Albury and Sands to collect from the Spanish Wells residents donations of food. In less than four hours the shallop was provisioned with tamarind pods, dried fruit, smoked fish and fresh water. Rations set aside for the expedition to Virginia had been halved by the relief effort, but no one objected.

Throughout the remainder of the last month of 1648, the people of Spanish Wells set to work preparing the shallop for its voyage to the northwest. A crude tarpaulin woven of palm fronds was fitted as shade from the sun and, at least to some degree, shelter from the rain. To the extent possible after providing relief to the cave settlement, the shallop was provisioned for a voyage estimated to take at least one week. The storage of water was a difficult problem to solve. Two pigs bladders were already in use as water vessels. In addition, the thickest part of large fallen tree had been laboriously hollowed over period of weeks, alternatively using small fires and the settlement's only chisel. The 'barrels' lid was fashioned from the same tree. Coconut fiber rimmed the lid, making it nearly watertight. When all three water vessels were filled, and assuming they did not fail en route, the crew of nine would have approximately one 50 gallons of fresh water.

As the last few days of the year ebbed away, the new one roared in on a persistent north wind. The seas crashed and foamed over the Devil's Backbone for three days, never resting. Finally, on January 2, 1649, Sayle and his crew of eight men rowed away from the south shore of St. Georges island and through the channel into the bight. As the sun breached the horizon to the east, the gentle westerly curve of Eleutheria took shape before them. Profiting from a whispering eastern breeze, the crew raised the canvas and stowed their oars. The shallop glided smoothly along the shoreline of the neighboring island as if the sun's early rays rising from the east were somehow propelling them westward.

9 SALVATION AND EXILE

Bermuda Council, summer 1649

We upon sufficient grounds, reports and circumstances are convinced that our Royal Sovereign, Charles the First is slain, which horrid act we detest, and unwilling to have our conscience strained with the breach of oath to our God, and to avoid falling into a premunire, acknowledge the high born Charles, Prince of Wales to be the undoubted heir apparent.

* * * * *

"Davey!," cried Henry Rowan from the hillside overlooking the path along the narrow southern inlet and bay. "I've got something to show you and Fishy Jack. Are ya headed home now?"

"Aye, Mr. Rowan. I was just having some sport with Toothy Jill. She's been helping me herd minnows into the trap."

"Wait there, I'll come down to ya," yelled Rowan as he loped down the steep hillside. As he drew closer, David could see that Rowan gripped something in his right hand.

"What do ya think of it?, asked Rowan as he held out what was clearly a harpoon, but a very odd one indeed. "I've been workin' at it all week. Finished her off this morning. What do ya say we take her aboard the dinghy this morning?"

David stared intently at the object, suddenly realizing from what it was manufactured.

"It's a chain!"

"Aye, I'll wager the first ever made into a harpoon," smiled Rowan. "You yourself, Davey, salvaged this length from the *William*. It was too short to be of any other use."

David reached for the spear-like thing, instantly appreciating its balance. Looking closely now, he could see that Rowan had somehow folded each link over onto itself and hammered them all into a paralysis, each binding the other in reworked metal. As a whole, the unit flexed nicely. It was more flat than cylindrical, and its tip was cleverly wrought from two unfurled links shaped into a point then doubled back into a barb.

"How did ya do it, Mr. Rowan?"

"Ah well, I had first to make a great heap of charcoal, as tall as you are yourself, Davey. Then I spent the better part of this week sweating like a plow horse as I hammered away at them links. I'm fairly sure she's stout enough for good sized fishes."

"But what did ya hammer it on? There's naught but soft limestone around here."

Now there you're wrong, my boy. I found me somethin' that came in handy, to be sure. Out towards the end of west island, I found an old gun, a four pounder, just lying atop a big coral head. Couldn't tell it was a cannon at first, mind ya, it was that crusted over. Mr. Sands helped me haul her ashore. It's cast iron, not bronze, so we reckon it hasn't been lying out there all that long. She's far and beyond her use as munitions, but she makes a nice anvil nonetheless, especially now that I've got her flattened out a bit on top."

David, clearly itching to see the cannon, asked, "where did ya haul the gun to, Mr. Rowan?"

"Well, we hauled it as far as we could, which is barely four paces from the water's edge. It was one thing to float her strapped to a dried up old tree trunk, it was another to get her up the beach. So that's where I set up my smithy," chuckled Rowan.

* * * * *

Rowan, Jackson, David and Toothy Jill set out aboard the dinghy in the late afternoon, allowing the sun to raise itself well into the sky and overcome the chill left behind by the previous night. Jackson was almost too excited to feign skepticism about the functionality of the unorthodox spear. Despite the chilly January water temperature, he was determined to slip over the dinghy's gunwale and give Rowan's creation a try.

"I know just the devil we can test your harpoon on, Henry," said Jackson. He's a big old fella that twice got off a hook and now knows better than to get his ownself mixed up with fishin' lines. Big brownish striped grouper, probably thirty pounds or so. Sits all day in his hole and never comes out but to feed on somethin' crossing in front of his parlor. He's not a stone's throw from where ya say ya hauled the gun ashore, so we can take a look at your smithy as well," Jackson said to Rowan.

The wind was favorable for the passage westward along the south shore of St. George's Cay and its western neighbor. The small craft soon swung northward into the channel lying off the end of the neighbor before veering east along the Devils Backbone. Jackson busied himself tying a small loop of crude line through a natural hole in a large lump of limestone.

"Pigeon Davey here may not need any assistance sinkin' to the bottom, but I need a little help, even though I've lost some blubber over the past few months," said the old sailor as he finished constructing his diving weight.

He showed Rowan the handiwork, explaining, "I just slip my foot through this tight loop on the stone, ya see, then down I'll go feet-first and hopefully end up standin' just to the side of Mr. Grouper's little cottage. Then I just take my foot out of the loop, grab it with my left hand, and if the big fella's in his hole, I take a jab at him with your harpoon in my right."

The dinghy bounced along over the light chop, heading roughly north-east until Jackson asked to take the tiller.

"I'll take 'er from here, Pigeon, I know exactly where Mr. Grouper's lays his table and takes callers."

Once over the coral head, David and Jackson lowered the sail and Rowan manned the oars, keeping the dinghy relatively still over the target. With no ceremony, Jackson stripped to his knee breeches and slipped quietly over the side."

"Whoa now!" he whispered to Rowan, "I'll have to admit the water's a bit colder than I'm accustomed to in my old age. Go ahead and hand me the sudden death, Henry," and a name was born for the small harpoon. Jackson took the weapon in his right hand, keeping his left firmly on the gunwale.

"Alright, Davey, here's my foot." he said holding his left foot up beside the hull. "Slip the weight on it."

David quickly did as he was told. Jackson took a dozen long, deep breaths and then quietly slipped below the surface. The chop was a little too heavy to allow David and Rowan to see him from the surface. Less than a minute later, Jackson suddenly broke the surface and immediately exclaimed, "I t'ink I got 'im! Stuck him real proper like, and without much fuss."

Down he went again, this time rising to the surface with the large grouper in tow, the spear lodged just behind its formidable block of a head. Rowan leaned over the transom and hauled the fish aboard, careful not to bend the spear, while David helped Jackson back into the boat.

"Move aside, gentlemen, old Fishy Jack's got to have a go at the oars before he dies of chill. Which way to your smithy, Rowan?"

Rowan pointed ashore towards a broad expanse of tall pine trees, "Just head for the pines, Fishy, over there to the east."

* * * * *

After a "tour of the works", as Rowan described his charcoal pile and old Spanish gun, the three hoisted sail and set off again towards the channel separating the neighbor island from yet another further to the west. As they passed the last beach and rounded the rocky point, slipping from shallow turquoise waters into the deeper, azure blue channel, Toothy Jill, perched in the bow as usual, began to bark frantically. Davey spotted the cause of her excitement before Rowan and Jackson. "A sail!" cried the boy. There, dead ahead!"

Jackson, his eyes not what they used to be, squinted into the distance, unable to confirm David's report. But Rowan did, "Aye, it looks to be a small pinnace, maybe twenty-five ton."

Frustrated with the dinghy's slow, tacking progress into the wind, Rowan and Jackson each took up an oar. The dinghy closed rapidly on the pinnace as it approached cautiously from the southwest under the power of its jib only.

As they reached the end of the channel, a figure appeared on the pinnace's bow waving a black hat in broad arching motions. A minute later, Davey called out, "It's Captain Sayle! It's the Captain, Fishy! He made it!"

"Are ya sure, Pigeon? We must be sure the vessel's friendly or we'll pull the dinghy up onto the flats where they can't follow," said Jackson.

"No, I'm sure," cried Davey, "there's Mr. Sands! And there's Mr. Roberts. It's them, Fishy!"

Rowan nodded his agreement and the two adults began to row a course that would intercept the relief ship.

In what seemed like hours but was truly only fifteen minutes, they came alongside the pinnace and were greeted by an uproarious cheer.

"Tie her right there alongside, Fishy and climb aboard," called Sayle. "Do ya suppose we have enough water to enter the bay from the south channel?"

"Aye, Captain," responded Jackson, it'll be a fine high tide in about an hour and I imagine this fine vessel only draws about five feet."

A short, ruddy faced man with a strong Irish lilt responded for Captain Sayle, "She draws just over six feet fully laden, that's right."

"You'll fare well then, but only because of the high tide, ya understand. Are you the captain of this ship?"

"Yes I am. I hail from Nansemond County, in the Virginia Colonies. Your Captain Sayle did a marvelous t'ing making the crossing in that open boat," he said, pointing astern at the shallop under tow.

In an hour, the pinnace lowered her jib and foresail as she neared the narrow, north-south channel leading onto the waterfront of St. George's Cay. The crew used the shallop to tow the larger vessel into the slender bay as the people of Spanish Wells gathered along the shoreline waving and cheering.

* * * * *

To the relief of all, the captain of the pinnace agreed to take Butler and his men to Virginia. Their departure was jubilantly celebrated in private, and somberly blessed in public. The colony remained split, however, some settlers remaining on the north shore of the main island, Eleutheria, and some taking up permanent residence on St. George's Cay. With the delivery of provisions, those who'd suffered most grievously at the cave settlement began to gain strength. The hardiest of the settlers soon put to use the half dozen muskets and supply of shot and powder brought from Virginia. A pig was taken only paces from the cave. Pigeons and water fowl were shot among the nearby mangroves. For the first time since the

William broke apart on the reef, a luxuriou sense of "freedom" welled up in the settlers' hearts.

Activity blossomed everywhere in the cool winter air and it carried on through into the warm spring. With a supply of proper tools, John Saunders set to work building a twenty three foot shallow-draft sloop, which would function well for a number of purposes, including fishing.

By May, with the assistance of many of the St. George's Cay settlers, Saunders had nearly completed the project. Her rigging was constructed and assembled as the first upwelling of summer heat forced a dramatic shortening of workdays. In mid-June, Saunders floated his creation in the bay. Jane Saunders christened the sleek new vessel "Grace." Throughout the steamy months of July and August, the little sloop provided welcome relief to those lucky enough to sail her on breezy days. She also allowed the settlement to nearly double its fish harvest.

The ministries of Reverends Copeland and Goulding transformed from missions of grim perseverance to missions of high spirit and dedication. The ramshackle shelters dotting St. Georges Cay and the north shore of Eleutheria transformed into actual dwellings, some even resembling respectable cottages. Patches of earth choked with vine and weeds were transformed into garden plots and diminutive orchards. The population of domestic animals transformed from one, Toothy Jill, to half a dozen, thanks to the goats brought from Virginia.

For the first time, the settlers felt their departure from Bermuda was less like exile and more like opportunity. For the first time, they felt more like "Adventurers" and less like survivors. God, it seemed, had tested them and they were now being blessed with His mercy.

* * * * *

Jackson burst through the door into Sayle's parlor, only then realizing he'd failed to knock. Before he could retreat, Margery Sayle waved him the rest of the way in.

"Whatever is the matter, Mr. Jackson?"

Jackson's breath was quick and labored. It was clear that he'd run to the top of the hill where the Sayle's house was perched.

"A ship, ma'am," sputtered Jackson. "A ship headed straight for the reef. Please fetch the Captain, if ya will."

In a moment, Sayle emerged from his small chambers where Jackson immediately confronted him with the news. The two quickly exited the cottage with Jackson leading Sayle by the elbow. They scrambled as fast as they could up the "look-out," a tall tree pressed into service in that regard by having ladder rungs spiked into its stout trunk. Once they stepped onto the small platform in the tree's canopy, Jackson pointed toward the western-most point of Eleutheria. There to the east and less than a mile offshore, a merchantman ship approached.

"God save them, Mr. Jackson, they will surely run upon the reef if they attempt to make the channel. Go quickly now to Mr. Saunders' sloop and try to draw them off. Likely she's come from Bermuda."

As Jackson scurried noisily down the hill toward the bay, he all but concluded in his mind that it would be impossible to sail the sloop out of the bay, then northward up through the channel and then easterly along the shore quickly enough to draw off the ship. If the crew of the approaching vessel did not conclude on their own that passage through the reef could not be accomplished, at best the ship would be gravely damaged. More likely she'd be lost.

As he neared the bottom of the hill, Jackson spotted David gazing up at him.

"Davey," yelled Jackson, "quick-like, race ahead to the sloop and start readying her to sail! Find Saunders as well if ya can!"

At once, David sprinted down the bayside path with Toothy Jill yelping excitedly alongside. In just over two minutes the boy and dog covered almost a quarter mile. As the sloop drew into sight, he noticed with relief that Saunders was already aboard her bailing water from the previous night's downpour.

"Uncle Saunders! Fishy's coming for the sloop! There's something the matter but he didn't say what!"

"Alright, Davey, pull me back in by the bowline there while I finish with this bailing."

David snugged the line so the bow nudged the shore, then he jumped aboard and began rigging the sail.

Jackson huffed his way aboard soon after.

"What's got into ya, Fishy?" asked Saunders.

"There's a ship approaching. Heading straight inta the Backbone and I'm afraid it's too late to wave her off."

No further words were necessary among them. Jackson shoved off from shore and used a paddle to pull the sloop's bow around to the east. The breeze was northerly, which meant it hardly reached the sheltered southern shore of St. George's Cay. The sloop's progress down the bay toward the inlet was almost unbearably slow.

Finally clearing the eastern end of the island, the unobstructed breeze immediately stiffened and the boat darted forward. The north wind, however, forced them to tack several times as they made their way up the deep channel separating St. George's Cay from the main island. They would be blind to the approaching merchantman until the sloop passed the western tip of Eleutheria, Gun Point.

"It's in God's hands, whispered Jackson into the warm breeze. She'll be upon the reef now if she didn't see it. It's been nearly an hour since we shoved off."

Saunders said nothing and concentrated on speeding the sloop along the best he could. It was agony. Each minute that dragged by increased the weight of doom in the air. A green turtle swam alongside, seemingly without a care, and lazy nurse shark dozed under a grassy sea bank, oblivious to the anxious men floating above her.

Finally, Saunders performed the last required tack and the *Grace* rounded the point.

"It can't be," exclaimed Jackson in a voice almost too hushed to be audible.

There with her bow safely in the bay was the merchantman. With a few more heaves of the kedge anchor line, her crew pulled the ship well clear of the Devil's Backbone. She floated passively in the aquamarine bay with sunbeams dancing all around her hull.

Now skating sharply eastward on the north wind, Saunders maneuvered the sloop within hailing distance of the ship. The longboat that had run out the ship's kedge anchor rowed alongside the sloop.

"I'll be stewed in my own gravy!" yelled Jackson, "Is that you, Mr. Ridley?"

A dark man standing in the bow of the longboat let out a deep rolling peal of laughter. "Aye, Fishy, but it's not just me, there are sixty of us come to join ya!"

Saunders piped in, "But Ridley, how on earth did ya manage to breach the reef? It's as fearsome a hazard as any I've ever seen. I'm sorry to say, the *William* was taken to pieces just a little ways east of this very spot."

"Ah well," began Ridley, I've an eye for these sorts of things, ya might say. Although Reverend Copeland will assert the hand of God guided us through. How is old Copeland, by the way?"

"He's as fit as a butcher's dog," laughed Jackson. Why I saw him yesterday splittin' enough wood to burn up the Devil himself."

Ridley again broke out in hardy laughter. "What do you men think?" he asked Jackson and Saunders, "Where should our little ship anchor for the time being?"

"I tell ya it's a plain miracle ya came to this spot, Ridley. Our settlement is just yonder to the west on that wee island, St. George's Cay, and there are others not a stone's throw west of here where we lost the *William*."

Ridley smiled, "Perhaps not so much a miracle as ya might think. We spotted smoke from the far end of your island earlier today. Someone clearing land?"

"That it likely was," said Jackson pointing to the west. "We've got many a garden plot down on that end. Always beatin' back the vines and whatnot, so fires is common."

"Let's get your ship into the channel, Ridley," suggested Saunders. "Have yer captain raise a foresail and then follow right in our wake. The tide's well up and there's no real hazard at this point if ya stay on our course."

"Very well," agreed Robert Ridley as he took up his oar again. "You three," began Ridley, but then amended his statement after noticing Toothy Jill standing on the bow of the sloop; "You *four* will know quite a number among our ship's compliment. Reverend Nathaniel White is aboard, as is Charles Sweeting. You'll likely also recognize Stephen Painter," he continued, pointing toward the faces peering over the merchantman's rail.

The crew of the merchantman, *Dover*, raised enough sail to make the ship navigable. By now, the entire population of the Spanish Wells settlement was lined up along the island's eastern point, many waving hats and shouting welcomes. The *Dover* was well known among the former Bermudians, so there was no mistaking the fact that those aboard her arrived with good intent. As she moved south of the point, the canvas was quickly lowered and the anchor dropped, swinging her bow northward into the wind. In time, the narrow inlet leading to the south shore of the island would be dredged, allowing for deep draft vessels, but now only the Dover's longboat could make the passage. All during the remainder of the day, both the longboat and the *Grace* ferried new settlers to the south shore.

It was immediately apparent to the people of Spanish Wells that their brethren were woefully under-provisioned.

* * * * *

Reverend White and Charles Sweeting sat at Captain Sayle's roughhewn dining table, which his son Thomas helped carry outside and set up under the stars. A light supper of sweet potato, cold crawfish and goat cheese was served by Margery, while Thomas poured small cups of sea grape wine for the visitors. At first, Sweeting and White responded politely to Sayle's questions about the *Dover*'s passage between Bermuda and St. George's Cay, the health of the ship's compliment, the weather and other niceties. Now that Margery had cleared the dinner plates, Sayle softly broached the subject of the *Dover*'s apparent shortage of supplies.

"You say the *Dover* is already emptied of her cargo, Mr. Sweeting?"

Sweeting looked for a moment at Reverend White, then back at Sayle. He could see that Sayle was asking an indirect question, but he resisted the impulse to provide Sayle with an indirect answer.

"Sir, on the 21st day of August, the Council withdrew what little protection they'd afforded the Independents, so we had to leave Bermuda, and leave as quickly was we could," explained Sweeting. "We provisioned as best we could under the dire circumstances. Perhaps worst of all, sir, the Council forced us to pay an extraordinary fee for our own exile. The leasing of the *Dover* has bankrupted most of us."

Reverend White continued. "You see, Captain, a death warrant was issued against King Charles, signed by some of your investors I might add, and Cromwell saw to it the warrant was executed. When the Bermuda Council received the news, their response was to swear allegiance to the slain king and exact what revenge they could upon our number."

Sayle reached across the table and softly placed his hand on White's thin shoulder. "Reverend, we have been under-provisioned since we lost the *William* over two years ago, but we have persevered in the name of our Lord. I have no doubt the Lord will provide what we need to persevere anew."

133

* * * * *

The *Dorset* pointed her keen bowsprit into the gathering squall as if she were trying to pick a fight by jabbing a finger into the chest of an opponent. The departure from St. Georges Cay was as uneventful as the *Dorset*'s sudden and unexpected departure from Bermuda had been frenzied. As the ship's captain, John Flowers, understood the matter, the ship's shareholders had exacted a heavy toll from the passengers forced to flee Bermuda under threat of reprisal for the king's execution. Flowers was a fair man and he resented playing a part in any transaction that could be regarded as usurious.

The whole thing gave the captain indigestion, so he tried not to think about it. It did trouble him deeply, however, that his pious passengers were so lightly provisioned for a voyage into the unknown. Having now seen for himself how meager an existence Captain Sayle's party had carved out of the shallow soil, limestone and treacherous Bahamian shoals, he was even more concerned about the prospects for his passengers' survival.

Flowers was a nonjudgmental sort, not prone to draw bright distinctions between Anglicans, Presbyterians, Independents or any other religious sect. He'd always found the so-called 'puritans' to be not much different from the Royalist Anglicans, notwithstanding the fact that many Anglicans despised the puritans on principle. Over the years, Flowers a sailed with many a pilgrim and Royalist alike. He remembered Robert Ridley from a run he'd made to Barbados in 1635, when Ridley was only thirty years old. It seemed to him there'd been an Albury on that voyage as well, and also a Timothie Pinder. Yes, he remembered. While ashore on St. George's Cay, a man by the name of David Albury presented himself. Flowers also met a boy whose surname was Pinder.

Young master Pinder and his guardian, Benjamin Jackson, boarded the *Dorset* the day before Flowers ordered her back north to Bermuda. Jackson presented a veritable fortune in ambergris he and the boy gathered from the surrounding beaches, and in return they asked very little. Flowers pictured the transaction now in his mind's eye.

"Davey here, is a fine scholar, Captain Flowers," Jackson said. "Perhaps you've a book or some such papers you could spare?"

Flowers was touched by the old sailor's shy request. He reached up to his bookshelf and almost immediately spotted what he was looking for. He handed the boy a play written by William Shakespeare entitled *The Tempest*.

"Young lad, I want you to read this for Mr. Jackson, will you?" Flowers asked.

"Yes, Captain," the lad responded, as he reverently took the book from Flowers' outstretched hand.

"There is no man more deserving of the tale than Mr. Jackson," continued Flowers. "This play was inspired by the description of Bermuda written by Mr. Jackson's old shipmate aboard the *Sea Venture*, William Stratchey."

"Ya don't say!" Jackson responded, "I never knew Bill to do any writin'. Why that's a grand t'ing ya tell me, Captain Flowers, and I t'ank ya for it."

"I have something else for David," Flowers said. He then walked to his desk, opened the cover, and withdrew a beautifully bound book.

"This is a fine new log book I purchased from Captain Babb of the *Hopewell*. Not a word has yet been writ in it, David, but I think perhaps you should follow in Mr. Stratchey's footsteps. You're in the midst of an adventure, for better or worse, and you too may inspire a work like *The Tempest* someday. So you take this book and save your thoughts in it. I'll give you enough ink and quills to last until you fill every page."

Rain from the squall began to spatter against the sails above and the change in conditions drew Flowers' attention tenuously back to the present. A line from *The Tempest* flitted across his consciousness: "We are such stuff as dreams are made on, rounded with a little sleep." It astounded Flowers how much tenacity of mind and spirit some of the puritan families of Bermuda stored in the marrow of their bones. It seemed that Sayle's company had manifest their longing for a religious sanctuary in the same way Shakespeare's Gonzalo had done for dry land in Act I, Scene I of *The Tempest*: "Now would I give a thousand furlongs of sea for an acre of barren ground, long heath, brown furze, any thing. " It seemed to the captain that if any people deserved to find a fruitful sanctuary, it was they, the settlers of Eleutheria.

As he stood there on the quarterdeck next to the helmsman a bluish flash of lightning branched raggedly across the approaching dark clouds. At that moment, Flowers resolved that when next he sailed for the Massachusetts colonies in the early spring, he would inform Governor Winthrop of the dire situation brewing in the Bahama Islands. He knew such an announcement to the Bermuda Council would have no effect, but perhaps it was in Winthrop's power to assist.

10 EBB AND FLOW

21 July 1649

I am David Pinder. Fishy Jack calls me Davey sometimes Pigeon Davey sometimes only Pigeon. I had good parents but they was blowed up in the church back in Torrington Devon England. There is no church here on St. George's Cay but Reverend Copeland says someday there will be many. Truth is I don't know if he's right on account of our island is particular small. I come here with my friend Fishy Jack when I was 11 years of age. First I was to work for Captain Sayle and the congregation but then Fishy took me and learned me how to fish. We also go turtling but Fishy don't like it because the turtles always cry tears when we pull them out of the sea. Once when we lived in Bermuda we harpooned a swordfish as big as Fishy, me, Mrs. Newbold and Mr. Newbold all put together. That time I had to keep Toothy Jill away from the line so she wouldn't get pulled overboard and drowned maybe. Toothy Jill is a good friend like Fishy is. She can dive conch like me. I mean dive under water and all. She's a dog. But I don't care and Fishy don't care. Fishy says she is our kin but not to tell the reverends. Fishy said to me again today that we got to eat by ourselves away from the others on account of there's so many peoples now on the island and not enough barrels and whatnot brung from Bermuda. Captain Sayle went to Virginia too, but he only brung back foods for 70 in the small ship. Now we got many more which the Dover brung. People, not barrels. Mr. Ridley found a way through the Devil's Backbone which is our reef we fish. Mr. Ridley's got a rock named for him wot points pretty much to his channel. I wish I found that channel. That's the first page almost all filled up. I must write a smaller hand if I'm to save all my thoughts in this book. Captain Flowers give it me. He also said I could have all manner of ink and quills as he was mighty gleeful to have the whale puke me and Fishy give him. Now there ain't no more light so I'm to bed.

At first, there was no resentment. On St. George's Cay. At first there was only charity. At first the provisions brought by Sayle from the Virginia Colonies were distributed equally, regardless of whether the recipients were newly arrived or long-suffering. Slowly, as the ache of hunger and discomfort of cramped living conditions intensified, so too did baser survival instincts begin to germinate in the minds of even the most pious settlers, at first subconsciously, later with careful premeditation.

A piece of green fruit, lonely at the end of a scraggly guava tree, might have upwards of one hundred secret human admirers, carefully watching and accounting for each day's growth, each week's contribution towards ripeness. Ever day's catch of fish was anticipated by all. Every pair of eyes carefully traced the progress and location of the settlement's two small boats.

Again, the young boy and the old fisherman began establishing small caches of dried fruit, tamarind pods, and turtle eggs. This time, they also constructed secret little enclosures to hold their "livestock" both above water and below, land crabs held in pens on dry land, conch held in pens among the shallow shoals. Again, those born to the sea and schooled in the ways of the tropics, like Jackson, Sands, Rowan, Saunders and Ridley fared far better than those who'd immigrated more directly from England.

28 August 1649

Didn't it blow! Such a storm as I never imagined. Fishy said he's seen gravely worse back on the Bermuda Islands, what he calls Somers Island when he forgets to say Bermuda. Then the sea come right up and spoiled all the sweet water in Mr. Sands cistern. Then two of the goats got throwed in the bay and perished. Them what built dwellins on the point were placed in dreadful peril with the sea pouring in and all manner of frights so Fishy, Mr. Sands and others fetched them up here on our hill. Most everything got blowed off the trees and Mr. Rowan says that's a severe happenstance. And he's right cause there ain't no sugar apple to be found anywhere now. Me and Toothy Jill looked. I won't miss the tamarind nearly so much as them sugar apples what Fishy says are stunning popular among lads such as myself. So now there's even scarcer stores than we had before. Some of the seed got spoiled in the water too. Still and all, Fishy says we ain't in nearly so bad a shape as we were when the William struck the reef. We must repair our hut again, but seems like we do that regular anyway. Mr. Saunders saw the storm coming and he got the Grace hauled way up the hill and tied her down. We done the same with the dinghy. During the worst of the tempest on the second day the shallop got flung in among the mangroves and now she's stuck fast. Captain Sayle says she's not harmed and we'll haul her out fine. None got hurt in Spanish Wells, though some is powerful melancholy about the loss of cargo and whatnot. Today Mr. Saunders and a crew set out for the cave to see about them that dwells about there. Mr. Lowe says the sea likely didn't rise over the dunes and go into the cave. There's a lad I know over there his name is James Seymour. He's sickly a lot. Fishy told me the Lord looks after them what can't look after themselves. He was speaking of James I know. Yesterday Toothy Jill went all by herself to seek out Jane, which she never done before. Fishy says storms rile a dog's spirits and Toothy's one to worry about them what she likes. Today me and Fishy went fishing but it was no good. We eat some eggs on the beach. Then we helped Cpt. Sayle and his sons remedy the Governor's Palace is what Fishy calls their cottage. Me and Jane walked the span of north beach and Jane told me we wouldn't be able to promenade much longer because I'm getting growed up. Said it was the reverends what were particular about such things. It don't seem like Reverend Copeland would forbid beach combing with Jane but Fishy said don't be so sure so now I'm mournful. Now is time for prayers and then I got to sleep.

* * * * *

"Fishy," whispered David through the dark morning chill.

"Still too early, Pigeon, so there's no sense in crowing just yet," grumbled Jackson from his hammock.

"But I've never seen a hunt before so how am I to sleep?"

"View it this way, Davey, every time we go fishin' it's a hunt. T'ain't no difference if yer after game on dry land or under the sea."

"You're sayin' so, but you know as well as I that we don't fire muskets at yeller-tail fishes."

"True, enough Davey, but that don't mean we need to stay wakeful all the night speakin' of such differences. Go to bed. Or at least lay there and be still so ole Fishy can rest his bones."

It was two days until Christmas, the third Jackson and David would spend on St. George's Cay. In the morning, a contingent of men, led by Captain Sayle himself, would set out in the shallop for a beach miles to the south across the sound where the tracks of at least four feral pigs had been spotted the day before. Sayle was determined that each settlement, the one on St. George's Cay and the one on the main island, would have a Christmas eve feast followed by a day of worship and celebration for the birth of their Savior.

"I'm gonna look about for land crabs 'cause I can't sleep none," huffed David.

"You do that, Pigeon, and best of luck to ya. Sun won't be up for at least two hours so ya ought to be able to gather a peck of the devils before then," mumbled Jackson as he threw his arm over his eyes.

Toothy Jill, curled in her corner, let out a deep sigh, hauled herself to her feet, then circled in her nest four times before lowering herself again with a loud huff.

"Stay here then," said David to the sleepy dog as he walked out into the night.

He looked about the hilltop in the pale blue light of a quarter moon. All the fuss about land, he thought to himself, but it was the sea that mattered. What would he do with twenty-five acres of land besides plant more sugar apples? How would a few bushels of fruit and sweet potatoes make anyone rich? It was beyond him. Deciphering what was valuable to people back in England seemed both impossible and irrelevant. What sense was there in treating whale puke like gold when it was fresh water that meant the difference between life and death.

It didn't make any difference he decided. This place was his home now and he loved it dearly. Yes, many were going hungry and most seemed desperate, but the sea had always provided David and Jackson sufficient nourishment and one never knew what the beach would capture on any given day. Last month, a whole whale washed ashore. A group of men led by Robert Ridley rendered less than half of the blubber and produced enough oil to light thousands of smoky lamps. The bones were magnificent as well. They'd carved two fine little harpoons from a single jawbone.

Fishy said someday their sea would toss a Spanish ship full of silver and gold ingots onto the reef. Then there'd be books and all manner of finery the sea couldn't provide. Until then, David was not only content, he was happy.

* * * * *

23 December 1649

Today a wild pig nearly eat Daniel Saunders but Mr. Albury struck him the pig on the head with his cutlass and that was that. The pigs on the main island are powerful devilish and they got tusks what they use as ordnance. This particular beast was angry at having been plugged in the chest with a musket ball. Fishy said he the pig was dead when he went after the younger Mr. Saunders but didn't know it to be so at the time. Captain Sayle did fell another pig not far from the one what didn't know he'd died. That pig knew right sudden he was dead and there weren't no protest. Then on the way back to St. George's Cay I fell into sleep and dreamed that first pig was after me. Fishy said my limbs were going twitch such as Toothy Jill's do at times and the men aboard got mighty gleeful at the sight. I don't remember thrashing but I do remember that devilish pig running for me. We went first to the main island settlement and give them their pig so they could have Christmas dinner. Then we went home and the men drenched boiling sea water on our pig and scraped him off all proper and clean. The men dug a fine big fire pit and commenced to making a large bed of coals. Then Mr. Sands set up the spit he say is like the Frenchmen do and that whole pig's now cooking slow. He the pig gets turned over so as not to catch fire I suppose. It's something bad to smell but Mrs. Sayle says it will smell real fine by and by. Wish we had sugar apples but they got blowed off the trees. Jane Saunders says she has sea grape jelly for me and Fishy and I am glad for that. Last night I couldn't sleep so I caught me a large compliment of land crab which I will give to Jane on account of the jelly. Now I smell the pig again and it do smell pleasanter. Tomorrow me, Fishy and Toothy are going out to the place where the William sank to *see if anything buried in the sand got unburied by the Northers what blow in winter. Fishy don't much like going in the water this time of year but I don't mind too awful. Still got ever so many pages in this book Captain Flowers give me. For Christmas I will read the book about Bermuda to Fishy, though I looked her over and the words are dreadful vexing.*

The Christmas feast came and went. The winter crops that followed were few. A cabbage was a great luxury, a handful of indian corn a fortune. Sweet potatoes assumed greater trading value than gold itself. Hunger was the spice that overpowered every meager meal.

By the end of January, many among the settlers ceased all activity save for the gathering of anything and everything edible. The flour was long gone now and bread a distant dream. Those initially disinclined to unfamiliar foods developed undiscerning pallets. Lobster, which the settlers called crawfish, no longer turned stomachs. Conch meat formerly used only for bait, now appeared in thin chowders.

When the weather permitted, all four boats fished day and night. There was always something to eat, but never enough to stifle omnipresent hunger. In mid-February, the two nanny goats with the lowest milk production were slaughtered. By March, sea birds began finding their way into stew pots along with more palatable pigeons and ducks.

By April, Sayle began considering another open-boat voyage to the Virginia Colonies. He mustered the same crew of eight and by vote the men decided that August 1, 1650 would be the day they set sail.

17 July, 1650

Today I had cider from a barrel brung by Mr. James Pen and Mr. Abraham Palmure who come all the way from the city of Bostown which Captain Sayle says is away in the North at a place called Massachoosit. It was strong but I didn't say so and asked for more. Fishy said no on account of the reverends also being aboard. Mr. Pen and Mr. Palmure was sent by Governor Winthrop who is "deceased" is what Reverend Copeland calls dead. He deceased on 26 March 1649, only before he did, a ship's master told him our settlement was dire underfed and also we ain't got building stuffs. So Mr. Winthrop went about the people what live there in Massachoosit and collected coins from them that wished to help us here on St. Georges Cay and on our main island. By and by Mr. Winthrop's men used up the money to buy all manner of cargo and then hired out Mr. Pen and Mr. Palmure's nice pinnace. Mr. Saunders says she's no more than 27 ton I don't know how he can know. Now we have all manner of luxury. We got many blankets which suits me fine I suppose but I think them in Bostown don't know how fine warm the climate is hereabouts. Captain Sayle got given real glass for making church windows which will be grand but first we need a church. There is also much salt fish which tickled Mr. Albury to no end. He laughed so hard he got pains in his stomach. The cider is something that "the Governor" (is what Mr. Pen called Captain Sayle) will stow away in his house which Fishy calls The Palace. All and all it was mighty good to have Mr. Pen and Mr. Palmure show up as they did. Mr. Ridley and Mr. Sands have set to work on a letter of thanks to send back with them.

All the men are also about the main island felling braziletto dye wood and hauling it to the beach, then they use the shallop to tow the logs and such over to the ship brung by Mr. Pen and Mr. Palmure. Mr. Ridley says braziletto wood is of great value so we don't have to be beholding. When they load 10 ton of the stuff, back it will go to Bostown where it will bring a good price. Then the pounds sterling will be given like as a gift to the school Governor Winthrop was restless to build (before he deceased) called Harverd Colledge. Fishy told me when we were fishing this morning that soon there will be other ships coming and things will be much changed. I don't know what to think of that. It's nice to have luxuries I suppose. Jane got new clothes and was glad of them. Toothy Jill got a mighty thigh bone from Mr. Pen's cook and later she made friends with Mr. Palmure's dog. Fishy says them two are married now. Today I thought about my uncle Reverend Allsap and how he stepped off into the sea and drowned on the way to Bermuda. I reckon it's best he's in Heaven cause I'm vastly certain he'd not like it here on St. George's Cay.

* * * * *

Throughout all of the difficult times, Jackson kept his word to Captain Sayle, assuring David appeared at the Captain's door every Sunday morning. David too kept his word, helping Sayle in his dedication to the Copeland congregation. The latter part of each Sunday was reserved for David's religious instruction. The catechism that Captain Sayle presented David in Bermuda was now well-worn and moldered.

This Sunday afternoon as Sayle opened his front door and bid the boy goodbye, Margery approached from behind and placed her hand on the captain's sleeve.

"Husband, the boy sounds more like Mr. Jackson every week that passes. You must challenge him next Sunday about his manner of speaking."

Sayle nodded his head, attempting to appear somber, but a smile nevertheless forced its way onto his face."

"Yes, I'll speak to David. The lad was clearly well schooled in Devon and I'm sure the same was true while he was his uncle's ward. His speech has roughened because he admires Jackson so."

Margery was less amused. "I am sorely distraught to hear the boy describe the landing of a large fish by exclaiming: I clicked the 'ole clapperdogeon right out of his watery libkin and didn't he then turn the hackum right sudden!"

Sayle was a man of God, to be sure, but his tolerance for rough language was fortified through decades at sea with men who'd spent much of their time in taverns until financial stresses (*low tide* as they said) forced them to sign on for another voyage.

"Yes, the description is colorful, Margery, and I'll make a suggestion for temperance in that regard. I do not believe the roughening of his tongue places his soul in peril, but he must remember from where he comes, notwithstanding the primitive nature of his present-day surroundings."

* * * * *

5 August, 1650

Today Capt. Sayle and Rev. Goulding told me I must heed to the way I speak. I ~~ain't~~ don't think I speak ~~no~~ different from earlier. Fishy says listen to the Captain and Reverend Goulding so I guess I will. ~~It ain't~~ It's not that I don't want to, it's just I don't hardly ever speak to ~~no~~ anyone but Fishy and we speak sea talk on account of us always being at sea fishing and such. As well I need to do as Capt. Flowers said and save my thoughts in the log book and it's likely sensible to write down the proper words such that the thoughts will come out right. It is stunning hot today it being summer. Fishy and ~~me~~ I spent much time in the water this morning and in the afternoon we had to pull the dinghy up on a beach in the shade and flee the irksome sun. When the climate is fierce hot I think about Devon and the awful cold then I ~~ain't~~ I am not dissatisfied.

18 September, 1650

Toothy Jill had her pups today but only three of them. I am so merry and Fishy is too. Jane wept and she wants a pup desperate so Fishy said she could pick one out. It will be so splendid grand to have pups about. Fishy says the male pup must be named Toothy Pete and I reckon that is a fine and good thing. She is the best sort of mother Toothy Jill is. Fishy said it pleased God to give her only 3 pups which is right and proper so she don't become overly weary in rearing them up. I will tell James Seymour over at the cave that Toothy had her pups as he was fiercely interested in the matter. Today also was pleasant because Fishy found a piece of whale puke big as a goat. It will buy all manner of luxury he says and maybe more books. The book about Bermuda and a storm is a puzzle but I read it to Fishy much as I can even if Mr. Shakespeare does prance about so with his words. Now and again he writes something fetching. For example there's a freakish sort of fellow what's called Calaban in the book. He said something pleasing about Bermuda which me and Fishy liked and here it is:

Be not afeard; the isle is full of noises, Sounds and sweet airs, that give delight and hurt not. Sometimes a thousand twangling instruments Will hum about mine ears, and sometime voices That, if I then had waked after long sleep, Will make me sleep again: and then, in dreaming, The clouds methought would open and show riches Ready to drop upon me that, when I waked, I cried to dream again.

This Calaban was goodly familiar with the island just like Fishy Jack and always could find food and suchlike. Fishy says all the rot about spirits is a falsehood and it don't take no special knowledge to plot a course through something that just ain't there. So no credit to Mr. Calaban for any such nonsense.

Post script - I named my pup Miranda from the book. Fishy says it's a good name and not to trouble with placing a 'Toothy' in front of it.

22 September, 1650

Today I learned of a woeful event which was the passing of a boy James Seymour who stayed back at the cave with his mother and father. He was sickly as I wrote down before but I am sorely overcome by his passing on account of he was a boy younger than me. Reverend Copeland speaks of returning to Bermuda which is also troublesome to my conscience. It ain't There are many besides Rev. Copeland speaking of leaving Eleutheria.

Capt. Sayle says he will not leave and I am glad of that. Fishy and me are pleased with our island and our land what Capt. Sayle will give to us though I don't know how we will prosper from it. Mr. and Mrs. Sands say they will never leave and they are strong of will. Mrs. Sands is with child again and Fishy says a babe will be good for the settlement. Mr. Albury told me today he fears John Saunders will send his sister Jane back to Bermuda to be safe. I can tell Mr. Albury wants to marry and be with Jane and that would be the grandest affair which I know our Lord in Heaven would favor.

Christmas Eve, 1650

Fishy Jack compels me this night to write some in the log book. Of late I ~~ain't~~ have been saddened and not in the mind to do so as many of our party left for Bermuda aboard a ship what come last month. The ship raked much salt far south of here and stopped on its way back north. Fishy says Bermuda waters is too deep to establish salt works and our islands hereabouts have many good and shallow salt ponds. So ships will be passing regular it seems. The master of the salt ship said to us that Josias Forster is Governor again in Bermuda and Fishy said that weren't glad news to any who might be witches as Forster has a powerful dislike of such folk and burns them up frequent. There is much fruit about the place this winter and I already fetched some early oranges and brung some home for me and Fishy. There was a surgeon aboard the salt ship and Fishy went and had his irksome tooth drawn. Capt. Sayle give him a great tankard of cider afterward which was for the tooth. Before he got his tooth drawed Fishy traded all of our whale puke with the master of the salt ship so now Fishy says Christmas tomorrow will have many luxuries though he won't tell of them. Jane and Mr. Albury are to be married in the Spring so Jane does not have to go back to Bermuda. Mr. Albury hauled a hundred pound of braziletto seed aboard the salt ship and traded with the master. Fishy says we'd be well to collect the seeds too but we're always fishing so I don't know how we would do so.

Now it is Christmas morn and Fishy was true about the luxuries. We have a wondrous new fishing net as fine as ever Fishy has seen. I have a pair of boots that are so grand I will never take them off my feet. Fact is we have all new clothes. Fishy give to Capt. Sayle a tin full of tea which the Captain did fuss over for some time afterwards. It's almost time for Christmas services and I am to help Reverend White now as Rev. Copeland went away. Fishy said he is worry laden because the reverend will be poor and without means back in Bermuda.

11 SERENITY

Jackson sat propped against a palm tree in the sand, a gloriously dappled sunset blossoming to his left amid magenta rimmed clouds. Toothy Jill's grey muzzle rested on Jackson's bandy thigh, her blue eye a bit more cloudy than the brown one. He stroked the dog's silky head and pointed with the other hand down the beach where the silhouettes of a man, a woman and a dog were framed by the red setting sun.

"There's your little one, Toothy, only she's growed up now."

Toothy Jill raised her head and sniffed the air. She then lifted herself from the soft sand and trotted away towards the silhouettes. The pup placed into Jane's care, now four years old, romped towards her mother. The Sands family cared for and loved the male from the same small litter, a smaller reincarnation of Toothy Pete. Miranda, the smallest of Toothy Jill's puppies, was always by David's side, day and night.

David Albury and his wife, Jane, stopped now in front of Jackson.

"Stay seated, Fishy, no need to get up."

"Ah well, the sun has almost finished her performance so I might as well make a move. I see little Toothy Jen is in fine form. Ya no doubt spoil her as much as ya do that little girl of yorn."

"Yes, in fact I do. Bess is not the jealous sort, Fishy, so I see no reason not to spoil them equally. Our Bess says she and little Jen are best friends and I never heard a truer thing. I thank you every day for giving me one of Jill's pups."

"Well it ain't everyone I would trust but I know your heart, Janey. Mr. Albury," Jackson continued, "you are a fortunate man and I'm glad we hauled you out of the *William*'s flooded companionway those many years ago on account of how well ya look after your wife."

Albury shook his head and began to chuckle while Jackson dissolved into his nearly toothless grin.

In the nearly four years since the majority of settlers returned to Bermuda, life on St. George's Cay had proceeded at a languid pace, punctuated by the excitement of an arriving ship or the passing of a storm.

While prosperity evaded the company, hunger retreated far back into the shadows. The company's Articles and Orders, while not implemented in every respect due to the settlement's small population, were followed in principal. In 1653, Jackson had, in fact, supervised a salvage in accord with the Articles. A respectful relationship had, in fact, been forged with those few ever-roving Lucayan Indians who survived Spanish decimation. Religious tolerance remained the settlement's cornerstone and in early 1654 Sayle himself welcomed into his home a small congregation of Quakers banished from Bermuda.

The settlement, it seemed, was now the preferred dumping ground for Bermudan undesirables. The exiled Quakers were only the first of many to be shipped south to that "little island" where the banished would scratch out an existence from barren rock and shallow ground.

* * * * *

21 April, 1654

I oft times wonder whether old Capt. Flowers remains alive. I should like to show him how much of the log book I've filled with thoughts since it was given me back in 1649. Out of decency, I would not speak to Capt. Flowers of our low opinion of Mr. Shakespeare's tale of Bermuda. Fishy Jack and me don't much go in for yarns of a sort one can't cypher and ole Shakespeare's book is a right blunderbus. Fishy says if he ever saw Mr. Shakespeare he'd punch him in the boltsprit and kick him in the bunghole just to show what a load of tripe his version of Bermuda be. By and by we come upon another wrack bigger than the last one, and all lives lost. Me, Fishy, Mr. Sands and Mr. Albury just commenced stripping her when up comes a pack of Spaniards bent on having the salvage themselves. Them being fitted out with cannon and such ,we parted ways quick and now have only a gaping big cavity in our sail to show for our efforts. Fishy says there's no value in fighting with Spaniards and we'd likely get the pox from them if we did , what with their low ways and such. We did manage to take away a very fine little 3 pound gun which if we don't use ourselves should fetch a goodly sum.

2 October, 1654

My pup Miranda and me are just returned from a voyage of which I must write afore my thoughts grow thinnish. Thanks be to God, the 3 pounder we got from the Spanish wrack, and Mr. Saunders, for I am now master of a sprite little sloop of 21 foot. She is quick as a bird on a smooth reach in the sound and Miranda rides her bow like as to challenge the world. I named her Rose for my Ma back in Devon before she was deceased. I provisioned her with sweet water and suchlike and off we went, Miranda and me, sailing south along the west coast of the main island. Fishy said be mindful of the weather and tide but otherwise he were not troubled of danger. She is long our main island and Miranda and me explored the whole western shore maybe 100 mile or more. About half way down there's a harbour any ship would be grateful for. We camped there two days, though Miranda didn't much like the sand fleas, and walked about the hills. On the way out the harbour under a rocky head I fetched up a crawfish big as a Miranda almost and what a pair of horns, near three foot long. I brought them back to Spanish Wells to show Fishy and didn't his eyes pop! Also we skinned two fine sharks of which I will give one skin to Mr. Saunders. Miranda had both them shark livers and was gladdened mightily. The best thing was I met a fine Indian away down south and talked about the Lord to him like as to please Rev. White. I don't know how much Godliness soaked through but my friend the Indian sure did take a liking to the Rose and he had a gleeful time learning to sail her. His canoe weren't a bad vessel itself and was a pleasure to paddle amongst the shoals and mangroves. On the way back home me and Miranda stopped at the very thinnest point in the island and strolled about the rocks. The sights there are such as must be awful rare in the world. It's only a few paces from the one side of the island to the other side and maybe someday the great waves on the east will break right on through to the west. It's like good and evil faced off, the crashing dark sea roaring to get at the peaceful bright waters of the sound. I reckon I'll go back there frequent as it's in my mind now to do so.

12 DIASPORA

November 2, 1656, Bermuda Council

Upon the 2nd daie of November 1656 there was consultation held by the Governor and all his counsell about the conspiracy and plott that the negroes in this Island had contrived for cutting off and the distroieing the English in the night which being cleerely manifested then it was ordered that they should come to a triall by a marshall court whereupon there were sumoned downe to Georges these gentlemen following who were appointed for their triall viz:

Capt William Wilkinson
Capt Stephen Paynter
Capt Horatio Malary
Capt Godherd Aser
Capt William Williams
Capt fflorentia Seymer
Leiftenr Gualtier Abbott

Leiftenr John Rawlinges
Leiftenr John Rivers
Leiftenr Myles Rivers
Leiftenr John Ffox

Their Proceeding is as ffolloweth. Imprimis, it being put to the vote whether Blacke Anthony, Mr Richard Hunt's negro, according to evidence given in doth stand guilty of that plott and conspiracy against the English to cutt them off and destroy them. It was the unanimous vote and consent of the court that the said Blacke Anthony was Guilty.

Cabilecto, M Gilbert Hills' negro, Ffranck Jeames, Mr. Devitt's negro man, Black Tom, Capt Thomas Burrows' negro, and William Fforce, were all convicted in nearly the same words.

It was put to the vote whether Black Robin, Mr. Wiseman's negro man, were guilty of the conspiracy and riseing up against the English to destroy them. It was judged by the generall vote that he stands guilty as an accessory not as a principal. In the same terms Tony, Capt. Christopher Lea's negro.

It was also put to vote whether Blacke Jacke, Longson's negro, and Black Harry, Jonathan Tumor's negro, and black Tony, Capt Lea's negro are guilty of the conspiracy against the English. It is observed that by their confession they were instruments of the discovery of the plott in generall the Court therefore doth judge them worthy of favour of life.

Nevertheles there were 9 severall negro men condemned by the Court aforesaid yet there were only 2 of the cheife actors executed, namely, Black Tom the servant of Capt Thomas Burrows, who was put to death at Georges Gallowes, and the other Cabilecto, servant to Mr Gilbert Hill, who was executed upon a Gibbett sett up by the Gouernor's appointment upon Coblers Hand.

William Fforce, condemned as accessory, was carried to a Gibbett sett up at Heme Baye where it was hoped he would have confessed the plott amongst the negroes. And although he was putt to it to the uttermost yett confessed nothing so as the Governor gave orders to the sherriffe and Fforce was repreived and after sent away to Eleutheria with the rest of the free negroes who besought the Governor that they might be banisht to that Land rather than to the Indias which request his worship with his counsell did condescend unto and were afterwards shipt away in the Blessing bound thither.

* * * * *

Copy of a letter dated 14 Oct 1656 sent by Capt Limbrey who arrived in Bermuda the 7th of November 1657

By the Elizabeth and Anne, John Stowe Master, we sent you a letter dirrected to Mr. Nathaniel White minister at Eleutheria enviting him and all those with him as many of them as are willing to returne from thence to the Somer Islands and assigning Mr White ye house and gleab land at the ourplus for his reception upon arrivall but having received no account either from you or them Wee now pray you the Governor and councell by your next letters to send us an account of the delivery of those letters and the effect of those said invitations there upon.

* * * * *

There haveing been much debate betweene Capt. Richard Locker and his Eleutherian passengers about damage and average of the Rebecca and Anne att length it was concluded that nevertheless all former orders made between Captain Lockyer and them that upon the payment of 20lb in ready money and 15 lbs in Ambergreece of the best sorte at 25s p ounce That the ffreighters and passengers and merchants shall have liberty to discharg and unlade the said shipp and take of her goodes which money and amber is in consideration of damag and averages And upon this agreement all differences and engagements about the said ship are to cease betweene them and the said owners and ffreighters The ffreight and passengers 1 only excepted There not being present money in the handes of the ffreighters Capt Lockyer is content to stay untill the 19th day of this Instant month and the ffreighters doth promise to make payment.

* * * * *

On November 15, 1656, in St. George's Bay, Bermuda, the ship called *Blessing* defied its name as she took aboard a compliment of wretched and fearful exiles. William Force, a terrible raw brand upon his right cheek, clattered up the gangway in irons. He was a tall, well-constructed man with skin the color and shine of blackstrap molasses. He held is head high and if he heard the jeers hurled from the wharf they were powerless against his pride. Other free black men followed Force up the gangway, a few in chains, but most walked freely, clutching scant possessions and small children.

William Force was a man who cherished every second of his freedom and to him mankind's greatest sin, of all those perpetrated around the world, was the institution of slavery. He was accused of fomenting a slave rebellion. Two slave co-conspirators were summarily executed. A wave of panic swept over Bermuda and now the *Blessing* was to carry almost every free black Bermudan and a handful of alleged slave co-conspirators south to Eleutheria where they were to live and toil in exile.

Several families of Quakers also quietly shuffled aboard, hated not only for their religious practices but also for their sympathy towards black slaves. Even in a setting of bucolic passivity that was Bermuda, intolerance seemed to hang in the air like acrid smoke. The *Blessing*, the same ship that on June 18, 1609 departed the filthy wharves of London bound for Jamestown carrying puritans refugees, now carried a new wave of religious exiles to Eleutheria.

Brandishing a cutlass, the *Blessing*'s first mate approached William Force.

"You'll do well not to resist, you black devil. You so much as think about making trouble and I'll carve both your ears from your head."

Force looked the mate directly in the eye and smiled broadly. "Why should I make trouble? I'm a free man bound for a land named for freedom."

* * * * *

Twelve days later, the *Blessing* appeared on the horizon to the north of St. George's Cay. By late afternoon, it was clear the ship was making for the island. Captain Sayle ordered the shallop be readied with a crew of six.

As the shallop made its way through the channel off Ridley head, the *Blessing* lowered her remaining canvas then dropped anchor in a light blue patch of water. She immediately lowered her longboat and several men could be seen scrambling overboard. Captain Sayle stood in the shallop's bow and waved towards the *Blessing*'s quarterdeck. Her master appeared a moment later waving a response. He then boarded the longboat and its crew rowed southward to meet the shallop.

"Captain Sayle, I presume!" a stout man hailed from the approaching longboat.

"Yes," cried Sayle, "You be Captain Harding then. I recognize the *Blessing*. You are welcome here. If you'll ready your tow line, we'll assist your vessel through the reef and show you to a fine anchorage."

The longboat from the blessing now rowed close alongside the shallop and Harding reached to shake Sayle's hand.

"I doubt sir, that we shall be welcome when I inform yea of the passengers aboard. I've shipped three score of free blacks, a number of convict slaves and some Quakers as well."

Sayle and the crew struggled to mask their surprise. All eyes turned in unison to the deck of the Blessing, as if in disbelief. Captain Sayle quickly recovered his composure and spoke.

"There are no slaves here, so those aboard who were regarded as such in Bermuda shall be free men so long as they dwell among our islands. In every respect, they and everyone aboard is welcome, so long as they comply with our ordinances. God judges men, not I."

Harding nodded slightly. "I'm pleased to hear your words, Captain. I've had no trouble during the voyage with any aboard my ship and I suspect there shall be none once they are ashore. My passengers are no doubt anxious to step on dry land, so if you please, show my ship to her anchorage."

* * * * *

By the end of the day, November 29, 1656, the *Blessing*'s cargo of exiles, together with everything they owned and all the provisions they'd marshaled, lay scattered about the St. Georges Cay waterfront. The weather was cool and dry, a gentle westerly wind rustling the palm trees. As if fearful their very footsteps would ignite a conflagration of dissent from the island's inhabitants, the exiles remained huddled together along water's edge.

As Captain Sayle strode down the hillside towards the crowd, William Force looked up from the group of black men he was addressing. He rose and straightened his waistcoat, apparently preparing to greet the Captain. A Quaker gentlemen sitting not far away also rose and strolled over to the man in the waistcoat. Sayle extended his hand as he drew up to the two men. Force reached out and with a decisive grip, shook hands.

"I am William Force. This man is Mr. Thayer and he is a friend to me and all who were aboard the *Blessing*."

Captain Sayle nodded to both men. "My name is Captain William Sayle. You are welcome here and we shall do what we can to make you comfortable. Am I to understand that you two gentlemen are leaders among this group?"

Thayer was first to respond, "We are *representatives* you might say, Captain and in behalf of our brothers and sisters we thank you for your welcome."

"Perhaps you will join my family this evening for a meal at my lodgings. We no doubt have much to discuss and it would be our pleasure to provide you as much information about your new environs as we're able to provide. I will send my son Thomas for you before the sun sets."

Force smiled, but then winced slightly from the pain of the still-healing brand on his right cheek.

"The pleasure shall be ours, Captain. Your Mr. Sands has already been kind enough to share a source of fresh water and I wish to assure you at the outset that our number shall be frugal in regard to its use."

"Thank you, Mr. Force. I have assigned Mr. Saunders and Mr. Rowan to conduct a census of your party so that we might present plans for billeting the women and children in our dwellings. I'm afraid we will not immediately be capable of accommodating the men."

Thayer responded, "That is indeed a great kindness, Captain, but we wish to cause no disruption and we are reasonably provisioned to care for ourselves."

"Your deference is greatly appreciated, Mr. Thayer, but we are all Christians here and it would be to our great satisfaction if we could be of any assistance, no matter how modest."

After the exchange of introductions and platitudes, Sayle left Force and Thayer by the waterfront to meet with John Saunders and Henry Rowan. At first glance, the party from the *Blessing* did appear reasonably well provisioned, so the situation was far from critical, but much planning would be required both in regard to immediate needs and future objectives.

* * * * *

The meal served by Margery was nothing less than a feast and both Force and Thayer ate well after having endured nearly two weeks of sea rations. Several fine hogfish were served, along with half a dozen pigeons. Two precious cabbages, not quite fully grown, were also sacrificed.

"That was as fine a meal as I have ever tasted, Mrs. Sayle," offered Force, raising his tankard of cider in salute.

Margery smiled and demurely exited the dining area.

"I cannot say we dine like that daily, gentlemen, but our islands here provide sufficient game and the sea is fruitful to those who understand her ways," Sayle qualified.

Upon Sayle's subtle hint, the men pushed their chairs away from the table.

"Captain Harding kindly provided me a supply of tobacco and enough clay pipes to last a lifetime. I suggest we stroll along the north beach and enjoy a smoke together."

The men walked casually down the gentle slope, across a small flat expanse and onto the beach, gleaming under a nearly full moon. The westerly breeze was now softer and the lightly rippled water glinted before them like shattered glass.

Sayle pivoted to the east and pointed. "Our main island there, Eleutheria, is about three miles at its widest, but runs approximately one hundred miles to the south. Not more than a mile or so beyond that point our ship, the *William*, was lost upon the reef. It was a trying time, gentlemen, as we lost almost the whole of our supplies. Beyond the main island lies a fine harbor with a deep-water channel, then a chain of three islands running north to south, then the open sea."

Sayle then turned and pointed west.

"On this heading we have our small island, which runs about two mile in length, then another island of similar size, then yet another with a fine natural harbur. Our St. Georges Cay affords ready access through the reef and is well sheltered from the north winds."

"And you say there are other settlers to our east, on Eleutheria" asked Thayer.

"Aye. When the *William* was lost we took shelter in a cave not one hundred paces from the very beach. Some, planters for the most part, have remained in the area, though it is unsafe to shelter a boat there for any length of time. Those that remained behind are more inclined to the earth than they are to the sea."

Force had been silent for some time, but now suddenly cleared his throat.

"Captain, I mean to tell you that we, the free blacks and slaves among us, were poorly treated in Bermuda. I am accused of organizing a slave rebellion and as a consequence, I and my fellow free blacks are now banished to your islands. Mr. Thayer and his brethren too were sorely mistreated and I know not what his aims here be. But as for the blacks among us, slaves and free alike, I wish humbly to ask you for a grant of land in which to form our own settlement. To be sure, I am vastly grateful for your hospitable welcome, but I wish to cause no rift among your people. I must speak honestly as well that we would relish the chance to live as a free black community, to work together under the common purposes fate and mankind have thrust upon us."

Sayle peered intently into Force's dark eyes and was silent for an uncomfortably long time. When he finally spoke, his voice broke slightly and he hesitated again. After several puffs of his pipe, he began.

"First be assured, Mr. Force, that slavery is not tolerated here and no man that left Bermuda in those bonds shall wear them evermore so long as he remains in these islands. Second, I am sincere that you and your number are welcome on St. George's Cay or anywhere you may prefer to settle. We could begin to build the first dwellings right here on this spot if it were your wish. Contrarily, if it is your wish to live apart and in your own way, we shall not hinder such effort and in fact will do everything in our power to assist you. I ask that you discuss all possible plans with the ones you represent and we shall thenceforth endeavor to help you plot the chosen course."

Force nodded politely, "Captain, we've passed the last two weeks discussing the matter in a thorough fashion and many a vote has been taken with always the same result. If you will allow us, we will establish a settlement of our own."

"Very well then, Mr. Force, tomorrow our shallop shall be placed at your disposal together with a crew, and you are welcome to conduct a survey of suitable sites. As long as the shallop and crew are required, you shall have at least that assistance."

"I thank you sincerely, Captain. We shall use your shallop as briefly as possible. Is it possible to commission among any of your settler's the construction of one or two small craft.?"

"Yes, you may speak to John Saunders of such matters. You likely know Mr. Saunders by reputation, as he owned a very fine boatyard on St. George's Bay in Bermuda."

7 December, 1656

Fishy, me and Miranda has been all week aboard the shallop and the Rose on account of momentous happenings. The Blessing and her Master, Captain Harding, made shore at Spanish Wells on 27 November. Come to find out the Blessing was hired out to transport over three score of settlers what Bermuda had no liking for. We got more Quakers, no surprise, but we also got nearly all the free black Bermudans who's lately been sorely mistreated by the Council. And there's a story behind that. Off the Blessing come a fine and strong black gentleman by the name of William Force. He's a right captain by nature that one. Well, he got weary of them on Bermuda what believes they can own a man and hold him slave. A number of slaves our Mr. Force knew and spoke with time to time rebelled and the word is there was blood. Two of them involved was hanged by the Council and all manner of other blacks was rounded up and forced to leave

Bermuda on the Blessing. Captain Sayle says he reckons Mr. Force feels together both sorrowful and glad that they was banished, sorrowful that everyone was mistreated on account of the rebellion and glad on account of coming to freedom, Eleutheria. So Mr. Force tells Captain Sayle he and his number wish to start their own settlement and not be beholding to any man. The Captain says not to be troubled about slavery as we don't believe in such around here. But Force he wishes to cut it on his own so his party never has to be worrisome again about being rounded up and shoved off. Captain says very well and he orders the shallop crewed so Mr. Force can wander about searching for a place to settle. By and by he and his party decide on a piece of ground down and nearabout the thin part of the island I wrote about before. There's a narrow cut in the shoreline to the west and boats must pass thought it and across the bay to reach Mr. Force's parcel. And I mean to tell it's a grand and rousing thing to shoot through that cut on a current looks just like a raging river. I feel like a cork in a water spout when I take the Rose on through. The land about there is flattish and the bay is dread shallow in some spots, but the soil is passable. It is well sheltered for the most part and there are numerous and diverse small fish can be netted easy. There is good fruit as well. I don't know about the supply of sweet water but Mr. Force looked the place over real proper and he seems like a man knows what he's doing. Well then we passed the better part of a week ferrying people and cargo down to the spot which Fishy now calls Bogue on account of it is devilish hard to pinch into the wind and land when its blowing from the east. We had all of our boats ferrying constant. It was a grand scene when finally all were transported and the cargo was ashore. We lost a nanny goat overboard the Rose on the last run and wasn't it precarious to get her back aboard! The crew of the shallop, the crew of the Rose (me and Miranda) and the crew of the Grace all camped down there that last night and it were cheerful with music and all manner of celebration. One of Mr. Force's friends killed a pig right off and roasted him up on the beach. I aim to frequent the new settlement in my sloop Rose as the folk are friendly and I wish them well. Miranda was feared at first but now she is partial to them too. We found some whale bones cast up on the eastern shore and that is always good cheer though not for the whale.

24 December, 1656

It pleased me this morn to take aboard the Rose our Captain Sayle and Rev. White. We sailed on down and through the cut to visit Mr. Force and his party. It were something to see how many trees they felled and what all they have done to build things up around there in such a brief spell. We had prayers well attended and a fine meal in a long dwelling they did raise these last weeks. Captain Sayle presented a fine gift what was a cask of honey and a great wide net that many on

St. George's Cay all worked upon. Mr. Force was powerful taken and he presented us with a great heap of salt they'd raked from I don't know where. I wanted to stay longer but we hastened to leave upon the outgoing tide so as to clear the cut and return to our island for services. And glad that we left when we did because we barely landed in time. Rev. White was fidgety the whole way back but we couldn't make way no faster as the breeze were northerly. Miranda, Fishy and me had such a fine evening after services and tomorrow we will spend with Jane and Mr. Albury. Mr. Sands says he will bring Toothy Pete the Second by for a visit as the whole Toothy Jill family will be present. We aim to search about for another wrack soon as possible as we have grown accustomed to luxuries round about Christmastime. If we don't find one Fishy says there will be a ship soon and we can trade more whale puke which Mrs. Sayle says I must call ambergris.

31 December, 1656

When I wake in the morn it will be the year 1657 and don't it seem almost a dream. Fishy and I spoke at supper about these past years, near ten of them from the time we come here and lost the William. Nowadays Fishy is weary more than he were back then as he is aged. I don't know what will become of him when Toothy Jill passes and she is right elderly. Regular we give her minced fish and turtle eggs on account of her teeth being poor

168

and her eyes too is failing. She still do love to fish though and we give her a nice crate to ride in so as not to get tossed about. Most changed of all is our Spanish Wells people. Ships come now frequent from Bermuda and some now and again from Virginia. Most takes salt back. But the cargo they bring accounts more for the changes I spoke of. The Council up in Bermuda do send all manner of folk here as punishment for things they done, mostly in Bermuda but sometimes also in England and elsewheres. And I don't just mean worshiping different. I mean things such as stealing, or assault, or not paying debts, or sins such as adultery and such. It seems in some ways that Capt. Sayle accepts the Council treating us like a prison. I don't know what to think other than it seems unjust we should have to live alongside criminals and highwaymen. There are a few women hereabouts lately that Jane says I must not so much as greet in passing or I'll be in hot tar with the Reverends. I don't know how we can have all these new folk about the island and yet we can't so much as tip a hat to them. Things is not so clear as in times before. Then there is the biggest change of all. Captain Sayle and his family, Thomas and all, are to return to Bermuda aboard the Blessing in March. He says things are much changed there and he has more work to do for the good of us all. These matters of who can do what and when and where on Bermuda do not concern me and I am weary of that talk. Here among these islands is my home and I intend to stay without regard to the wind what blows in

Bermuda. I know there are others feel the same way such as Mr. Sands. Fishy Jack will never leave which is all well because I don't want him to. I am full growed now for many years and it is good to set my own course. Fishy well taught me fishing and wracking and the ambergris business too. I see also that whales are plentiful and there likely is a living to be made in them some day. I reflect on the matter frequent and believe whales can be harvested with harpoons and not merely found dead and stuck fast on a beach. There may be sin mixed up in there somewhere as they are mighty creatures to be sure. But I suspect the Lord will show me the right course by and by.

4 April, 1657

With Captain Sayle and his family all gone away there is now dwelling in his house a man named Curtis. He means to make a go of wracking and Fishy and me bear no grudge against him trying. Though the Captain is gone Fishy reported to Curtis that he Fishy Jack was put in the charge of wracking operations by Captain Sayle his own self. Curtis acknowledged such and swore unto us that if he did find a wrack Fishy Jack would direct the stripping of her and be paid for his self and for the settlement.

* * * * *

We hearing by certeyne Spaniards which Mr. Justinian Martin brought into our harbor the 24th of July being distrest at sea that ther hath lately bin a great shipp & great store of Riches in her wreckt at sea neare some of the Bahama Islands And by their report is likely to be recovered and obteyned. It is thought fitt not to neglect any opportunity for the recovery thereof for the benifitt of the Lord Protector the honorable Company and of the recoverers that shall aduenture therein it was therefore ordered That Capt. Richard Lockyer have a commission to go forth for the discovery and recovery of the said Treasuer And that the Spaniards being 8 in number be kept on shoare untill Wee heare further both of or Lord Protector and the honoble Company and their pleasures knowne therein. It is also agreed that the two men one Irish the other English with the Spanish Pilot shall saile forthe wth the said Capt. Lockyer and the others be kept as afore said untill wee have further intelligence of the truth of thinges only there beeing an Indian amongst these Spanyards which Mr. Martin desiers may be kept on his account and not to be disposed of untill further order from him. It was likewise promised that Mr. Martin aforesaid shall have a share or parte porportionable to his service in bringing the Spanyards to our Port if the designe doe prosper according to expectation. This was granted the rather because Mr. Martin did freely yeild up and deliuer to the Pilott all his instruments for navigation and dealt well with the rest in returning their clothes to them.

* * * * *

24 August, 1657

What a time of it we've had Fishy and me. These past months and in particular these past weeks has been like as if old Shakespeare his self dreamt up the story and all manner of folk in it. Along come in mid-July three more men took up residence in Capt. Sayle's house alongside Curtis. Them being Richard Richardson, John Williams and Aser Eley. All keen on the idea of wracking though none had ever done such. By and by Richardson wearies of the other three or there is a disturbance among them and off goes Richardson to the cave to live. Richardson's got a fine shallop so me and Fishy already showed him the entire north shore of Eleutheria and environs thereabout. Well then word comes of a wrack on the east shore of Thomas Mann Island just to the southeast of the long point on our main island. Off we go Fishy, me and Curtis to have a peck about and certain enough there's the wrack and she's a Spaniard. No sign of survivors. Back we goes to St. George's Cay. The boys Williams and Eley are right worked up about the whole affair and starts in conniving who best to get the most loot for us what know about the wrack. Fishy explains the lay of the land. First James Mann got to have his share on account of it's his parcel upon which the wrack lies. Then there's the share to the agent Fishy to keep for the settlement. Then there's the shares what go to them that works the wrack. By and by Fishy makes them to understand and reports that there's enough cargo and probably pieces of eight as well for every man and why get so worked up about it. Fishy also says there is sense in having Richardson work alongside for a share as he owns a very fine shallop. Finally Curtis, Williams and Eley agree and off we go to fetch Richardson aboard. Well don't Richardson start in on the same course trying to get more of a share than the others. Well now Richardson actually makes a fair argument that he's placing his shallop in service and at risk. More time passes and Fishy and I are worried about the wrack going all to splinters but eventual they all agree. Off we go again to the wrack bringing both the settlement's shallop and Richardson's shallop. Truth be told and no offense intended of Curtis, Williams and Richardson but never did Fishy and me see such green ones. There weren't no question that any of them do any diving as none can swim. So Fishy and me spend I don't know how many days grubbing about what's left of the holds and all about the scattered ruins while the lubbers stripped what they could from above water. Well didn't we come up with some pounds silver and pieces of eight! The first haul was 2600 pounds sterling. We put it all up in 100 pound bags and then Curtis, Eley, Williams and Richardson start in again scrapping! Me and Fishy was growing weary of it all but we went back to work and pulled up even more. By and by we divided the silver and gold (the lubbers took little interest in the gear we salvaged). Fishy says the best part of the whole deal is we'll never have to see Curtis, Williams, Richardson or Eley again as they're right anxious to leave our settlement and go spend their loot where there's something they can spend it on. Me and Fishy got enough coin now for any manner of luxury what visiting ships might bring. Fishy said I ought to go to Bermuda or maybe Virginia as it is time I take a wife. Jane and her husband David Albury speak of the same thing constant. I reckon I'd need to build a house and buy all manner of things to put in if I were to fetch a wife back here to St. George's Cay. It unsettles me to think of leaving the island on account of Fishy being aged.

10 October, 1657

Toothy Jill passed away this morning and I cannot write of it. Perhaps if my Faith in God were greater I would not be so distressed.

12 NEPTUNA

At a Council Table held at Georges the 21st of June 1660, Capt. William Sayle Governor, Captain George Tucker, Mr. Francis Watlington, and Henry Tucker Secretie being then present.

The case of Neptuna, the wife of Benjamin Downeham hath this day been taken into consideration, the which having been found guilty of Adultery, for that she hath (in her husbands absence) had a child begotten of her body by John Morgan, churugian, whereby she hath made herself subject to the sentence of death by the present Laws of England, nevertheless an opportunity of sending her away to Eleutheria by Mr. Thomas Sayle's ship being now presented. The Governor and Council, in favour of her life, have thought it fit, and ordered her banishment there hence in lieu of the execution of the Law as aforesaid, in the said Mr. Thomas Sayle's ship.

On the 23rd day of July, a wispy girl aged 19, stepped out of her dark cell and stood blinking in the brilliant Bermuda sunlight, her tiny baby clutched closely to her breast.

"I'm to fetch ya to the ship, miss. Captain Thomas Sayle's vessel," the shy sailor hoarsely announced.

The girl stood silent, still blinking in the pitiless sun. She was disheveled, dirty and had lately been convicted of a capital offense, yet still she appeared wholesome and arresting, as if she were an exotic plant in one of the many ornate gardens that dotted the island.

Without looking at the sailor she spoke her first words in many days. "My possessions, are they aboard Mr. Sayle's ship?"

The sailor now looked nervous. He was anxious to complete his errand. "No miss, none that I know of. Likely your husband . . . that is, likely Mr. Downeham ain't sent anything on account of he'd be liable for the cost of freight, ya see?"

The girl, formerly Neptuna Downeham, now simply Neptuna, or "girl" or at best, "miss," nodded passively. She shifted the baby in her arms and spoke again.

"I have all I need."

"Yes, miss," answered the sailor, "but you should know as well Captain Sayle the younger is a kind-hearted man. He'll do for the babe what he can. He's readied a decent berth for ya aboard and there be swaddling and such for the babe. A wash basin as well."

Neptuna was silent again, softly stroking her babies downy head.

"If . . . if I might say so, miss, I know certain it was Captain Sayle the Governor what saved your life. I heard him speak to the younger about ya and there weren't going to be no argument that yea should be taken aboard and away from here."

The girl looked into the sailor's face for the first time. Her pale blue eyes were now steady.

"I am told it is a place named for freedom which doth seem a cruel slight does it not?"

"I don't know much, miss, but I have sailed to Eleutheria and I can tell ya it is as free a place as I've ever seen whilst ashore. It ain't like some of them dens scattered about the Caribe Sea. It ain't Hispaniola or worse. I suspect it'll suit ya better than the end of a rope."

Thomas Sayle was issued orders for a trade mission in 1658. In the spring of 1660, he'd carried passengers and cargo from London to Bermuda and was now bound for Eleutheria with supplies for the colony. From there, he would cut braziletto wood, rake salt, harvest any whale or seal oil he could and, as always, search out ambergris at every opportunity. Once collected, the goods would be sold primarily in Barbados, though Jamaica would serve as an alternative market.

It gave him great pleasure, and a degree of solace as well, that he was in command of a ship carrying the same name as the one lost on the Devil's Backbone eleven years prior. As he approached Ridley Head, he took the helm himself.

"You may lower the remaining canvas, Mr. Ellis," Thomas called to the mate. "And you may lower the longboat thereafter."

Nathaniel, Thomas Sayle's brother, was now Governor of the settlement, but he was not a permanent resident. At present, Nathaniel was in London, as his father's Charter to the Eleutherian islands was under challenge. Yes, Captain William Sayle did appear to have a Charter, but a patent had never been granted to seal the deal.

"The longboat's over the side, Captain. Shall we run a kedge down the channel," Ellis asked.

"Not yet. Hail the Governor's shallop and wave her on through the passage. We will see if our ship'll move through under tow without kedging. I can scarcely feel the southerly this close into shore and I suspect she'll move ahead without breaking the backs of our oarsmen."

Under the strength of twelve sets of oars, the *William* eased through the narrow passage and into the open bay to the east northeast of St. George's Cay. Thomas Sayle was home again, gazing ahead at the island named for freedom. His nineteen year-old adulterous passenger, looked over the ship's bowsprit at the land of her banishment.

* * * * *

Neptuna settled herself into the longboat, shading her baby's eyes from a malicious noonday sun. Thomas Sayle then stepped agilely into the bow, tossing the bowline at his feet. He extended to

Neptuna a bundle tied into quarters with a hemp line.

"You take these, miss" Sayle said of the swaddling, "there is no need to leave them aboard."

"You are charitable, Captain. I pray you believe that were I able, I would make recompense."

Sayle did not respond and instead ordered the crew to their oars. As the boat pulled away from the *William*, the heat remained, but it was now feebly disguised by a languid southwesterly breeze. Long strands of Neptula's hair rose into chaotic flight. She wore no bonnet. She wore the cloths she'd been wearing when the Bermuda constabulary wrenched her from her home and into a St. George's Bay prison cell.

The gin clear water parted into shimmering eddies as the oars slapped rhythmically onward. A stretch of waterfront amateurishly playing the role of a wharf came into view. Thomas Sayle spoke again to Neptuna, almost in a whisper.

"There is little I can do for you here, you understand. My ship sails tomorrow and I do not know if I shall return. You may wish to seek out Jane Albury. Her heart is more open than some. She will not turn away from the needs of your girl child."

* * * * *

Sailing the *Rose* briskly down the channel, David spotted a longboat and recognized Thomas Sayle standing in the bow. He waved a greeting to the young captain, noticing a women seated statuesquely at Sayle's feet. Since early that morning, David had been fishing off Egg Island well to the west and so had no notice of a ship's arrival. There would be an opportunity to sell the barrels of whale oil he and Jackson rendered from a whale found dead on shoals to the northwest. Perhaps too there would be opportunity to purchase goods with some of the gold and silver salvaged from the wreck on James Mann Island.

The *Rose* drew quickly alongside Sayle's longboat, bringing the woman's face into focus. She was the most perplexingly lovely creature he'd ever seen. The *Rose* glided far down the channel before David realized he was holding his breath. The woman was young, that was clear. Her bodice was faded and threadbare, as was her long skirt, but her attire was finely wrought and would have been very expensive at one time. Her chestnut hair was tousled and sun-streaked, but she appeared to pay no heed. The hue of her acute blue eyes was foreign to the Caribbean surroundings, reminding David instead of the cold winter skies and a frozen rivers of Dover. Yet her gold rubicund face emanated warmth in a manner that reminded David of the young Lucayan Indian he'd taught to sail the *Rose* two years prior. She clutched a tiny bundle to her bodice, which might be a child, but she appeared to be alone. Her features were fine. He imagined her bones were as thin as sea urchin spines, yet she appeared as unyielding as the sea itself. She seemed at once tall and diminutive, fragile and resilient, forgiving and fierce.

Throughout the remainder of the day as he sat in the shade with Henry Rowan building crab traps, the vision of the woman in the longboat etched its way deeply into his mind.

* * * * *

Jane Albury looked up from her sweet potato patch to see a woman sitting in the shadows of a pigeon plumb tree about a hundred paces away, apparently attempting discreetly to nurse a baby. The path to the Albury home was thinly established in the sandy soil, shaded for the most part by tall trees. It lead nowhere else but to the Albury's cottage and so it was the first time in Jane's memory she'd seen anyone along the path whose journey had not ended at the cottage door.

She continued weeding the potato patch waiting for the stranger to finish with her baby and approach closer to the cottage. But instead, the woman rose slowly to her feet and began walking down the path in the opposite direction of the cottage.

"Sister!"called Jane to the wispy apparition. "Will you join me for a moment?"

The woman stopped and stood in place for a while, then walked towards Jane. Her stride was somehow both passive and determined. Her small frame belied the magnetic manner in which it drew Jane's attention. Something had keenly attracted Jane's gaze to the stranger, though another stranger may have gone unnoticed tucked away in the shade of the pigeon plum tree.

"Sister, you are newly come on Thomas Sayle's ship?" asked Jane as the woman halted in front of her.

"Yes, I arrived aboard his ship. It was Governor Sayle made it so." The woman's speech had a foreign lilt, something of a lowlands dialect, Friesian or Hollandic perhaps.

"*Governor* Sayle? You say Captain William Sayle is governor of Bermuda once again?"

"Yes. He occupies the Governor's seat on the Council," the woman responded.

"Are you as the others who come here of late? Are you sent here to our island as a sentence? What is your name? Tell me, sister."

"My name is Neptuna."

"And your surname, what are you called?"

"I was once called Downeham. I was born Van Allen."

The response seemed peculiar to Jane. In fact, everything about Neptuna seemed uncommon.

"And are you banished here? Did the Governor send you here to serve a sentence?"

"I am told my sentence was death and yet I live. I am told this place is freedom and so I understand I am free."

"Neptuna, are you alone with your baby? Are you *here* because you are alone with a baby?"

"Yes. Twelve months ago a violent man forced my daughter upon me, yet now I would die today if it meant her life would carry on another day. My husband placed me before the Council where the English Law was laid upon my case."

"Have you means, Neptuna? How will you care for your daughter?"

"On the voyage I formed a resolution; it is the only resolution within my mind's power to conceive. As long as I remain alive I will be able to nourish my girl. And so I will live."

Neptuna turned on the sandy path and began to walk away. She'd only taken a few paces before looking over her shoulder and speaking. "The ship's captain, Captain Sayle, he told me I should seek out Jane Albury."

"Sister," Jane softly relied, "you have found her."

* * * * *

5 August, 1660

Today the rains and great rushes of wind blowed across Spanish Wells and I watched our

180

cistern fill to brimming in less time than it takes Miranda to prance down our little knoll. We stayed home the morning through but it were odd being idle so we, Miranda and I, set out to walk about in the freshening rain. Something drew me directly along to the Albury's cottage and I was not surprised to see the cause. The women from the longboat were there in the cook-shed. And true it were a babe I saw yesterday in her arms. I wish I'd paid heed and proper attention to all the learning Captain and Mrs. Sayle tried to place before me, for I now lack the words to speak of this women, Neptuna. My eyes took her in yesterday and today my ears. As I sat with David in his cottage, I could hear Neptuna speak to Jane out behind. The voice of Neptuna is like song and she is spare with words. Yet the few words she does utter hold me so.

* * * * *

"Davey, have ya lost yer wits? Ya cannot speak to the woman. There ain't no one ya can ask to court her, boy. And ya *must* know why she come to be here on this island. There ain't a soul hereabouts that don't know she's an adulteress, lad. I tell ya again, it would please me to pay your passage to Bermuda, or Virginia or Barbados or wherever in the wide world ya wish to go and find a proper wife. She's out there Davey. Do ya not remember me telling you of my Caroline?"

"I remember well, Fishy. I remember exactly what you told to me. In all the wide world God sent your Caroline to a spot in the middle of the sea where you lived. So too might God have sent Neptuna to me here in Spanish Wells."

"Davey, lad, I told ya them t'ings and I believe them to be true. But I also believe God does such t'ings only exceeding rare. Ya should not expect He hatches the same plan daily, for yer then bound to run yer heart upon a reef."

David nodded. He rarely disagreed with Jackson, but he persisted to some degree.

"I'll not say God brought her here for me, Fishy. I say he *may* have done so. It seems to me He may also be setting my course to cross hers. Yesterday, when I sailed into the waterfront from Egg Island, and today when I walked to the Albury's cottage for the first time in half a year. These things speak to me, Fishy."

Jackson breathed a deep sigh and shook his head. The two men sat quietly together while the sun set and then Jackson looked up again at David.

"You've grown into a fine man, Pigeon Davey. Will ya do somethin' for me?", he asked.

"I'll try, Fishy. I always try."

"Go to David Albury. Ask David to have Jane bring this Neptuna to the point tomorrow at sunset."

* * * * *

"Girl, what ya say cannot be so," Jackson whispered. "Speak the name again. I want to be certain I heard ya proper."

Neptuna stood facing Jackson as the huge red sun balanced on the western horizon like a passageway to heaven itself. Jackson squinted hard, staring intently at the girl's features, trying to dispel what he believed must be a mere illusion.

"I was born Neptuna Van Allen. My father was Captain Cornelius Van Allen of the ship, *Hemels Gate*."

Jackson shook his head slowly side to side then broke into a broad, toothless grin.

"Neptuna, girl, I served with yer father on many a voyage. He is the finest captain and the kindest man I know. I pray he lives as I'd be greatly saddened to hear otherwise."

"No, sir, he lives no longer. The masters of *Hemels Gate* forced him to sell back his shares at a four-fifths discount, and then they put him ashore in Bermuda. I was born on the *Hemels Gate* and was fourteen years of age when they made us to leave the ship. My mother died when I was born and I have no memory of her."

"Your father, Neptuna, why did they send him ashore? And how did he die?"

"He would not carry slaves. There is no other reason. For them, that one reason was enough. We had no means to live and my father was a proud man. It ate him. Being ashore ate him until there was nothing left. An old man, his name was Downeton, took me and made me his wife."

Jackson looked down the beach as the sun disappeared from view, painting the underside of a cloud gold, red and orange before the approaching night could protest.

"This Downeton, he is not the father of your baby, is he?"

"No, a man named John Morgan is the father. I would have killed him if he had not taken the knife from my hand. I have no malice now, only revulsion. My daughter will never hear me speak his name I beg you never to speak it yourself."

Jackson looked the young woman directly in the eyes as he responded. "You've no fear of that, Neptuna. All the t'ings what happened to ya in Bermuda need not follow you here. We live in a simple way on this island. There is no Council, no judgments are made by them what don't know ya. I knew yer father well and through him I know you've a good heart and most important, a pure soul."

He paused for a moment, collecting his thoughts. "I raised a boy, now a man, by the name o' David Pinder. I mean to tell ya he is a good person like yerself. And I tell ya so because ya may see him about the place. He may come calling, that is to say."

Neptuna showed no sign of having heard Jackson. Her eyes were turned towards Jane, who stood out on the point holding the baby.

* * * * *

"Pigeon, ya must understand the girl has suffered much these past five years, that's all I'm saying. I'm not askin' ya not to court her, I'm just tellin' ya what I know. Ya must not pursue the lass. She will come to you or never at all."

David nodded, but in his mind he was uncertain he understood what Jackson was trying to say.

"Neptuna's father was the kindest man I ever met. She likely wasn't prepared for the sort of men she run up against once her father was gone. So you keep that always in yer mind, boy."

9 August, 1660

I caught a fine dorado fish and brung it up to the Albury's cottage. I went and put it out back in the cook-shed and she were there with her babe. Jane come out back and was gladdened by the fish. She said to me: Mr. Pinder I am pleased to introduce you to Neptuna Van Allen. She and her baby daughter are new to Spanish Wells. I took off my hat and said I was pleased to meet her. Then I asked what was the name of her daughter. It were plain I done something wrong, as Neptuna looked straight down to her feet and was silent. Jane she looked quick at me and shook her head ever so little. Then Jane asked about Fishy and I said he were well but some bothered by the heat. I was nervy about saying something else wrong so I left. But it were curious what Miranda done. She goes up to Neptuna and puts her chin on the girls lap. And there was the first time I seen Neptuna smile. She stroked my Mirada's head. My Mirada has a way of looking direct into one's eyes and she done this with Neptuna. I said goodbye and walked out the cook-shed and it were 10 minute or more before I realized Miranda stayed behind with Neptuna and the baby.

* * * * *

David and Jane Albury boarded the *Rose* and sat beside David as he trimmed the mainsheet and guided the sloop eastward through the channel. The three were attending prayer services at the cave with others who'd survived the wreck of the *William* in 1647.

Without being prompted to do so, Jane suddenly spoke of the mystery surrounding Neptuna's reluctance to speak her child's name, if the child even had a name.

"I do not know why she never speaks to her baby by name. And I have not asked her, as it is clear to me she has her reasons."

David himself had not stopped pondering the question since his visit to the Albury's cottage weeks before. "Perhaps she feels she surrenders a part of the child by speaking her name to others."

Jane's hand flew to her lips as she gasped. "You astonish me sometimes, David. I believe you are right yet I do not understand how you could know such a thing."

David Albury smiled and patted David on the shoulder. "That's my Janey, always underestimating the hearts of men."

"I do not underestimate the hearts of men. I underestimate their intellect," Jane responded with a giggle.

24 September, 1660

Miranda speaks to the girl as I cannot, yet there are no words between them. I say her name, Neptuna, and my Miranda starts to dance about. I say "you may go to her if you wish" and she is off. She returned home yesterday wearing the most fetching collar woven from sweetgrass. Fishy said Neptuna first wove a collar for me only I cannot see it. Today I found a late turtle nest on the main island and took two dozen eggs from it. I covered the others as the she turtle had done. I wondered if Neptuna has seen, as I have, the little hatchlings make their way to the sea for the first time. It is a marvel how the Lord guides them. When I brought the eggs to the Albury's house, Neptuna was there under the pigeon plum tree with her babe. I called to her that I brung eggs for their supper and she rose to see. She asked me where I found them and I told her. Then she done

185

something surprised me. She asked if I might take the Alburys and her to see the nests when they begin to hatch. It were like she'd looked into my mind. I asked her if she'd ever seen the little ones take to the sea and she said that her father had showed her a hatching many years ago in another sea in another land. I said I would keep an eye on the nests and would be pleased to organize an outing on a night when the moon was shining strong. Now I shall wish for many hatchlings this season as it will delight Neptuna.

* * * * *

The year 1660 slipped quietly away. Peter Sands and William Barnette, two of the original shipwrecked Adventurers, were called to Bermuda to testify before the Council regarding William Sayle's Charter and his claim to the islands of Eleutheria. Both Sands and Barnett testified to having seen posted on the cave wall a document bearing an ornate stamp, but neither could swear what the document actually was. Regardless of the doubts many harbored concerning the legitimacy of Sayle's claims, Sayle and his family continued to support the Eleutherian colonies with trade missions.

Neptuna gradually, almost imperceptibly at first, allowed David to step lightly into her life. Each Sunday, David accompanied her to prayer services led by Sweeting, the lay leader who'd arrived in St. George's Cay in 1649, outlasting every reverend who'd arrived with him and thereafter.

On a chilly evening in January, the Albury's, Neptuna and David dined together at the Albury cottage. The four sat together by an outdoor fire, the men smoking clay pipes and the women sewing a quilt. Jane and her husband rose at the sound their daughter, Bess, calling from the cottage.

"She's a one for bad dreams," said Jane. "She'll not go back to sleep unless both of us sit with her.

It was the first time David had been alone with Neptuna, but he could think of nothing to say, so the two sat there in the fire's glow, silent. Once again, Neptuna seemed to read David's mind.

"My daughter's name is Sina. I do not wish anyone to know her name who would brand her as the illegitimate offspring of an adulteress. I do not believe you will do so, Mr. Pinder."

"Thank you for trusting me with your daughter's name, miss."

"And you may call me Neptuna. I have no other name."

David softly shook his head, "I believe your father would wish your family name be restored. This man, Downeham, has no claim to you and his name is dead to me. But with your leave, I will call you Neptuna Van Allen."

Neptuna smiled faintly. "It warms my heart to hear it, Mr. Pinder."

"I would be pleased if you called me David."

The young women nodded, but did not pronounce his name.

"Tomorrow, would you join me on a voyage to Bogue? I have whale oil to deliver to the settlement. There is a man I would like to introduce to you. You may bring Sina, of course. And Miranda will be aboard as well."

"I do not wish to scandalize you, Mr. Pinder. I must decline your invitation."

David breathed in deeply and then responded, "There will be no scandal, Neptuna Van Allen, and those who would look for scandal mean nothing to me. Fishy says the ones who speak most of sin are the ones fall prey to it most often."

"He is wise, your friend. Did you know he served under my father?"

"Yes. Fishy was powerful fond of your father. I wish that I could have met him."

David reached to stir the fire and a shower of sparks swirled around his feet. He spoke again to Neptuna.

"Will you reconsider voyaging with Miranda and me to Bogue tomorrow? I believe you would benefit from a day in the sound aboard my sloop, the *Rose*. The moon will be full tonight and we will leave before the sun rises so we may catch the tide through the cut, a passage we must navigate to reach Bogue."

Neptuna hesitated for a what seemed hours, then spoke quietly, just as the Albury's emerged from their cottage.

"I will see you at the waterfront then, Mr. Pinder, one hour before sunrise? Sina and I?"

David smiled. "Yes," responded David, "yes, I'll be there with Miranda. We'll bring food and drink."

＊ ＊ ＊ ＊ ＊

The Rose skipped across the moonlit sound on a broad reach, a light trail of phosphorescence swirling away from the rudder Miranda uncharacteristically abandoned her place in the bow to take a seat amidships next to Neptuna. Sina peered serenely from the blanket in which she was wrapped, cooing contentedly with the motion of the boat.

Words seemed unnecessary when the scene spoke so well for itself, so the *Rose*'s passengers simply enjoyed the experience, each in their own way. When the moon set, it did so almost as if were diving into the sea like a gull. One moment it was there, the next it was not. When the sun's first rays reached finger-like over the horizon, Miranda roused herself and let out an excited yip as a flying fish buzzed by. A large stingray glided under the boat like a ghost while a flock of birds descended upon a school of bait fish off the starboard side. David handed Neptuna a cloth-wrapped loaf of bread and a small crock of goat butter. He took the knife from its sheath on his belt and extended it handle-first to his beautiful passenger. She cut a piece of the loaf, spread it with butter and handed it back to David, who smiled and accepted the offering. She then cut a smaller piece for herself.

"I have sugar apples too," said David, "though I don't know if you're partial to them. Fishy says I am too fond of them for a full-growed man. But I do love them and can remember back in Bermuda the first time ever I tasted one."

"Then I shall make you my honing drops. 'Honing' means honey in the language of my birth. Do you know where there are bees' nests?"

"Aye, there are many about the rock walls on the north side of the main island where we wrecked aboard the *William*. There we lived in a grand cathedral of a cave for a time. Honey was about the *only* thing we had," David quipped.

"You have been here in this place ever since?"

"Ever since and no desire to go elsewhere. This is my home," David said with a sweep of his left arm. "It provides everything for me and Fishy, it and the ships what pass through from time to time."

Neptuna fed Sina some sugar apple and then looked up again to David.

"You and Mr. Jackson are family?"

"Aye, we are family but not as ya might think. My parents were killed when I was a young boy. When my uncle also died, Fishy took me in. He taught me everything."

"He is a kind man. Did he teach you such kindness?"

"Fishy says it don't pay to be unkind to no man or animal. A man spices his own life like as it were a stew and there ain't sense in pouring lye into the pot."

Neptuna smiled at the affirmation.

"I see. And your stew is without lye, I'm sure. Sugar apples perhaps, but no lye."

The *Rose* plunged ahead in the chop like a porpoise. There were no more words for a long while. As they approached the cut, David finally spoke.

"This part of the voyage is always a joy. I remember once in Devon when it was very cold. My father took me upon the hill where a sweetwater spring froze solid. It was blue and grey ice right from the top almost all the way to the bottom. We slid down the ice on our hind ends and I never had so much fun being cold. I truly was adverse to the cold, ya see."

The *Rose* continued eastward through the mouth of the cut, her mainsheet trimmed tight.

"Now look over the side at the current, Neptuna Van Allen, and tell me if it don't look just like a fierce river. See how she drives us along! It's like flying in my manner of thinking."

Neptuna removed the scarf from her head, placed Sina in her basket and stood up in the bow holding the mast with her left hand. Strands of her sun-streaked hair instantly floated aloft landing briefly upon the shoulders of her bodice before once again becoming airborne.

"It's wonderful," she said softly, perhaps only to herself.

* * * * *

William Force walked down to the dock to greet the *Rose*. He took the bowline from David and tied it to the post.

"Good morning, Davey, and who are your passengers?"

"This, Mr. Force, is Neptuna Van Allen and her baby girl, Sina."

Force cocked his head quickly, "Van Allen, miss. Would you be related to Captain Van Allen?"

Neptuna reached for David's hand as she stepped from the sloop onto the dock.

"Yes, my father was Captain Cornelius Van Allen. He died five years ago in Bermuda."

"Yes, yes, I know he died and I was much saddened to hear the news. I knew your father, and there is not a man in this settlement who has not heard of him. His refusal to carry slaves cost him his ship and his livelihood. His sacrifice is not forgotten among us."

Neptuna brushed a tear from her eye as if it were a fly. She squinted into the sun towards the small settlement and then turned to look out into the bay.

David reached to shake Force's hand. "I've the oil you requested, Mr. Force. It's fifty weight not counting the barrel. Will ya help me heave her onto the dock and we can roll her from there."

The two men jumped aboard the *Rose* and soon had the barrel rolling down the dock.

"Besides the onions and cabbages, I've something additional to trade, Davey," said Force as they upended the barrel at the entrance to the long meeting house. "I think ya might be interested."

Force waved David and Neptuna up the three steps into the meeting house, then walked them to the back. He picked up a delicately woven basket from the corner and extracted a small object. Holding it up to the window, he motioned David over to see. Several pieces of eight glinted softy in Force's palm.

"I pulled these up in a crab pot I got snagged off the east shore of the island. The trap was lodged under the brim of a corral head so I backed well off and dragged it along the bottom until I was sure I'd cleared the coral. When I pulled it up, there was a bucketful of sand, and these," he said, pointing to the rough coins.

"You've a wrack there, Mr. Force. The Spaniards may already have stripped her, but perhaps not. Do ya mean to take a closer look?"

"Ah well, that was what I wanted to trade, Davey. I'll lead you to the spot and give you a third share in anything we recover if you and Mr. Jackson would help us with the salvage."

"Fishy do love a wrack and he'll be fiercely eager to help. He's getting up in age but he still goes over the side from time to time and he has a sense about how wracks break up and scatter about. Was the site south or north of here?"

"It was south, under the great cliffs," said Force.

"Well then, that's a long way around. We'd need to establish a camp and provision it for at least a week. Can you and your men do that aforehand?"

Force nodded, "simply tell us when, Davey, and we'll make it so."

"It won't be until the calmer seas, Mr. Force. This time of year it's a rage over there, as ya well know. But by and by it will settle down. Go ahead and establish the camp in one month, then we'll wait for a stretch of fine weather. The water must be clear, not all stirred up ya understand, or we won't be able to look about."

Since David had last visited the Bogue settlement, Force had taken a wife, Elizabeth. Introductions were made all around before David, loaded Neptuna, Sina and Miranda back aboard the *Rose* for the trip home.

"Come up to Spanish Wells when you can, Mr. Force. Fishy would be pleased to see you and meet your new wife. If you don't come yourself, send word when you've set up the camp, if ya please."

"Certainly, Davey. You'll hear from me soon. I wish you a safe passage back to St. George's Cay and please send my regards to Mr. Jackson."

* * * * *

"We must see about acquiring a few panes of glass," Jackson said to Davey as the two eat their breakfast. "We'd be wise to fashion a glass-bottomed bucket or two. Whatever Mr. Force found is likely scattered far and wide, what with the swells pounding as they do over there."

"It sounds like the ship whatt went down may have come up under the cliffs, so she would have been pounded to splinters in no time. And it's deep there too, ain't it Fishy?"

"Aye, that's the rub, boy. Too deep for 'ole Fishy and maybe too deep for you as well. We'll see, we'll see."

29 March, 1661

Today Mr. William Force sailed into our bay in the new sloop what John Saunders made for the Bogue settlement. She is as fine a craft as ever I've seen and Saunders probably deserves far more than what he charged for the making of her. She be about 28 foot, maybe a little more. Saunders done some fanciful carving along her gunwales and tiller and the Bogue settlers were terrible pleased. Mr. Force tells us the camp has been set up over on the east shore of Eleutheria on a beach not very far from the site of the wrack and there be some shelter there for the boats. He's set a tackle in the event we need to pull the boats up into the high dunes, but I don't think such will be necessary. Yesterday it were dead calm out on the Backbone and I rowed Netuna out in the dingy with one of the glass-bottom buckets Fishy and me made. To see her face so pleased was a wonder to my heart. She is now keen to learn to swim, but Fishy don't reckon I ought to speak of such things in public as women aren't normally engaged in them kinds of pursuits. But my weren't she pleased to see the world under the surface! Next time out with the bucket we will bring Sina. We stopped in the shoals for conch and Miranda showed Neptuna how she does dive like her sweet mother Toothy Jill done. I heed what Fishy told me of Neptuna. I love her as I knew I would, but I do not tell her such things. Someday she will ask.

12 April, 1661

It is pleasant to be in the camp with Mr. Force and his men. There is a man named Charles. That is to say he was named Charles when he was a slave. He come from the continent of Africa and my word the astonishing tales he do tell. He speaks of his family and his people going back to when he reckons time began. I listen and it is true, as true as the bible and I don't know how that can be. He says he is Christian and I don't know how that sets with the stories. But all the same I could listen to Charles speak for days and not hear enough of him. Fishy too liked the tales. He cautions that we must not repeat them as they are to stay amongst the folk who live in the Bogue settlement. I know this without Fishy saying so. But I will tell Neptuna one day.

16 April, 1661

I do not believe I will ever force the sea water from my chest again, that long I have been under the surface. A piece of eight there then another a hundred paces away. The Spaniards what struck upon these cliffs were dashed in a frightful manner. The sea rages here in a way that cannot be understood on the western side of this rake-thin island. I see no ship at all, only the sparsest remnants, bones not among them. I know not why I dive this wrack but that I wish Mr. Force well. I have gold and silver aplenty keeping my sweet potatoes and tree roots company, loot what Fishy and me pulled from the waters off James Mann Island. As I sit here I know with clarity I will use them riches to build a home for me, Neptuna, Sina and Miranda. There is a place west of Spanish Wells on the neighboring island that is for us. I will teach Neptuna to swim, away from the eyes of others. Sina, my daughter, will grow up with the name what my father give me. No man will stand between me and my family. We will live here in these islands, the rest of the world be damned.

14 REFUGE

Once through the south channel, Jackson pulled the tiller to port directing the bow of his newly-built skiff in the opposite direction. The skiff bobbed along the southern shoreline of the sister island. Over the past several months the island unobtrusively assumed a name of its own in Jackson's mind. It was now Davey's Island.

He passed a tiny shallow bay set amid a flat, overgrown landscape, then gradually the land rose as if the island had shrugged its shoulders. The coastline here was a rocky shelf studded with jagged limestone daggers, the remnants of may layers of limestone left dry by a receding sea. The sea bed over which the skiff glided was grassy for the most part. A turtle paddled by, its elegantly mottled shell large as a café table.

A manicured hillside approached, its newly planted fruit trees looking somewhat self-conscious bordered as they were by established braziletto and *lignum vitae* trees. At the crest of the small hill, an appealing whitewashed cottage faced south. The four steps giving way to the cottage's simple, Bermudan-style veranda shone like a toothy grin in the morning sunlight. At the bottom of the hill, a set of steps carved into the soft limestone sea wall lead down to the water.

Jackson passed the homestead and continued west for a few moments, then came about to starboard on a heading that would lead him to the mooring set about thirty feet from the steps leading up to the property.

As he'd done thousands of similar times, Jackson lowered the mainsheet and glided deftly to the mooring. He threaded the long bowline through the float and allowed the southwest breeze to blow the stern of the skiff around to face the steps. He then played out line until he was close enough to step comfortably ashore. Once standing on the bottom step he threaded the bowline through an iron ring sunk into the stone wall. He synched the line until the boat drew several yards closer to the mooring, then tied the line off securely to the ring.

The refuge David built for Neptuna and Sina was nearly complete. As Jackson's bandy legs carried him huffing up the steep hillside, a giggle filtered its way down from the veranda.

"I hear me some kind of vermin up there," called Jackson, "per'aps a ship's rat made his way ashore!"

The giggle intensified and Sina's resolve to hide quickly evaporated. She danced down the steps and cried, "Fishy it's Sina! No rat, do ya hear!"

"How am I to know it's you when ya sneak about like a shadow? Where's yer ma and pa, did they finally have enough of ya and sail away?"

Sina's childish indignation blossomed into a spirited volley of protests and a heated demand that Jackson follow her immediately so she could present evidence to the contrary. She lead Jackson through the open door and across the plank floor and out the opposite door. There in a garden plot Neptuna knelt carefully weeding her young plants.

"Thank you for coming, Fishy. Jane found you at home then?"

"Aye, she did. She said you needed some help about the place."

"I cannot lift the lid off the cistern to check the water level and it's been so dry of late. Could you help me?"

"Yes and I'll show ya what yer clever husband done so you don't have to do no lifting. He's fixed things so all ya need do is slide the lid over with a lever."

Jackson showed Neptuna the small hole David bore into the top of the cistern near the heavy lid and the lever and fulcrum he'd constructed to move it.

"Ya merely place this block right between the lid and this hole here. Then ya situate the lever in the hole and push it against the block. See there?"

He pushed the lever against the fulcrum and the heavy stone lid slid easily open several inches. A strip of light illuminated the water below, perhaps four feet deep.

"You've plenty of water for yer plants, girl. It's high above the spigot there on the downhill side of the cistern, so yer garden will flourish just as you and Sina have in this place Davey built for ya."

David had sailed north to Abaco the week before with four men to investigate rumors of a wreck somewhere near Green Turtle Cay. He'd spent a sizable portion of his share of the salvage from the James Mann Island wreck buying needed materials and household supplies. Another wreck might replenish his dwindling reserves of hard currency.

Neptuna sat with Jackson on the veranda. As was her nature, she felt no need to engage in small talk. The two sat silently enjoying their closeness, watching Jackson's skiff float on the turquoise water below.

She thought back to the day it first occurred to her that watching Sina and David together reminded her very much of her and her own father. The little girl's first word, 'doggy' was uttered to David as he called Miranda from the Albury's front door.

She thought of the first swimming lesson David gave her, right where Jackson's boat was now moored, the excitement of floating for the first time, the novel feeling of warm water enveloping her body like a silk shroud, the stinging pain of opening her eyes underwater and the delight of seeing the tiny tropical fish swimming around her feet.

She thought of the moment she realized she'd been waiting all day for David to visit the Albury home. She thought of how worried she'd been when he'd sailed south to work William Force's wreck.

She thought of the first time she'd asked David not to leave.

19 May, 1663

When this log book is full, will I save my thoughts in another? When I'm gone from this earth, I know Sina will carry forward thoughts of me and thoughts of Neptuna. When Fishy is gone, I'll carry thoughts of him so long as I live. Did

Captain Flowers know my life would be made precious by Neptuna? Could he have seen our family take shape solid as a great rock yet billowy as a summer cloud? Neptuna is with child and I am afeared every moment of every day. If I lose her I lose myself forever. Fishy survived the loss of his Caroline, but I know I am not strong enough to live without Neptuna. This is a simple truth.

11 October 1663

This morning I was given another daughter by Neptuna. Jane is here and for that I am greatly relieved. But I am vexed more than ever about providing for our family. I love these islands but they are hard. When it were merely Fishy and me, such things as money had no great attraction, though we liked our luxuries at Christmastime. When I look about me I see we are alone here and must care for ourselves. Like the turtles Neptuna and I love to watch nesting on the beach, I must bury eggs in the sand for our future. I must bury eggs in the sand lest the sea take me under and away from my family. Tomorrow I aim to speak to Peter Sands and John Saunders about whales. I would not be prideful and hunt such great creatures were I not so worried about the welfare of my family. Neptuna has chosen this evening to name the new baby Hopen, Hope in the English language.

15 IRONS

1667 Letter by Robert Norwood, one of William Sayle's original investors, to the Royal Society in London.

If they be struck in deep water, they presently make into the deep with such violence, that the boat is in danger to be haled down after them, if they cut not the rope in time. Therefore, they usually strike them in shoal-water. They have very good Boats for that purpose, mann'd with six oars, such as they can row forwards and backwards, as occasion requireth. They row gently up to the Whale, about or before the Fins rather than towards the Tayl. Now the Harping-Irons are like those, which are usual in England in striking porpoises, but singular good mettal, that will not break, but wind, as they say, about a mans hand. To the Harping-Iron is made fast a strong lythe rope, and into the socket of that iron is put a staffe, which, when the Whale is struck, comes out of the socket; and so when the Whale is something quiet they hale up to him by the rope, and, it may be to strike into him another Harping-Iron, or Lance him with Lances in staves, till they have kill'd him. This I write by relation, for I have not seen any kill'd my self. I hear not that they have found any Sperma Ceti in any of these Whales; but I have heard from credible persons that there is a kind of such as have the Sperma at Eleutheria, and others of the Bahama Islands (Where also they find quantities of Ambergreese) and that those have great teeth (which ours have not) and are very sinewy.

* * * * *

It took more than two years for David, John Saunders, Peter Sands, Henry Rowan, Joshua Roberts, Edward Harris and David Albury to build the boats they'd need to hunt whales. Nearly a hundred years before the whalers of Nantucket attempted to tie a harpooned whale to a boat, the men of Eleutheria planned to do so. In each of the four, sturdy boats, Saunders set into the bows short, stout pylons around which the whaling lines would be wrapped. The boats were fitted out for six pairs of oars and carried a single sail aloft.

Peter Sands voyaged to Bermuda and with Governor Sayle's assistance, commissioned the making of dozens of harpoons from the finest iron that could be found. Sayle also assisted the Eleutherians in the purchase of hundreds of yards of strong line, lances and rendering pots.

In spring, the whales would swim northward past James Mann Island to the east. That island and its sister to the south, Harbour Island, would be used as staging grounds.

12 April, 1665

Day before yesterday we set out from our camp setting a course north of the spouts we spotted southeast about a mile out. We sat quietly in their path and Peter Sands' boat rowed easy alongside a great black fellow who looked like he could swallow all of us in a gulp. We rowed alongside Peter's boat then crossed over the great beast when he sounded. He could not dive very deep though, as the water was strewn with coral heads and was no more than eighty feet. When he rose again Sands' boat was on his port side and we were off his starboard. We hesitated at first and he sounded again. While we rowed along to keep pace with our whale, all of us agreed that when next he breached we would let loose two irons at once. He did then rise and Sands called to us to let fly. I will never forget, though I will try forever to do so, the volume of blood that spouted from his great billows. He sounded again and as he did we played out line so quick it burned scars in our gunwales. When he breached again we tied off the lines, the whale pulling us forward fast as a horse can gallop. Pink and red clouds burst from his blowhole as he swam, yet he did not die. Our third boat come alongside the wounded animal and hurled another iron into his heaving back. Down he went again nearly carrying our first two boats with him. We cut our lines before being dragged into the deep but my boat was swamped and fell back. When the whale breached again, the third boat tied off its line while Sands' boat sunk yet another harpoon. This time our whale heaved over on his side and come to a stop. Our boat now bailed, we joined the others who were warding off two large sharks. It was an hour before we could tow our whale into the surf. The sharks had eaten well, but still most of the whale's flanks were saved. We have rendered oil for two days and nights now. At night it's a ghastly scene and I wonder what my daughters would think of their father. My Neptuna was born to the sea. She come into life aboard the Dutch ship Hemels Gate, but I wonder too if she would look upon her husband in the same way were she to see this camp. We are all of us soaked in oil and blood. It is a hazard to wash in the sea as a great trail of blood runs down the beach into the water where the sharks do gather like devilish flies. We are tormented above by the more earthly kind of flies. Mosquitos as well. But these barrels of oil will protect our families. They will buy provisions and armaments. They will allow us our independence and they will allow us to worship our Lord in a new church, built with the revenues of our terrible labor. May God forgive us.

2 May, 1665

We passed the last two days ferrying our barrels of oil to Spanish Wells. We will load empty barrels in the morning and make our way back to camp. I cleaned myself best I could. We all of us scrubbed with sand and sea water and were grateful for a driving rain as we passed Ridley Head. My Neptuna, Sina and Hopen greeted us at the waterfront. Fishy fetched them in his skiff. The girls are some excited by the barrels stacked and ready for the next ship, as I have told them the barrels carry gold. Neptuna reproached me in her silent way. She does not approve of our children being drawn to money and in this she is right. She is right in all manner of things that I am too slow to understand. Yet she do love me nonetheless. It is a marvel all of my own. We sailed together from the waterfront around to our home. When the children were to bed, Neptuna and I sat for a long while on the steps leading down to the water. The moon was high and we could make out the grand sweep of the main island to the south and east. She does not ask me of the whaling. She's knows somehow I do not wish to speak of it. She knows always what is upon my mind. I am 30 years of age. Fishy is 74. My Neptuna is ageless.

27 May, 1665

It were a shock to find Captain Sayle arrived at St. George's Cay aboard the Blessing, although it is no longer called Blessing. The Captain, together with John Dorrel and Hugh Wentworth have purchased the Blessing and renamed her Recovery. I seems the Captain did in 1663 name Mr. Wentworth "Husband in the Islands on Behalf of the Adventurers About the Whale Fisheries." Their purchase of the Blessing, now Recovery, and her fitting as a whaling vessel be fine fortune for *us here in Spanish Wells. We did sell all of our oil to the Recovery for a goodly price, though part of the bargain was that we help the Captain's crew careen the Recovery before she sailed. We struck the whale camp ten days ago when our barrels were all full. So it is that we have learned to kill whales without ourselves dying in the process. We have all agreed to hunt whales next spring. I am glad to be away from it. I believe God did give these creatures the ability to surmise their own deaths and it haunts me. I have fished since I was a small boy, but these whales are far greater and wiser than fish. I held a whale's enormous blood drained heart in my arms and it spoke to me.*

"Papa wake up! I've a fish on my line!"

David propped himself up against the *Rose*'s ribs and gently took the dancing line from Sina's hands.

"Good girl. Did ya bait that hook yourself?"

"Yes you fell asleep reading the storm book."

"I did fall asleep, didn't I? Miranda too. Don't tell your Mum or she'll think I've been taken ill. She worries more than a rabbit. Look here, girl, a nice little yellertail. Are ya ready to go back home? We've a nice basket of fish there to show for our labor."

Sina nodded her blond head as she stroked Miranda's smooth muzzle. "Let's make a fishy pie tonight!"

"That's a fine idea. We can use the rest of the onions."

"Hopen doesn't like onions, Papa. She's a baby."

"Well she'll have food what's proper for a finicky girl of two years and we'll eat all the fishy pie ourselves. Home then?"

"Yes, but I want to pilot the boat to our house," chirped Sina.

"Ah, our house. Do ya know what Miranda in the storm book says about a house?"

Sina shook her head, "What, Papa?"

"She said this, child:

> *There's nothing ill can dwell in such a temple:*
> *If the ill spirit have so fair a house,*

Good things will strive to dwell with 't.

Sina smiled at her father. "You built our fine house with all good things in it, Hopen too."

David stroked the girls ivory white hair, and spoke again.

"The house Miranda spoke of in the book is the house that carries one's heart and soul around the wide world. Our bodies are also our homes. Yours is such a fine temple no bad spirit would ever come near it. Good things will always dwell inside you, daughter. Your mother saw to that."

* * * * *

"Fishy calls you Pigeon from time to time. Why is that so?", asked Neptuna?

David exhaled and smiled wistfully, the Jamaica rum loosening his desire always to prune his rough speech into neat hedgerows.

"It were a sea name what he give to me long ago, the time we sailed from Portsmouth with my uncle, the Reverend Allsop. I was powerful intent on listening to what Fishy had to say about the sea, and Bermuda and living amongst others, so I nodded and ducked my head bird-like while he told his tales. He reckoned I looked like a pigeon, ya see? I was a nervy kind of boy and I don't know what would have become of me had not Fishy took me in. It was the going to sea with him every day what calmed me."

"And your parents, David, you say they died together in a church, but you don't explain such a dire happenstance. How did they come to die in a church, Davey?"

David looked into his wife's ice-bright eyes and propelled himself back in time to the night his mother lifted him from his bed and dashed across the rain-soaked farmyard into the neighbor's doorway. He felt the warmth from the fireplace on his left side as he lied curled on a musty sheepskin. His ears and chest felt the concussion from the exploding church as it rippled across the fields, into the farmyard and under the cottage. The next morning the widow Agnes told him the church was gone, his parents were gone, everything was gone, but he would stay there safe in the cottage. Then his scarecrow uncle had come, announcing the sale of Goliath and Simon, the oxen responsible for the family's great hopes and tall pride.

"I don't know exactly how they died. It was the war between

King Charles and Oliver Cromwell. I remember my uncle telling me the Royalists established their powder magazine in the church basement, and there was an explosion. My father was held in the church for some reason, and my mother went to search for him."

Neptuna rose from her chair on the veranda and knelt by her husband who sat in the matching chair. The soft night air of their island smelled of the sea and of their garden. She placed her head on his knee and wrapped her arms around his legs.

"David Pinder, I was sent to you."

* * * * *

24 April, 1667

This be my third season killing whales and I do believe my last. I am away up in the Abaco islands now two months and the absence of Neptuna, Sina and Hopen lays me low. The Recovery is here and Mr. Wentworth hath told me that he and Captain Sayle were blown by a storm into a grand and deep harbour whilst voyaging to the Carolina colonies. There are many soft beaches to accommodate the careening of vessels, as we must constantly scrape away the ship worms that are so powerful hungry in these waters. This island is named for Captain Sayle and he reckons it will soon be the principal settlement in these our Bahama Islands.

16 CHANGING TIDES

Neptuna stood on the veranda watching David tie up the *Rose* then walk up the steep hillside. He'd been so saddened by the death of Miranda the month before, she worried his heart would break entirely. Now Fishy was taken ill again.

At the point where the steps carved into the limestone sea shoreline ended, she'd built stone steps set into the hillside while David was whaling the year before in Abaco. As he approached the veranda, she called out.

"Jane was here earlier. She says that Fishy is taken ill again, David. I think you should go to him now without delay."

To David's ear, Neptuna's accent had not faded in the least since she'd come into his life in 1660. It was 1668 now. Sina was almost ten years old and Hopen nearly eight. No other children had come

"Aye, I'll go now to his cottage. It's the fevers again, I'm sure."

Neptuna nodded, "Yes, this is what Jane told me."

The summer months seemed to bring on Jackson's frightful chills and fevers. He was seventy-five years old and would be fit as a man half his age if not for the fact that some demon appeared intent upon boiling him alive from the inside out.

David had taken Jackson to Sayle Island in June to trade for powder and shot, but the old man started to shake with fever hours after they'd made port. David settled the old sailor in the sloop as best he could and set out for provisions. The settlement seemed only to be populated by riffraff and whores. Hugh Wentworth was ostensibly in charge of the place, but chaos seemed to be the blueprint for the colony.

David hadn't been away from the waterfront for more than a quarter hour before he was approached by two men kitted out in ostentatious regalia unfamiliar to David.

"You, boy," called the elder of the two, "we'll have a word with ya!"

They approached reeking of stale rum, pig fat and black powder.

"You're not from here, I can see," said the other one, his hand resting on the butt of a pistol. "Where do ya hail?"

"Northeast of here, Eleutheria," responded David.

"Ah well, a damned farmer then!" bellowed Elder.

"Not so much farmer as fisherman and wracker," explained David. "I've been in these islands since 1647."

"By God ya don't say, boy! Then ya came from Bermuda," spat Pistol.

"Aye, we sailed from Bermuda, yes."

Elder was overcome by a rattling cough which he eventually quelled by a long drag at a rum bottle produced from a coat pocket. "All that time sitting on yer arse up on that shite pile of an island; ya must be raving. Well today, boy, is yer lucky day. We're taking on crew to join Captain Morgan against the mongrel Spaniards in Cuba. He's eight ships so far and ours will be nine and ten. Join us aboard and you'll have your fair share of the loot, enough to keep ya in grog the rest of yer life," he cackled.

Pistol, looking much agitated by the mention of money, added, "Aye, we'll all have enough to live like randy kings afterwards. Why the devil would ya fart around hopin' and preyin' a wayward Spanish dog drives his ship upon your piss-pot of an island when ya can take matters into yer own hands!"

"We're told by Governor Sayle there's a treaty with Spain," said David."

"What in blazes does that poncy bastard know about Spaniards," roared Pistol. "They don't know nothin' in Bermuda. T'was the governor of Jamaica what give Captain Morgan the letter of Marquise. What's he to do? Let the poxy Spaniard dogs overrun his island? No, the thing to do is exactly what he done: call in the privateers!"

Elder, not sensing much movement in the prospective crewman

spiced the deal further. "Any black bastard ya find and capture will be yer's to keep. If ya don't want him, I hear their fetching thirty pound sterling up in Bermuda."

Pistol saw it was no use and his anger now bubbled to the surface. "Damn yer eyes you miserable coward! We're givin' ya the opportunity of a lifetime and ya stand there like an old milk cow chewin' her cud. Are the rest of ya on Eleutheria daft as yerself?"

"There are twenty families in our settlement and among them not a single fool. I've got business here today so if you're finished flapping your lips I'll be on my way."

Elder snickered, "By all means, miss, we'll let ya get back to yer catechism. Or per'aps you're off to buy yerself a new bonnet fer Easter. Don't forget to stop in church on the way."

Pistol roared with laughter and grabbed the bottle of rum from Elder, downing most of the remnants in a gulp. "I've heard there's a perfumery just opened in town so you'll be wantin' to stop in before ya head back to yer bunghole of an island."

David and Jackson sailed from Charles Town richer for powder and shot, but poorer for the experience. The settlement was not the sort of place Captain Sayle envisioned when he'd formed the Company of Adventurers. David told Jackson of the encounter with the would-be recruiters for Morgan's fleet of privateers.

"There'll be trouble in these islands by and by," Jackson foretold. "The Spaniards won't stand for attacks upon their settlements. They're the kind of creatures what takes a pound of flesh for every insult."

True, Charles Town was rapidly becoming a mecca not only for banished Bermudians, but also for privateers. Though many claimed to be wreckers, like David and Jackson, the wreckers of Charles Town were rumored to be much less scrupulous in their methods. Some did not appear to refute reports that they'd lured Spanish ships onto shallow shoals. Survivors reported to be aboard wrecks seemed sometimes to disappear into thin air.

Regardless of the relative veracity of the stories, the Spanish presence in the Caribbean was very strong and it was difficult to imagine the empire standing idly by while English privateers declared open season. To the Spanish, the English settlements in Charles Town and Eleutheria were rapidly growing in infamy.

* * * * *

As David guided the *Rose* into the Spanish Wells waterfront, Peter Sands waved him over to an upturned barrel serving as a table. Sands handed David a pint of English cider and urged him to sit.

"I thank ya Peter, but I can't stay. I'm going to look in on Fishy. He's the fevers again."

Sands smile disappeared immediately. "I'm sorry to hear, Davey. I'll check up on him when ya return to your home."

They drank their uncomfortably warm cider in silence for a few moments, then Sands looked up from his tankard.

"Have ya heard the latest?"

"If ya mean on the political side of things, no, I haven't."

"Well," continued Sands, "Charles the Second granted to the Carolina Lord Proprietors our little islands here, and also Abaco, Sayle Island – what they call 'Providence' nowadays – Inagua and all the land between 22 degrees to 27 degrees north. So now we must all pay one pound sterling whenever the King sets foot here," chuckled Sands.

David's head cocked slightly to the side, "Well, I suppose we need not worry about setting aside silver, as it's fiercely unlikely he'll be visiting any time soon," he smiled.

When David knocked on Fishy's door, Jane Albury appeared.

"He's improved a little, Davey. But he was asking for you when the fever was fearful high."

David walked through the cottage and out onto the back porch where Jackson lay in his hammock, always the sailor.

"Why Hallo Pigeon, what brings ya here?"

"You bring me here you old goat. You've got Neptuna all nervy again with yer fevers."

"Ah *that*," sputtered Jackson, "why that's part of living in the warm climes is all. Fevers is good fer ya. Purifies the blood they say."

He sat up in his hammock and dangled his legs over the side.

"I've somethin' for Sina and Hopen."

David smiled and began shaking his head.

"Ah, you're a right Spartan, you are, boy. Girls need their little treasures; you ought to know that by now. Now, look there on the table. I got them from Captain Williams last week."

David looked down at the tabletop where two porcelain figurines lay, one of a white pony and the other of a dog looking very much like Miranda.

"You're determined to spoil those girls before you push off."
"My calling in life, boy."

* * * * *

13 March, 1669

Last evening were a rare pleasure. Neptuna and me are not ones to chatter late into the night, but we did both enjoy our visitor and his tale. We found at our steps down to the boat one Captain John Russell, late of the wracked ship, Port Royal. There he was standing upon our steps by himself having just sailed around our island in a skiff he borrowed from John Saunders. It were near sunset and we asked him to supper. I had a tuna big as a goat what I caught four mile out and Neptuna's garden is now a wonder of sweet potato and all manner of victuals. Come to learn Captain Russell's ship were caught in the storm what blew in from the nor'east on 12 January. They were thrown up upon Munjake island nearabouts Abaco and all made it to shore. There weren't water or food and conditions were frightful bad for all. Worse of all, the Port Royal had took on a carpenter who was dead set opposed to working. He did so delay and dither that Capt. Russell began to lose men to the dire conditions. So our Capt. Russell do take up the damnable carpenter in the ship's dinghy and maroons the devil on another island by his self. Then back goes Russell to Munjake and he himself builds a boat. Then he sails said boat here to St. George's Cay. Yesterday, he puts the crew aboard one of our boats and off they go to Providence (what we formerly called Sayle Island). Meanwhile, our Capt. Russell sails about our small island and it pleases him greatly. He sees our house, it being the only one hereabouts, and makes himself known. We did much enjoy supper with the Captain and the children were proper and quiet all the while. Announces Capt. Russell that he intends to put a bid in with the Lords Proprietors for our island, that much he likes it. He is a man of some substantial means despite the loss of the Port Royal. He says he does not intend to be a landlord to us and our home and land would be ours as far as he was concerned. We are glad for that and perhaps we will soon have a neighbor of fine and good stature. I believe the name Russell Island suits the place.

* * * * *

"Why it's little John Albury," David pronounced as the boy walked up the steps to the Pinder home. "I hear you've turned fifteen years of age this very day," David added as he shook the boy's hand.

"Yes sir," the tall, smiling boy answered, "I've been fifteen the whole day through and it pleases me greatly."

"Why so, John? Is today so very different from yesterday?"

"Yesterday I was a year younger than Sina and today we are the same age."

"That's one way of seeing things, to be sure. Come into the house. I've a peck of crawfish for your mother and father and something for you as well."

David led the boy from the veranda into the small sitting room.

"The crawfish be out back in the kitchen, but first this," he said, reaching for a spool of finely woven line. "Fishy Jack learned me long ago how to fashion fishing line out of a horse tail. I happened upon one – a horse tail – last month on Harbour Island," he said, patting the fishing knife on his belt.

"I thank you Mr. Pinder," said the boy, feeling the soft and pliable line in his fingers.

"I thought if you're in no hurry to get back home we could try that line out together."

"No hurry at all. Can we . . . ."

"Can we bring Sina, ya mean? The answer is yes, boy. Sina!" called David out the back door. "Let's go out for a short pleasure cruise with your beau!"

Sina appeared in the doorway, furious and red-faced.

"Papa! I'll never go out fishing again if you continue to speak such nonsense," she hissed.

John Albury smiled shyly from the corner, but knew better than to say anything.

Hopen skipped into the room followed by Neptuna.

"Let's *all* go out in the *Rose*. It's John's birthday, so we should celebrate a little. No more work today."

As the sail filled with the easterly breeze and he steered the little sloop towards Meeks Patch Island, David could not suppress a wide grin. The sight of his family together always instilled a sense of amazement in the man, once an orphan. Hopen, now a lanky thirteen year old with her mother's sun-streaked chestnut hair, stood in the bow, ever anxious to spot her favorite animal, the porpoise. Her thin, tanned hands clutched the gunwale as she peered over the side with her blue-green eyes.

Sina and Neptuna sat together on the middle bench through which the mast ran. Sina's form was sturdier than Hopen's, her shoulders very straight and broad. Her skin tone was the darkest in the family, her tanned hands and face making her blond hair seem even lighter. She was more Norse in appearance, while Neptuna and Hopen's features were more Dutch.

Now that Jackson's health was frail, John Albury, the son of Jane and David Albury, frequently served as David's crew aboard the *Rose*. They'd passed many hours at sea together, fishing the reefs and deep water near and far. The boy was curious about anything and everything to do with fishing. He was also convinced that someday he would come upon a Spanish wreck that would make him a wealthy man.

"What would ya do with the money, John?" David had asked.

"I'd marry your daughter," John answered without hesitation.

The *Rose* skimmed over the bright clear waters, dotted with huge starfish and the shadow of the occasional turtle. David came about and tacked toward the channel that separated Russell Island from its neighbor further west. When they made the channel, David struck the sail, dropped anchor and distributed baited fishing lines. As usual, Hopen was the first to land a fish. And as usual she did so with relish, quickly setting the hook, then deftly working the line in with her elegant but capable little hands. She was competitive, by nature and no sooner had she removed the Bar Jack from the line than she was baiting the hook and tossing it overboard for another.

In two hours, the *Rose* was littered with flopping fish. As David sailed her back towards home, the afternoon sun gilded the crests of small waves with gold.

Sitting next to David by the tiller, John Albury spoke. "Thank you for the line, Mr. Pinder. It's the best I've ever used."

"You can thank the bobtailed horse what lives on Harbour Island."

* * * * *

4 March, 1680

It is hard for me to ponder my girl Sina as a married woman. It is hard also for me to ponder Fishy Jack's 89 years! He attended the wedding aboard the Recovery entirely deaf to the words spoken, as his hearing has now abandoned him. My Neptuna were so happy for her girl the tears did flow the whole while. And I know too she be relieved that the stain she imagined would follow her daughter never did. All here look up to Sina, as she's as fine and strong in every manner. I am to blame for the loss of my daughter in marriage to John Albury. If I'd not taken the boy wracking with me after the Norther blew past here in January, he'd not have a share of the fine salvage we come upon. But all and all he is a diver by nature and he earned everything he got fair and square. He were some disappointed the wrack carried no treasure but was in high spirits indeed when we sold the goods down in Hispaniola for a mighty price. It were a Godsend Captain Sayle willed the Recovery to our settlement. It do raise the hairs on my arms when I see her tied up at the waterfront. We got the channels dredged such as she can go in and out, even through the south passage. My new son in-law has built a nice cottage down on the point in Spanish Wells, too low to the water for my liking, but Sina is greatly pleased. She writes letters to her friend in Boston who she met aboard her father's ship, the Welcome, when it came into port here. Sarah is her name. I ask Sina if she is lonely in our little settlement and she says she is not. She does love John Albury, that be certain, and he the same of her. This is a thing that gladdens my heart greatly. I wish the same of her sister. And of Hopen? Hopen learns the children in Spanish Wells to read and write and she is paid for it. She will now live with Sina and her new husband in town. Neptuna and I are saddened but we say nothing to the children. They must do for themselves now. All these years later I mourn the loss of Toothy Jill and my Miranda. I cannot bear the thought of having another dog in the home as it would only remind me of my loss, but Neptuna is determined I should find a pup to bring up. Perhaps she is right.

We buried Fishy Jack at sea this morning. All of us boarded the Recovery at sunrise and we took her out through the Ridley Head passage past the reef what kept me and Fishy and all of us survivors alive those many years ago. There weren't a Reverend anywhere abouts. They've all gone away, although they talk of some fella perhaps coming to Harbour Island. There's always such talk. Mr. Sweeting said some mighty fine words over Fishy as we committed him to the deep. It be rare deep out where we brung the Recovery. Fishy liked them blue waters. And so I am come from great happiness to great sadness. My Sina and John, my Hopen, and my Neptuna were all there aboard Recovery. They was greatly concerned about Papa which is what they call me. I am peaceful with the passing of Fishy. I mean not to hide from the truth that he were my father. In times past I felt powerful guilt thinking such a thing, as I loved my father back in Devon. I loved my mother, Rose as well. She is with me always. But Fishy brung me up these many years and he were the one what fed me by hand sometimes when circumstances were so grave. I remember them little bundles of fruit what we dried and buried all over these islands of ours. I remember in them times Fishy pulling a liver out of a fish, and dividing it for me and Toothy Jill. I remember like it were yesterday Fishy and me finding the tamarind tree. I remember him giving me that sugar apple away back in Bermuda. I remember everything yet I remember so little of my true father. I don't know what becomes of a man after he draws his last breath. I only know I want to live my life such as Fishy done.

Another Pinder has come to Spanish Wells! His name is Daniel Pinder and his father is Timothie Pinder of Bermuda. He has with him a lovely wife named Elizabeth. He arrived at our house bearing a letter from his father. I must admit I do not recall Timothie Pinder from my time in Bermuda though Timothie writes that he remembers me well, being as I was all the time with Fishy Jack. Timothie reckons we are related, both of us having folk what come from Dover area back in England. So right away Neptuna says to Daniel that he must go back into the village to fetch Elizabeth and they must stay with us until they are established. We enjoy their company and Daniel is of great assistance fishing, especially pulling the nets. Yesterday we sailed to Harbour Island to look about. Elizabeth came along and she took a strong liking to the place so it seems they may settle there instead of our Russell Island. Harbour Island is a beauty, to be sure, but too far away from the reef for my liking and too long to get to the open sea unless one risks keeping a boat on the east side. On the way home we dropped the anchor off the long point of the main island and there in the wee cove facing north were a large mass of ambergris bobbing by the rocky shore. It were a *goodly find. I also dove there for it were hot in the sun and I come up with a huge crawfish what scared poor Elizabeth near to death when I tossed the monster into the boat. Daniel thought it were great sport and soon Elizabeth were laughing as well.*

* * * * *

In 1682, the flood-tide of privateers on the island of Jamaica suddenly receded with the appointment of Sir Thomas Lynch as Governor. His predecessor, Thomas Modyford and his Bahamian contemporary, Roger Clarke were cut from the same profiteering cloth. Under pretext of Spanish harassment, both Modyford and Clarke were quick to issue letters of Marquee to the many privateers eager to make their fortunes at the expense of the many Spanish galleons sailing past Cuba and into the eastern Caribbean Sea.

But times were changing in Jamaica. Staid plantation owners now outnumbered raucous sea captains. The Jamaican town of Port Royal, once the privateering center of the universe, was now essentially closed for business. Many of the privateers who'd plied the waters around Jamaica and Cuba now migrated north to Charles Town on the island former known as Sayle Island. The ease with which Governor Clarke issued letters of Marque, for the right price of course, threatened the ever-tenuous peace with Spain.

The boundaries between privateering and piracy blurred. Letters of Marque issued for commissions of three months were forged into commissions good for three years. Fortunes were made by ships' captains and politicians alike. In 1682, Roger Clarke was recalled from Providence for his eccentric style of leadership, in which personal gain was plainly the principal pursuit. But the damage with Spain was done.

* * * * *

Holding the bowline for balance, Neptuna stepped from the *Rose* to the wharf while David adjusted the anchor line placed over the stern. He looked up at his wife waiting for him in the cool December air and brilliant sunshine. She smiled and brushed a lock of chestnut hair, streaked here and there by grey, behind her ear.

"We'll be late, David. Let's be on our way."
David gathered up the canvas sack full of ducks he'd shot that morning and leapt ashore.

"Late for what, girl? It's not even midday and Sina said plain that we'd have our Christmas dinner in the late afternoon."

"But we must clean and pluck the birds. We must prepare the coals. We must dig the sweet potatoes. We must bake the pies. Do you think Christmas dinner prepares itself?"

David smiled, "You Dutch are slaves to the clock, Neptuna. Here in Spanish Wells there is no need for such strictness. We'll eat soon enough."

"I know you David Pinder, you'll claim you're starving to death in an hour."

David smiled again and took Neptuna by the elbow as they walked east towards the point. John and Sina's cottage lay nestled among palmetto trees and nosegay frangipani. The clapboards gleamed white in the sun, making the red shutters look like startled eyes. A toddler, digging in the sand by the front door looked up suddenly then dashed into the house. A moment later Sina and Hopen appeared in the doorway, both wearing white aprons.
Neptuna stepped from the main path onto the paving stones leading up to the front door.

"You two look like you've been cooking already," she said as she reached out to embrace Sina then Hopen.

"We've been making the pies, Mumma," said Hopen.

"Elsie says she wants a sugar apple pie like Grandfather."

"A girl after my heart," said David as he reached down to scoop up the little girl.

These are good times, thought David as he sat on the low seawall cleaning his ducks. John Albury was a good man. Sina was happy. And the little girl, Elsie, was a marvel. Hopen would be married in April to the captain of a large three-mast Bermudan sloop, which plied between Abaco, Eleuthera, New Providence and the Virginia Colonies. Captain Harris would provide well for Hopen and she was not bothered in the least by the ten years that separated their ages.

6 May, 1683

We have all of us just returned from a grand adventure aboard Captain Harris' sloop, the Persistence. Following our Hopen's marriage to Captain Harcourt Harris, Persistence, with Hopen aboard, sailed on commission to Barbados where she took on four families of planters and all their freight. She then sailed back to St. George's Cay where Neptuna, John, Sina and me joined Hopen and her new husband on a crossing to Charleston in the Carolina Colony. We loaded four ton of braziletto wood at New Providence and then made our way across the banks and into the great current what flows northward along the coast of America. It were the finest of thing to be all of us together aboard a fast and handsome vessel bound for a place none of us had ever laid eyes upon. We come aground briefly on a sandbank at the entrance of Charleston Harbor despite having taken aboard a pilot, but no harm done. It were moving to see the town all laid out along the peninsula. The pilot told us Captain Sayle died at the place his party first landed which was called Port Royal. Then Sir John Yeamans took command and moved everyone to Albemarle Point on the west bank of the Ashley River. It were only three year ago the Lord Proprietors adopted the 'Grand Model' what called for the building of a town of a particular nature on Oyster Point that would serve all the plantations of the Carolina Colonies. In that short time the town is much grown. There be perhaps

3500 people here, many of them slaves. Luxuries are everywhere and we are all of us excited to be in such a place. The port is well laid out and there are so many masts rising into the air it looks like a forest from afar. It will be a great port city someday, to be sure, but the muddy water distresses me. I like to be able to see what I'm sailing over. There are deer skins piled everywhere about the port and I am told the Indians hereabout trade them. Neptuna purchased for me a fine pair of deerskin breeches and I for her a pair of the softest shoes I ever did touch. The first night we dined ashore upon a large haunch of deer which did seem the best meal we'd ever tasted, but it did not sit well with us. We have traded with a planter for diverse kind of seed which he commends for sandy soils such are ours. By and by two weeks did pass and Captain Harris completed his trading at the port. He took aboard a fine cargo of dried Indian corn, deer skins, salted meat, and rum which he intends to sell throughout our islands. The crossing to New Providence were fast and Captain Harris sold the rum within an hour and most of the salted meat as well. We anchored in the harbor overnight and were off to St. George's Cay in the morning. I am gladdened to be home, but Hopen is off again with her Captain. This time to Abaco.

17 ALONE

Cuban governor Jose Fernandez de Cordoba shouted so loudly he lost his voice for three days. The English swine, wallowing in their sty called Charles Town on the Island of New Providence, would pay. He'd written a letter to the king describing the privateers of the Bahama Islands as proven pirates. He'd then issued a commission to Spain's corsair, Juan de Alarcón, to burn the English settlement to the ground.

Off the island of Andros, seized Alarcón a sloop and its master, William Bell. At penalty of death, Bell was forced to act as pilot for ' Alarcón's two barcos luengo through the eastern channel into the port of Charles Town. As the sun began to rise in the November sky, landed 150 men a half a mile from the town. He then ordered his corsair ships bear down upon the six vessels anchored in the harbor.

Alarcon's men converged upon the town like crows. The sounds of musket fire echoed through the sandy streets while cannon fire lit up the harbor. Screams rising in the throats of women were cut short by Spanish steel. Everywhere the people of Charles Town ran, the Spanish soldiers were aready there. Black residents were presumed slaves and instantly became property of the corsair. For the most part women and children were merely kicked aside as the soldiers ran from building to building, looting first, then setting fires.

The 10-gun New England frigate Good Intent, captained by William Warren, and another anchored vessel managed somehow to escape across the bar, leaving the Spaniards to complete their pillage of the remaining four ships. Governor Lilbourne leapt from his bedroom window and ran for his life.

Half of the town was in flames by mid-morning as blood pooled in the gutters drawing clouds of black flies. Former Governor Roger

Clarke attempted impotently to raise a defense but was quickly wounded and captured. After a brief inquisition, he was carried to the center of town, impaled upon an iron spit and roasted while still alive, his arms and legs twitching insect-like for what seemed to be an impossibly long time.

By late afternoon, Alarcón loaded most of his plunder aboard the largest of the captured vessels and then assembled his men to sail again. By evening they'd left the harbor and were underway to the northeast.

* * * * *

David stood next to Hopen and Sina as the three waved the *Persistence* on her way down the channel. Hopen's round belly protruded under her bodice like a melon. She would have her baby in late March, or perhaps early April. For the time being, anyway, she would remain ashore. When the baby was old enough, Hopen, her husband and their child would again sail together aboard *Persistence*.

"Will you stay for supper, Papa", asked Sina?

"I would, girls, if your mother had come into town with me. It was different when Daniel and Elizabeth were with us, but now they're on Harbour Island, I don't want to leave your mother alone in the night."

"Will you bring Mumma and break fast with us in the morning then" Sina asked with a hopeful smile.

"We're off to Bogue in the morning. Don't ya remember?"

"Then we'll see you tomorrow evening when you return," Sina conceded. "You must wish Mr. Force well for us while you are in Bogue."

It was always a pleasure to see the *Persistence* off, as the occasion served as an excuse to spend time with his daughters. When David stepped from the *Rose* onto the steps he'd carved into the rocky shore below his house, he wondered how many times he'd done so before, and how many times he would do so in the future. Fishy had been blessed with a long life. David wished for a life long enough to see his grandchildren grown. What would the settlement look like in twenty years? What would tomorrow bring? His life with Neptuna was peaceful, the two of them ever mindful that each had saved the other in ways that were never spoken.

"Is there an odd Dutch lady lives in this house?" he called from

223

the veranda.

"There's a lady born on a Dutch ship here, but she's not odd in the least so you must have the wrong house," replied Neptuna.

"Well then I'll be off and I'm sorry to have troubled ya," David said, although instead of leaving he walked into the sitting room. Neptuna was leaning over the table lighting the oil lamp, her hair loose on her shoulders.

"A little more grey this year", thought David, but she looks like a women half her age.

"Did you see the *Persistence* away? Sina and Hopen, how are they?"

"Aye, we waved the captain down the channel together. The girls asked me to stay for supper but I can't bring it upon myself to leave you out here in the dark."

"I'm not afraid of the dark, husband. You should have stayed."

"Well *I'm* afraid of leaving ya in the dark so I come home fast as I could. What's for supper? Did John come by with the goat?"

"Yes he was here not half an hour ago. He came on foot along the path you cut. We've a half a haunch for supper but I've just now put it in the pot. It will be late by the time the stew is ready so you have some bread now."

It was past their normal bedtime when they finished their meal together on the veranda. The moon was a sliver and the stars a great swath of broken crystal strewn across the sky.

* * * * *

"Do ya remember your first voyage on the *Rose*?"

"Of course I do. We sailed to Bogue as we do this morning."

"No girl, not as we do this morning. There was only one of us in love on that first voyage."

"You are so sure of yourself, are you? I have loved you my whole life but it was not until I came to Eleutheria that I found you."

"Half the time I don't understand a word you speak," laughed David, "but I think ya might be saying you've grown fond of me."

"I'm saying that you've been in my heart since I was born. But you were not visible there. I could not know on sight that the one I loved was you until I had the chance to look into *your* heart and see myself."

David stared long into his wife's pale blue eyes before speaking again.

"You say things that are always true, Neptuna, and I am sorry to be so slow in understanding."

"You are not slow. We speak different languages. That is all. We both speak the English, yes, but there is more spoken from the heart than from the mouth. The words from the heart are difficult sometimes to understand."

* * * * *

"Hallo Mr. Pinder," yelled William Force from the dock. "Hallo Mrs. Pinder. You've been too long away. Come on quickly now, I've something to show you!"

Neptuna smiled broadly and waved to Force as he danced a little jig on the end of the dock.

"I see ya've been out in the sun too long, Mr. Force," called David as he brought the sloop alongside."

"Yes it's true I am a working man and do toil in the open fields. Someday perhaps I will be a wealthy man such as you and spend all my time sipping gold rum in the shade of a banyan tree."

"If that's what he does I wish he'd include me now and again," giggled Neptuna.

"What's got ya so worked up, William? Have ya found another wreck," asked David as he helped Neptuna onto the dock.

"Better still," responded Force, "and you'll soon see for yourself. Mrs. Pinder, are you up for a promenade overland to the next cove?"

"I'm not an old woman yet, Mr. Force, though you might have to help David along."

The three, led by the tall, handsome black man walked the half mile or so to the next cove. As they cleared the last small rise of land, a white-hulled sloop came into view lying on her side in the sand, the water barely three feet deep in the low tide. She had two masts and she was still flying canvas, which drooped waterlogged off her booms.

"Was there anyone aboard her?" asked David.

"No, not a soul. And there's nothing in her holds. Empty."

David stood staring at the vessel, which seemed to be in perfect condition, having come to rest in the soft sand and sea grass of the cove.

"Well it's salvage, all right. No one would have brung her in here purposeful like. I'd say she's yours, William. If there's word of a claim reaches Spanish Wells, we'll tell ya about it. But I would go ahead and start celebrating. Looks as though she's practically new."

"I'll pull her off the sand with my men, but I think I might be interested in selling her. Could you act as my agent, David? I'd pay you twenty percent."

"I may be interested in buying her myself, William. I'll ask around our settlement and see if I can come up with an investor or two."

"That would be grand, David. I can see you as a trader in your older years. Let someone else do the fishing."

"Well I like to fish, William, but aye, it might be nice to be a businessman part of the time."

Neptuna stepped up beside David and took his hand. "As long as you don't take to the sea and leave me behind."

"Never. Never. Never" answered David. "Let's go see Mrs. Force and then we should make our way home with the last of the tide."

* * * * *

David had planned to stay until the evening tide, but the sight of the beached sloop unnerved him. He said nothing to Neptuna, but it was clear to him the sloop had been boarded by hostiles and the crew perhaps killed. There was no other explanation for the vessel having grounded the way she did, under sail, undamaged, in fine weather. He wanted to be home with Neptuna safe in his house if there were pirates about, or even worse, Spaniards.

As the *Rose* emerged from the cut into the open sound, David swung the tiller to port and trimmed the mainsheet for the first of many tacks necessary to gain St. George's Cay when the breeze was northerly. Neptuna leaned against David's shoulder as they sat side by side on the bench seat. In the distance, a billow of smoke rose slowly over the forest canopy to the northeast.

"Is someone clearing land there, David?" asked Neptuna.
David squinted towards the northern horizon as the smoke rose higher.

"Looks like it may be so. That's where the cave settlement lies. But planting season is long over for the winter crop. Perhaps someone burning a new plot for next year."

The *Rose* pushed forward through the gathering chop as the sun rose in its November arch. Now another column of smoke climbed into the sky to the west of the first.

"Oh David, look. More smoke over there."

"Aye. It could be anything, Neptuna. There is no need worry just yet."

"But why would there be two fires?"

"It's not that hard to imagine two people burning off weeds at the same time, girl. We're still many miles away and things can look odd when it's just you alone with your imagination aboard a boat."

The two sat silently for another hour, but now the pall of smoke broadened across the northern end of Eleutheria and was spilling into the sound, carried by the northerly breeze.

Like a clap of thunder, the sound of a single cannon shot rolled over the water past the *Rose*. Neptuna sat ramrod straight on the bench squeezing David's hand tightly. Still she remained silent. Another hoarse roar emanated from the north, then a third. David gazed ahead unblinking, his knuckles white as ivory on the tiller. He brought the *Rose* about again and trimmed the sail tightly. There was nothing more to be done.

Now grey and black smoke suddenly darkened the sky over the Spanish Wells settlement. The cloud swelled rapidly in all directions then tapered to the south under the force of the strengthening breeze. But for the sound of the *Rose* making way through the clear waters, it was now quiet.

David placed his arm around his wife and willed the sloop forward. Again he tacked to the west, keeping his gaze fixed to the north. As far as he could discern, no smoke rose over Harbour Island. Nor did Russell Island appear affected. Neptuna remained perfectly still, straining her eyes and ears in the direction of home.

They'd left Bogue before noon, and now the sun was much lower to the west. In another hour, twilight would be upon them. If the breeze had been from the south, they'd have made port an hour ago.

"They'll be fine." The words seemed empty even as David spoke them, so he did not attempt to say more. Neptuna placed her hand on David's shoulder, feeling his tension-rigid muscles through the linen shirt. The columns of smoke further to the east diminished in volume, but further west St. Georges Cay was nearly obscured amidst the swirling grey, brown and black clouds.

By the time they reached the southern edge of Charles Island, twilight was giving way to darkness. As they entered the south channel, a red glow reached above the Charles Island trees to their right. Traveling into the wind, the sail began to luff and David quickly lowered it and took up the oars. As they cleared the channel and looked to the east, the ruins of the waterfront spread out before them. Smoldering heaps, the remains of cottages and outbuildings, dotted the point. The west wall of Sina and John's cottage still stood but was in flames, casting flickering light over the ashes and debris. The hilltop further west appeared now and then through the smoky haze, revealing the broken shapes of blackened homesteads dotted with glowing coals peering like reptilian eyes through the darkness.

A tall figure, silhouetted in the glow of red embers, approached the wharf as David shipped the oars and the *Rose* nudged into the berth. A hand reached down for the bowline and now David and Neptuna could see the hand's owner was Peter Sands. He took the line and made it fast, then bent to help Neptuna out of the boat and onto the wharf. David leapt from the boat and from the higher vantage point looked around at the devastation. He looked into Neptuna's tear streaked face and took her hand. They'd not spoken a word for over an hour.

Sands reached out with both hands, placing one on Neptuna's shoulder and the other on David's.

"I was on Harbour Island with the family. We were helping Daniel and Elizabeth build a larger cistern. We saw smoke from a fire and didn't think anything of it. But then there was the sound of cannon. I left my wife and children with Daniel. We agreed if trouble came to Harbour Island as well, we'd meet up again on the main island at Whale Point. I set out for the Backbone and when I got to Governor's Bay I could see what looked to be the *Recovery*, alone, well out to sea. There was not a soul about the cave and all the cottages were gone or were on fire. I beat well back into the bush calling out as I went, but there was no answer. I thought perhaps our folk had run into the forest to escape. Then I made my way here and found the same."

"The *Recovery*," David began, his throat as dry as straw, "do ya think they got away in her?"

"This I know, David, the ship I saw to the north was alone. I *think* we were attached by the Spaniards, and I *think* they came from the New Providence. Why would they ever come here first to this little settlement and risk one of our folk fleeing to Charles Town and sounding the alarm? They came from Charles Town and approached Spanish Wells from the south. Our Spanish Wells folk would have seen them coming. The main island folk would have been blind."

"But the fires started on the main island, not here," countered Neptuna.

Sands continued. "No, when the Spaniards arrived here at this waterfront, probably in longboats first, our folk had already fled to the *Recovery*. The Spaniards knew then they'd been spotted, so they would have made for their boats again, rowing hard to make the other settlement. They could always come back and do their burning later."

David looked out into the channel that separates St. George's Cay from the main island.

"Aye, our people would have pulled the *Recovery*'s anchor and moved her quick as they could through Ridley passage, then anchored again once they'd cleared the reef. They'd still be out of sight of the Spanish coming through the sound past Meeks Patch, so they would have ferried the cave folk aboard the Recovery under cover, thinking the Spaniards would appear at any moment."

Sands nodded his agreement and continued. "When the Spaniard longboats made to the east and into the main channel, they'd have seen the *Recovery* out to sea to the north or northeast. But they'd have pushed to the cave fast as they could not knowing if the settlers there had time to board the ship. When they made shore at the cave, they likely found everything left as it was, but all the people gone. Then they'd have started in on the looting and burning. After the cave settlement, they came back here and did the same."

It seemed to make good sense, but they could not be sure.

Netuna spoke up again. "But what if some of our people are hiding? Perhaps only a few made it to the *Recovery*."

"We must look, of course," answered Sands. "We can cover the south shore of St. George's Cay this eveing, then see if your home was spared. When the sun rises, we can search about Russell Island."

David looked again at his wife. Tears still tracked sporadically down her cheeks. He knew she was in agony. He was in agony. Sina, Hopen, Elsie and John were alive or they were dead. They had escaped or they were captive in the holds of Spanish ship. They were unmolested or they were suffering. Captain Harris was away in Virginia, only slightly more ignorant of his wife's fate than the three remaining occupants of the Spanish Wells waterfront.

They rowed the *Rose* the whole length of the south shore calling out every few moments until they reached the Russel Island landing. They then walked overland to David and Neptuna's cottage. It had been spared, probably because the Spaniards supposed it not worth their time to make another landing.

* * * * *

Well before the dawn broke upon the first day of ruin, Peter Sands stepped out on the veranda only to find David and Neptuna already wake. Husband and wife sat together, David in a straight back chair, Neptuna on a footstool beside the chair. Sands walked to the top step and sat down himself, staring out over the sound towards Meeks Patch Island.

David broke the silence. "The *Recovery* will not come back, Peter."

Sands did not turn around to face his friends, but muttered "I know" into the distance.

"Our men would not risk the lives of the women and children in returning to the settlements. For all they know, the Spaniards are encamped here. And even if that were not the case, they would only return to starvation. Everything is gone, the plantings destroyed, our stores looted. Joining William Force's clan in Bogue would put those settlers at risk of starvation as well, so they would not do so."

Sands now turned and spoke. "Nor would they risk crossing to Charles Town for the same reasons. No, they have set out for a safe harbor somewhere and will throw themselves upon Christian charity. It's the only course that insures their lives."

Neptuna began to weep softly against David's knee. The wind was now from the southwest and it rustled her hair, spreading it like a fan over David's thigh.

David reached down to stroke her head. "Neptuna, love, I will find them. I will bring them back, home to a new cottage I'll build for them. The privateers in Charles Town are driven off now, to be sure. The Spaniards will not return anytime soon."

"But how will you find them, David? Where will you search? How will you get there" Neptuna asked.

"Captain Harris will return in March with the *Persistence*, as he expects Hopen to deliver their child then. Before he arrives, I will prepare William Forces's newfound sloop for a voyage. Harris will provide a few crewmen from *Persistence* so that we may search with two ships rather than just his own. When I find our daughters, I'll sell the sloop as agent for Mr. Force. With my share of the sale, I'll purchase passage for Sina, John, Hopen and the baby. Or perhaps we can send word to Harris so we might return aboard *Persistence*."

Neptuna raised her head from David's knee and looked into his moonlit eyes. "I know you will find them, as I know your heart. You love us as only an orphan could, David."

Sands climbed to his feet. "I'll help you find them, David, and as God is my witness we'll all be together here again. I will never leave this place, these our islands, and I know you believe the same to be true for you and your family. God has blessed us handsomely and now tests our worthiness. You and I, and Neptuna as well, are born to the sea and we know these waters will always provide. We survived the wreck of the *William* and we will survive this test. We live as free men here in a place named for freedom itself. Our families will live free for a hundred more generations. In the marrow of my bones I feel these things will be so."

"They will be so, Peter. We will make them so."

January 6, 1687 letter from Massachusetts Colony businessmen,
Jeremiah Dunmer, Simeon Stoddard and Walter Gendal

To His Excellency, Sir Edmund Andros, Governor of Massachusetts:

Arrived at this town of Boston from Eleutheria, one of the Bahama Islands, many families having been spoiled by the Spaniards of all they possessed and driven off naked and destitute, who on their arrival here were like to be continued charge unto this place. Your Petitioners, considering the same, made application to the President and Council that if the interjacent land might be granted to us, who have each of us some land upon the place, that we would advance money for their support and supply and settlement on said land, Casco Bay. Were were pleased thereupon to have an order for removing said distressed unto that place, declaring they would recommend our request unto His Majesty for his royal favor therein. Whereupon we were at the charge of removing about nine families of the distressed people and have been at considerable charge in furnishing them with necessaries for their supply and support this winter.

June 8, 1687 letter from the Eleutheran refugees

To His Excellency, Sir Edmund Andros, Governor of Massachusetts:

Nicholas Davis, Nathanial Saunders, John Albury, and Daniel Saunders, in behalf of themselves, families and rest of the Company, humbly sheweth your Execellency that whereas we agreed with some gentlemen here, namely, Mr. Jerimiah Dunmer and Major Gidney of Salem, for the settlement of a plantation about Casco Bay, according to articles drawn up between us, we have performed our part, but inasmuch as these gentlemen have not performed their obligation to us, in which they were bound to supply us that we might carry on the plantation, we were forced to leave the plantation because we had not food to subsist there, to our great damage and undoing – for we are now in a far worse condition than were were before we went thither, not knowing what course to take to subsist, having worn out our cloths and wasted the little we had. Our humble petition to your Exellency is that we might have relief in the matter; for if we had forfeited our bonds to these gentlemen, as they have forfeited their bonds to us, the law would have been open to them.

19. AUTHOR'S NOTE

Who really existed? What really happened? Where did it all take place? This is a work of fiction, but its flesh hangs on a skeleton of historical evidence. Some moments along the chain of written history are blanketed with fog. For example, it is not known the exact date Captain William Sayle and the Company of Adventurers landed on Eleuthera (formerly "Eleutheria"). We know only that the Articles and Orders were signed July 9, 1647. In addition, there is no firm consensus regarding the exact place the Adventurers first landed, and where Captain Nathaniel Butler parted ways. Other moments are better documented, such as the Battle of Torrington, the explosion of the Torrington church, the expulsion of the second group of Independents from Bermuda and the 1656 slave rebellion. It is interesting that William Shakespeare's play, The Tempest, does, in fact, appear to have been based upon William Strachey's real account of the shipwreck of *Sea Venture* off St. George's Bay, Bermuda.

Historical figures such as William Sayle, Rev. Patrick Copeland, Governor John Winthrop, William Rener, Oliver Cromwell, General Fairfax, and King Charles I, lived in real life, of course. But clear portraits of their personalities do not necessarily exist.

This work of historical fiction is not a genealogical study, which might disappoint some of the families I wish only to honor. In creating characters for this story, I used many family names that were prominent in the first European migrations to The Bahamas. These same family names remain widespread throughout the islands. Go to the "main island" of Eleuthera, or Spanish Wells or Harbour Island and no doubt you will meet many Pinders, Sands, Higgs, Alburys, Saunders, Knowles, Roberts, etc. Nevertheless, the story's protagonist, David Pinder, is entirely fictional, as is Benjamin Jackson a.k.a., Fishy Jack. The three men who stayed behind on Bermuda in

1609 did not include Jackon. Those men were Robert Waters, Edward Chart and Christopher Carter.

There are sprinkles of historical 'truth' among some of the characters assigned familiar Bahamian names. For example, the Saunders family really did own an early 17th Century boatyard in St. George's Bay, Bermuda. My fictional character, David Pinder, marries a woman named Neptuna, who appears in actual court records from 17th Century Bermuda. Robert Ridley is, in fact, credited with actually finding a navigable passage through the Devil's Backbone.

It bears a special mention that William Force is a real figure from black history. He really was accused of fomenting a slave rebellion in Bermuda and he really was banished to Eleuthera aboard a ship called *Blessing*. There is tenable evidence Force, together with other banished free blacks and slaves from Bermuda, established a settlement in Bogue, likely the first free black settlement in the New World.

True also that the people of 17th Century Eleuthera were exceptionally resourceful and daring pioneers in the whaling industry. There is strong evidence to suggest they were harpooning whales and tying them off to their small whaling boats long before the more famous whalers of Nantucket even dreamed of doing so. And yes, despite Captain Sayle's advanced age, he too got into the whaling business. Nevertheless, I am unaware that Sayle ever willed his whaling ship, the *Blessing*, renamed *Recovery*, to the Eleutheran settlement.

One simply cannot help but appreciate the unique history of The Bahamas, filled with shipwrecked puritans, roving pirates, blockade and rum runners. I have loved these islands since my first visit as a small child in 1967. I am proud to be a resident of the Family Islands and I hope this book has given you a small glimpse into a very special place.

ABOUT THE AUTHOR

Tad Linn first visited The Bahamas as a young boy in 1967. He resides now in Spanish Wells. He is a former resident of many different towns, cities and places throughout the globe, but none so dear to his heart as Eleuthera.

Made in the USA
Charleston, SC
24 June 2014